Not
That Kind
of Guy

TITLES BY ANDIE J. CHRISTOPHER

Not the Girl You Marry
Not That Kind of Guy

Not That Kind of Guy

ANDIE J. CHRISTOPHER

JOVE
New York

A JOVE BOOK
Published by Berkley
An imprint of Penguin Random House LLC
penguinrandomhouse.com

Library of Congress Cataloging-in-Publication Data

Names: Christopher, Andie J., author.
Title: Not that kind of guy / Andie J. Christopher.
Description: First edition. | New York: Jove, 2020.
Identifiers: LCCN 2019051056 (print) | LCCN 2019051057 (ebook) |
ISBN 9781984802705 (trade paperback) | ISBN 9781984802712 (ebook)
Subjects: GSAFD: Love stories. | Humorous fiction.
Classification: LCC PS3603.H7628 N67 2020 (print) |
LCC PS3603.H7628 (ebook) | DDC 813/.6—dc23
LC record available at https://lccn.loc.gov/2019051056
LC ebook record available at https://lccn.loc.gov/2019051057

First Edition: April 2020

Printed in the United States of America
1 3 5 7 9 10 8 6 4 2

Cover design and illustration by Colleen Reinhart
Book design by Alison Cnockaert

To Gus,
who made me happy and remains a very good boy

CHAPTER ONE

BRIDGET NOLAN HAD DECIDED to marry Chris Dooley the day he took a piss in her kiddie pool. Like not a British "took the piss," but an actual piss. To her credit, she didn't decide to marry him until his mother dragged him away by the ear from said kiddie pool and took his Game Boy. It was his tear-streaked face while he apologized—with the sole purpose of getting his handheld gaming system back—that sealed the deal.

In her four-year-old mind, anyone who could apologize as beautifully as Chris Dooley—who cared that much about hurting her feelings—had to be a keeper. It didn't even matter that her dad had to clean out the pink plastic kiddie pool with bleach while cursing a blue streak.

The kiddie-pool incident was his first apology to her even though he'd already been the major source of consternation in her short life. Prior to the pool incident, he hadn't apologized for pulling her pigtail so hard the curl her mother had painstakingly constructed for her brother Jack's First Communion party went flat—and lopsided pigtails were definitely worthy of an apology. The lack thereof had made it impossible for her to stop thinking about him for weeks.

And he hadn't apologized when he poked her in the eye with his Super Soaker at her other brother Michael's birthday party a month later. He'd merely looked chagrined when Bridget's mom had "accidentally" thwacked him in the back of the head with *her* water gun. Even her mother's vengeance hadn't stopped her from thinking about him.

When she'd told her mother that Chris Dooley had taken over at least half of her waking thoughts, she'd said, "He probably just has a crush on you. Ignore it and he'll go away." But he hadn't gone away. And her thoughts of him had only intensified. The only solution would be to marry him. Maybe then she could stop thinking about him. It had certainly worked that way for her parents.

Her commitment to marry Chris had been deadly serious—much more so because she'd made it in the midst of her parents' divorce. Unlike the elder Nolans, she was *never* going to get a divorce. She would never rip a family apart the way hers was rent at the seams.

She'd finally started dating Chris Dooley officially when she was fifteen and he was seventeen. He'd finally started using her first name instead of calling her "Little Nolan," which constantly reminded her that she was the baby of the family, and totally below any interest of his that would include kissing.

However, even being her boyfriend had not decreased his rate of asshole moves to apologies. And Bridget had just eaten the apologies he gave her and starved the rest of the time. That's what a relationship was to her—surviving on crumbs. In a way, it made her understand her mother leaving. It wasn't like her dad emoted very much.

But she was stronger than her mother had been and would never give up just because a relationship wasn't precisely to her specifications. And she'd dated Chris for a dozen years to prove it.

She thought that he'd chosen her, just like she'd chosen him every day since he'd peed in her kiddie pool. She'd thought they were playing for keeps.

Until she realized that she did not want to play for keeps—definitely not with Chris. And maybe not with anyone.

All of her carefully laid plans about the kind of future she would have—where they'd live, how many children they'd have, and how they'd manage to pay off their student loans right in time to send their own kids to school—had gone up in smoke over about ten minutes. She'd nuked her whole life before her mashed potatoes had cooled off enough to eat.

After Chris left her apartment in a hurry, confused and full of the shame/rage thing that some guys did whenever things didn't go their way, she kind of fell apart for a while. She'd shed actual tears even though she'd previously thought that she was missing the gene that would allow her to feel sorry for herself.

Bridget expressing actual human emotions had thrown her dad and brothers off a bit. They didn't know how to handle her when she wasn't her put-together, perfectionist self. For a while, she'd noticed that they would exchange *looks* when she made it over for dinner or game night. When that happened—their roles reversed so they were the ones worried about her instead of the other way around—she knew she had to get her shit together.

After she'd dealt with the emotional and physical remnants of the future she no longer had or wanted, she hadn't looked back.

She was a Nolan, for Christ's sake. Nolans didn't wallow in the past. Nolans didn't cry over the demise of a romantic relationship—at least her father hadn't after her mom walked out on him. They bucked up and moved on.

A few months after the breakup, she'd decided that she was through with crying, thinking, and talking about the relationship. In fact, she was going to stop crying, thinking, or talking about *any* relationship. She wasn't any good at them anyway. In fact, romantic relationships were the only thing that she was really bad at. Maybe she got it from her dad. Once the idea that she didn't have to be in a relationship really sank into her psyche, it was simple to decide to focus on her career, her friends, her family, and herself. And no one else.

And, to be honest, she was kind of relieved. She was done doing the emotional labor for an overgrown baby man.

She was *happy* to be helping to plan her brother's wedding instead of her own. This brunch wasn't really planning—it was more of a war strategy session—with her brother's newly minted fiancée, Hannah, and Hannah's best friend, Sasha. They were both wedding and event planners, so this shit was serious.

And, to her surprise, she didn't think about what it might be like to be doing this with Chris. It had been so long since they'd broken up, she barely thought about him at all anymore. At first, he'd been sort of like a phantom, haunting her at odd moments. But when she focused on other things, she realized that she was definitely better off without him.

Bridget was grateful that they'd hit a cycling class first, because she'd needed to burn off some energy before diving into wedding planning. Not that Hannah wasn't beyond lovely and way too good for her middle brother. The whole thing just made her remember that she was a failure at relationships.

Bridget's future sister-in-law raised her glass. "So, here's the game plan—no hashtags, no fairy lights, not a single, solitary, fucking mason jar." She pointed her mimosa at Bridget and Sasha. "Just you two as my bridesmaids."

"Me?" Bridget hadn't known Hannah for that long, and she'd assumed that her bridal party would be populated by her college friends. Not being a part of the wedding party would also aid in her efforts to avoid running into Chris at the wedding. She could wear green and white and blend in with the giant floral arrangements with a magnum of champagne. She'd emerge for the toasts and then slink back into the greenery like that GIF of Homer Simpson disappearing into a hedge.

As a bridesmaid, she would have no such quarter. There would be the rehearsal dinner, the pictures, the dancing—thank God Hannah wouldn't do a big bridal party entrance at the reception—but there would also be the toasts and the smiling and the keeping her inflamed case of irritation toward her ex bottled up for hours at a time. She would probably snap at least one molar if she couldn't land at least one or two cutting barbs about how his suit game had deteriorated since she'd stopped picking out his clothes.

She didn't want him back, but his face had turned remarkably punch-worthy since they broke up.

"Yes, you." Hannah scoffed as though Bridget's surprise was ridiculous. "We have brunch almost every weekend and you're going to be my sister, for Christ's sake."

"Is this just for Jack's sake?"

"Well, he does make me see God on a regular basis." Hannah smirked, and Sasha blushed. Bridget just tried to keep her shrimp and grits down. "But I wouldn't invite you to be in my bridal party if you were an asshole. I'd make you be his groom's bitch."

Bridget shook her head, suppressing a laugh. Hannah was nothing like any of the girls Jack had dated before her, who were all fine. But Hannah was irreverent—bordering on crass—and Bridget loved the hell out of her. Hannah was the only kind of woman she could see her brother with in the long term. Her brother needed someone who wouldn't let him get away with anything.

Sasha leaned in. "Are you seeing anyone?" That seemed apropos of nothing right now.

"Of course not." Bridget had just told her family that she didn't have time to date. Which was true. She also prosecuted sex crimes as an assistant state's attorney. Given what she saw at her day job, she didn't have the inclination to meet strange men, even in public places.

"It's been two years." Like Hannah needed to remind her.

Sasha leaned in even closer. "Are you still in love with Chris?"

"No," she answered firmly. That was one thing she was sure of. Sometimes she missed being part of a couple. Missed having someone to text or call when something interesting or funny happened. She missed having someone to cuddle up with on a Friday night with Netflix. But if that was all she missed, she could just get a dog. A dog would probably be more loyal than a guy she'd wasted almost half her life on. "I just haven't met anybody worth considering."

That lie came out smoothly enough. She had no intention of meeting anyone ever. She would not fuck up her life again, just for the sake of someone to binge television and eat expensive cheese with. Even if a second salary would make it easier to afford said expensive cheese.

"Well, you need to meet someone before the wedding," Sasha said. "I simply won't have you sitting alone while Chris swans about with his 'flavor of the week.'"

"There are flavors?" Bridget had purposely not thought about Chris dating anyone else. It was the only thing keeping bees from flying out of her mouth every time she ran into him. She didn't want him back, but she hated the idea of him being happy. She was petty, and she accepted that about herself. But now that the topic had been introduced, she couldn't stuff the bees back down her throat.

Hannah's mouth flattened out and she shot Sasha a *look*. "None of them have lasted more than a few weeks."

Bridget barely contained her sneer. She'd gotten to know both Hannah and Sasha pretty well in the last couple of years, but not well enough to tell them that her relationship with Chris had put her off relationships—permanently. Before Jack and Hannah had met and fallen in love, Hannah had been in no-man's-land herself. Bridget had a feeling that if her future sister-in-law got a whiff of her extreme reticence about romance, she would descend upon her with the enthusiasm of the newly converted. "It's fine. We broke up . . . for a lot of reasons. I didn't exactly expect him to remain celibate."

She even leaned back in her chair to emphasize how cool she was with all of this. Totally cool with her ex-boyfriend banging anyone and everyone.

"But I agree with Sasha." Hannah was declarative. "We have to find you a date."

"I don't *want* a date," Bridget said.

Apparently, they were going to ignore her. "Most of the decent guys I know are gay," Sasha said.

"Other than Jack, I know married guys and professional athletes."

"I would take a professional athlete." Chris had always hated that he'd never been good enough at sports to make varsity in anything. Taking a professional athlete to a wedding would leave her ex feeling woefully insecure. It would make for a much more enjoyable evening on her part.

"I don't think you're ready for a professional athlete," Sasha said. "Chris is your first and only, which means you've never dealt with a guy who had a tight end, much less an actual tight end. Dating is actually insane. It's a whole lot of work with a regular guy—like you have to decide if you want to have sex with him the first few minutes of a date, because if he senses that you aren't down to go to Bonetown, then he won't call you again. But if you do have sex with him, you have to be very careful not to spook him into thinking that you want to marry him that day." Sasha hadn't paused to take a breath.

Hannah raised her glass. "And that's just with a regular guy."

"And I'm supposed to want to meet one of these regular guys?" Bridget doubted their utility even more after this conversation.

All three of them looked at one another for a beat before bursting out laughing so hard they all lost their breath.

Bridget supposed Sasha was right. Every time she'd been approached by a dude since her breakup, she'd been frozen in place. A deer in headlights. Luckily, she knew how to excuse herself quickly enough that she hadn't been run down yet.

"Do you know anyone at work?" Bridget groaned inwardly at

Hannah's suggestion. Even if her work wasn't the unsexiest thing ever, none of the guys at the office were desirable. For one thing, she found only two of them attractive—and only in the right light, if she squinted. But the killing blow was that they all knew Chris. In fact, she was pretty sure Jake was in Chris's weekend five-on-five league.

"I can't date anyone at work." It would be unprofessional. She had a reputation as a hard-ass bitch to maintain. Dating someone at work would compromise that. In the past couple of years with so many changes—getting dumped, her brother finding the perfect girl, and her parents getting back together after more than a decade apart—her work had been the only constant. "But I have a few months. I'll come up with something."

She paused for a moment, thinking before she revealed the next thing. "I don't think I want to date anymore."

"Like, at all?" Sasha looked concerned.

Hannah just nodded. "That's how I felt before I met Jack."

Oh shit. Hannah was now going to try to set her up with religious fervor. Honestly, Bridget would be more likely to change her mind if Hannah was trying to get her to repent and accept Jesus. At least Bridget would be good at religion. She'd had plenty of practice believing in that which could not be seen when she was with Chris. During the course of their relationship, she'd believed that time together would outweigh her growing dread at spending the rest of her life with someone who'd ceased to inspire anything in her other than mild disgust. She'd also believed that he knew her.

But Hannah wasn't going to try to sell her on Jesus—lapsed Catholics didn't do that sort of thing. Hannah was going to try to sell her on love like an ex-smoker trying to pry the ciggies out of her hands.

It absolutely wouldn't work. "Don't even think about it." Bridget pointed at her future sister-in-law. "I can see what you're thinking, and I'm not interested in it at all."

Hannah held her hands up. "Thinking what?" She even had the audacity to have an innocent look on her face.

But Bridget narrowed her gaze and stared down both of her friends. "I. Don't. Want. To. Be. In. A. Relationship."

"But don't you want partnership?" Sasha was still a romantic even though her dating life was a continuing disaster, right underneath issues of national and global importance on the horribleness scale. And if she wasn't such a genuinely nice person, Bridget would start her point-by-point summary on why it was completely illogical to continue searching for love when a successful conclusion of that search was not supported by any past evidence.

Instead, she simply said, "No."

"Really?" Hannah sounded surprised. "We're not judging you, but did Chris really fuck you up that much?"

"Chris didn't fuck me up at all, but our breakup clarified some things for me." Bridget paused, like she did before making an argument before a jury. "I just . . . I decided it wasn't for me."

"But that's like saying you don't like cheese after trying one— very shitty—kind of cheese." Hannah did sort of make sense— and yet . . .

"There is no bad cheese." At least Bridget had never hated a single cheese.

"The kind that has toxic mold on it?" Why did Sasha have to choose this moment to make sense?

"I don't know if Chris is really toxic . . ."

Hannah rolled her eyes. "What did he do, anyway?"

NOT THAT KIND OF GUY

Bridget chewed on her grits along with her answer. She hadn't told anyone in her family about the real reason she and Chris had broken up. Part of her was embarrassed about it, afraid that they would blame her for putting a perfectly fine relationship out of its misery. And part of her couldn't really name why they'd broken up. But her growing friendship with these two women made her want to try.

"He put a down payment on a house." She paused, and both women's eyes widened. "I'd never even seen it."

"It makes sense that you broke up with him, then."

Now that she'd started talking, it seemed that she couldn't stop. "No, I freaked out because—I just flashed forward to my future and realized that spending it with him would mean that I was tied to his boneheaded choices for the rest of my life. And then he broke up with me when I freaked out."

"The nerve." Hannah's voice was filled with venom—definitely for Chris.

"Yikes." Sasha didn't look like she had much more to say.

"I think it's totally reasonable for you to want to go to the wedding alone." When Hannah said that, Bridget was glad she'd trusted her.

"Unless you meet someone great." Of course, Sasha left room for hope.

Bridget sipped her mimosa to stop herself from saying something sarcastic.

AT LEAST SHE HAD work. There, she exerted control and she never lost. As an assistant state's attorney in the Special Prosecutions

Bureau, she prosecuted sexual assault cases and crimes against children. Although her work dealt with difficult topics, it was deeply rewarding. The people she got justice for were often afraid of seeking it, and being able to give them some measure of peace—sending the people who hurt them to prison—made her feel useful.

A lot of the friends she went to law school with worked at big firms. Most of them hated their lives, and they rarely got to see the inside of a courtroom. Bridget was in court at least a few times a week. And she was always moving and doing something different.

She knew she couldn't do it forever, though. Otherwise, she would end up as an embittered husk, smoking multiple packs of Camels a day. But she didn't know what she would do next—certainly not a big firm—but she had to find a job that would let her pay her student loans.

She loved her work, but she was going to be paying off her student loans until she was ninety—since her salary upon which her income-based repayment plan was predicated was way below the median income for lawyers. Like the basement of the basement without the median even in sight.

Although she could count on her dad to help if she asked—she hated asking. Her new lease on single life included not running to her dad just because she couldn't afford the same vacations and homes her former classmates now could.

Despite all the downsides to her job, she looked forward to going into work and rarely had that sinking feeling on Monday morning when she got into the office—except for today.

Her boss, Jackie, was sitting in her office. Jackie was only a couple of years older than her—even though the job was great, the pace of the under-resourced office burned people out. She was married, with two little kids and constant dark circles under her eyes. Sometimes she even had a tic. Jackie was much more ambitious than Bridget and had her eyes on political office, which meant that sometimes she butted in to Bridget's cases when the public was particularly invested.

They got along, but only to a point. And definitely not before coffee.

"What do you need?" She wouldn't be here if she didn't want something.

Jackie smiled at her. A bad sign. "I need you to take on one of the interns."

"Are you serious?" Bridget closed her eyes and put down her bag. "I don't have time to teach some baby lawyer anything."

"He's—"

Bridget wasn't even going to let her finish. "And I'm not bringing a man around my mostly female, traumatized complaining witnesses."

"You know that fellowship you applied for last year?" Jackie was referring to a fellowship for public interest lawyers from the University of Chicago, which would have allowed Bridget to pay off her student loans. It would have meant vacations with fruity drinks the size of her head *and* never having to hit up her dad to make ends meet. It would have meant freedom. But she hadn't gotten it.

"I recall." She was careful not to betray her disappointment to Jackie. They were colleagues rather than friends. "What does that have to do with taking on this intern?"

"His parents—the Kidos—fund it."

Oh fuck. The Kido Family Trust was a big deal and sort of explained why her taking on this intern and getting this fellowship was so important to her boss—it was going to make her look good. Jane Kido's father was a beloved former senator from Hawaii and had been a decorated soldier during World War II, when many fellow Japanese-Americans were interned. And Jane's husband, Brian, was the son of a famous Japanese photojournalist who chronicled the end of the war, and a Boston Brahmin heiress. If the United States had nobility, the Kido family would be among them.

However, Jane and Brian's son, Matt, had a reputation as a louche playboy. One that even Bridget—with her head perpetually occupied by her caseload—knew about.

"So, what you're saying is that, if I take on this little, rich shithead as my intern, I might get the fellowship this year?"

Jackie held up a hand. "I'm not saying that. I can't guarantee it, but I think it would go a long way."

"I'm not giving him any cases until I verify that he's not going to fuck them up." Bridget sat down, knowing she'd lost.

"Just make sure you don't call him a little, rich shithead to his face."

CHAPTER TWO

WHEN MATT KIDO WAS ten, he told his mother that he wanted to quit playing soccer. Since they were on their way to soccer practice when he told her this, she didn't take it kindly. She hadn't had *time* to take him to soccer practice; she had carved time from her busy schedule of manipulating global markets. She was not primed to hear that her son wanted to quit his one after-school activity. Then he made the terrible mistake of telling her that he wanted to quit because one of the other kids was making fun of him.

At the time, he'd been scrawny and short. He definitely wasn't the only Asian kid at his elite private school, but he was the only one with a war hero and senator for a grandfather on one side and an ancestor who had come over on the *Mayflower* on the other. Everyone knew who his parents were, which made him a target.

His mom had taken him to soccer practice and waited him out until he got out of the car and ran onto the field. He hadn't brought up wanting to quit soccer again.

For weeks, he'd thought that she'd forgotten all about the kids making fun of him—until they'd seen the main perpetrator riding his bike home from a game. She'd slowed down her SUV to a crawl next to the kid. Then she slowly—ever so slowly—knocked him off his bike.

The kid never made fun of Matt again. And after word spread about his mom's reaction, no one else did, either.

Matt had always been slightly embarrassed by that story—even after he shot up in height and filled out. He wished he had stood up to that bully himself. But he hadn't. It had always been easier to let his parents fight his battles for him.

Until recently. Like last-week recently. Like last week when he walked in on his girlfriend of three years having sex with one of their friends. In *his* condo. Even worse, most of their friends had known about it and hadn't told him.

He and Naomi were supposed to be summer associates at the same firm—along with several of their traitorous friends—for the summer. But the thought of spending twelve weeks having to see Naomi every day when he never wanted to see her again was intolerable. It was bad enough that they attended the same law school, that their parents were friends, and that he'd have to see her at alumni mixers and family events for the rest of his life. He just didn't want to see her when it was unacceptable to have a drink in his hand.

But he hadn't wanted to go to his parents for help. Not again, and not with anything having to do with Naomi. So, he took the second-most cowardly route—he ran away under the guise of doing public service. He'd abandoned his coveted summer associate position—the one that had perks like five-hundred-dollar lunches and firm trips to Switzerland—to be here.

And that's how he found himself looking at the most stunning woman he'd ever seen.

Matt had never seen anything like the woman leading the orientation for interns at the state's attorney's office. He looked around the room. There were seven women and two other men seated at the desks in the bullpen. The furniture didn't match, and the walls appeared to have been last painted in the early eighties, long before any of them were born. The place wasn't much to look at, but he was still excited.

Everyone else was staring at the woman in the front of the room, and he couldn't blame them.

Bridget Nolan had lush auburn hair, piercing gray-blue eyes, cut-glass cheekbones, and a voice that was better than a hand job. Jesus, he was gross. It was the epitome of inappropriate to be turned on by her describing doing interviews with arresting officers. She was trying to teach them to verify facts, not tie him into knots of sexual frustration.

Matt should be focusing on her words, not how the clacking of her heels against the concrete floor made his heart beat faster. Or the way her lean hips swung with each step she took. He was just lucky to be here and that no one seemed to know who he was yet.

He'd been prepared to walk in the door and find someone officially designated to pander to him. That's how it had been at every other "job" he'd ever had. He realized that it was part and parcel of being the scion of one of the most powerful families in the US, but it didn't exactly allow him to build up his self-esteem the old-fashioned way, the way his grandfather had, through hard work and sacrifice. He felt guilty for resenting the way that his parents had made everything in his life so easy. He felt bad that he felt bad about the fact that his parents were part of what made the world bad in general.

Although his parents had been puzzled by how he'd chosen to spend his summer, the move garnered him some grudging respect because it would look good for the family. But the more he listened to Bridget Nolan speak, the more he thought that some good might come of his summer in purgatory. He needed to prove that he wasn't some pointless trust-fund kid who had been shepherded through prep schools and the Ivy League, doing the bare minimum so that he could take over his parents' holdings and run them into the ground. Maybe performing well at this internship would give him a way to do that.

Maybe there was some purpose in blowing up his plans and finding himself sitting at a shabby desk in the open space where he and the other nine interns would work for three months under unforgiving fluorescent lights.

And maybe there was a reason that he was sitting here gobsmacked by the most gorgeous woman he'd ever seen. But that reason didn't have anything to do with his dick. He had to make sure that he was clear on that.

The dude sitting next to him leaned over and whispered, "Stop looking at her like that."

Matt looked over at the whisperer. In a rumpled white shirt and pleated-front trousers, he had the air of a slightly frazzled professor even though he couldn't have been more than twenty-five. Matt liked him immediately. Still, he couldn't exactly admit that he'd been ogling their boss. "Stop looking at who like what?"

"Bridget Nolan." The other guy rolled his eyes at Matt, which made Matt even more inclined to like him. He enjoyed it when people busted his balls because it didn't happen very often. "She's got the highest conviction rate in the office. She's a rock star—and a total fucking hard-ass who will eat you for lunch if you try to hit on her with your whole rich, pretty-boy thing you have going on."

Matt had to stifle a laugh. The Nerdy Professor next to him had him pegged and had given him valuable information about Bridget. "What's your name?"

"Brent Reisz." He extended his hand for a surreptitious shake. "And you're Matt Kido."

"Are you stalking me or something?"

"Nah, I just do my research so that I don't end up looking like an asshole on my first day."

When Brent said that last thing, Bridget's searing gaze snapped over to them. Matt felt his face heat, knowing that he was about to get eaten alive. And he didn't mind a bit.

"Something more interesting than what I'm saying up here, gentlemen?"

Brent stammered until Matt said, "Sorry, Ms. Nolan."

Bridget rolled her eyes at him, and Matt probably fell in love right then and there. "It's only Ms. Nolan if you're nasty—or if you're trying to interrupt my spiel.

"Each of you will be assigned to work with one prosecutor over the next three months." Bridget paused in front of him, and he stopped breathing. "You'll have a special student admission to the bar so you'll be able to conduct preliminary hearings and take testimony in front of the grand jury. You'll have a few cases going at once so that you can get some experience, but you'll be closely supervised."

Then she smiled at the group. It hit him like a punch in the nuts, even though it wasn't directed at him. He'd never had such a powerful reaction to anyone before. Other than the fact that she was drop-dead gorgeous, he didn't know why this woman in particular made him feel as though his skin was too tight for everything inside. There was nothing about her that was overtly sexy or provocative. And this was the most inconvenient time and circumstance for him to develop a crush.

He couldn't exactly ask out a woman who was in charge of his internship program for the summer. Not only was it creepy, but she couldn't say yes. And he couldn't use any of his usual methods for impressing a woman. She didn't seem like the kind of girl who would care about a sexy car—of which he had many.

Besides, the last thing he needed was a new girlfriend before his old relationship had even gotten a proper burial. If circumstances were different—maybe if she wasn't his boss—she might be the perfect candidate for a rebound.

But he wasn't going to let himself think about that.

Having a hard-on for the head of his internship program when he couldn't do anything about it wasn't ideal. But he could try to avoid her. He'd work with another prosecutor all summer who would report to Bridget on his progress. He'd steer clear of her at social events, and he'd get a great evaluation at the end of the summer. By then, this crush—along with the feeling that he'd reverted back to a hormonal state prevalent in middle school—would pass, and he would never think about whether Bridget Nolan had freckles everywhere ever, ever again.

She looked at him as he had that thought, and his stomach sank. She smiled directly at him and said, "Matt Kido, you're with me."

After the orientation session, Matt had to race to keep pace with Bridget as she showed him around the office. They were about the same height with her in heels, but she moved much faster—with a purpose. He, on the other hand, had always been what could be generously termed a slowpoke. Methodical and thorough, but slow.

He tried to keep up with what she was saying, but he would most definitely have to ask someone where the bathroom was.

MATT FINALLY FOUND THE bathroom before lunchtime—or what would be lunchtime if this office actually seemed to have a lunchtime. Here, it appeared that the attorneys shoveled food they'd brought from home into their mouths while their eyes stayed glued to case files—if they were in the office at all.

When he'd stopped by Brent's desk to see if he wanted to go check out the light of day, Brent told him that he wasn't meeting his supervising attorney until the afternoon. Also, his possibly new friend had gotten the memo about bringing lunch from home.

He was on his own. But, on the bright side, he found the bathroom while on the hunt for vending machines. He also found Bridget staring at the paltry selections. She didn't acknowledge him.

"No one told me to bring lunch." When she jumped, he realized that she hadn't even noticed that he was there.

But once she clocked him, she slowly turned and looked at him, one brow raised in skepticism. "Do you need someone to tell you to brush your teeth and pick up after yourself?" She didn't wait for him to answer. "Perhaps you don't belong in law school if you can't meet your basic needs?"

Matt's first instinct was to get defensive. She didn't know anything about him, and yet she was treating him like he was an annoyance. And yet, she kind of had a point. He knew that this summer wasn't going to be about schmoozing law partners who were probably friends with his parents over lobster lunches. He could have guessed that he would have to fend for himself in terms of food if he'd thought about it. But he hadn't thought about it.

He scratched the back of his head, something he did when he was nervous. And she made him nervous. Her attention on him was something he liked, but it made him uncomfortable. A people pleaser by nature, he didn't like being in trouble. And, though he couldn't know how at this particular moment, he knew he was in trouble with Bridget Nolan.

With most beautiful women, he would crack a smile and offer to take her out somewhere nice. Circumstances and the hard look on Bridget's face made him think that would be the *worst* thing he could do.

Instead, he turned to the vending machine. "Pringles or Cheez-Its?"

That made her laugh a little, which tasted like a victory. Either that, or he was really hungry. "Pro tip—those Pringles have been there for months. Which they should be, because Pringles are gross."

MATT'S DESK FOR THE summer was right outside Bridget's office. He could see her working inside, chewing on her pen and alternately tapping it on the yellow legal pad.

She hadn't spoken a word to him all day. Thinking that he could make up for the rough start they'd had on his first day, he'd brought her a cup of coffee. His limited office intel—an empty cup with her name and order on it in her trash—told him she drank a latte with whole milk.

He'd been so proud of his instinct to brownnose his way out of the doghouse . . . until she took a sniff of the coffee, looked at him pointedly, and threw it away.

Then she'd taken a stack of paper off her desk, sauntered over to his desk, and dropped it without even looking at him.

He watched her walk away, despite himself. Her gray wool skirt suit was just . . . a lot.

When he flipped his attention away from the sway of Bridget Nolan's hips, he saw the note she'd left on the top of the stack.

MAKE COPIES

CHAPTER THREE

BRIDGET DIDN'T FEEL GUILTY very often. Not because she was perfect by any measure or imagining, but because she made a conscious effort not to do anything to feel guilty about. Also, she'd hated going to confession before her First Communion. Having to tell some old dude about putting her Legos right next to her brother Michael's bed so that he would step on them upon waking wasn't a picnic. He'd totally deserved it because he'd cut all the hair off her favorite Barbie, but the priest made her say a lot of Hail Marys regardless.

So she wasn't sure how to assuage the oily feeling of guilt that hit her when she saw Matt's face as they were leaving a police interview a few weeks after he started to work for her. She'd only meant to scare the police officer who came in after having misplaced a rape kit. As soon as he called her "miss," she kind of lost it and threw him a glare that would have made a less oblivious douche piss his pants.

She launched into a Julia Sugarbaker–esque speech that was wasted on the police officer, who cared about getting his collar, but not enough to ensure that the chain of custody on the evidence was unimpeachable in court. Unfortunately, the only person she succeeded in putting the fear of God into was Matt.

And, to her surprise, she felt bad about that.

When her boss had told her that she would be saddled with some rich dilettante over the summer, she'd decided to punish him for slowing her down. If he was only in this internship to waste her time, she was going to make him feel it.

She should have known when he made copies and straightened out files for weeks without complaint that she'd been wrong—or maybe quick to judge. But because changing her mind was anathema, she'd doubled down, intent on icing him out, because it wasn't like he could be *that* helpful to her for three months. He was just an inconvenience that she had to bear for the sake of getting out from under her student loan debt.

Her need to keep him compartmentalized as a burden had nothing to do with the fact that he was almost overwhelmingly attractive. It was utterly unrelated to the fact that she always knew when he was approaching because of the delicious way he smelled. Really, she couldn't help but notice that. It was different from the antiseptic, almost hospital-like scent of the office.

She shouldn't be thinking about the way he smelled at all. But if she had to think about it, it should be reminding her that he smelled like a rich guy—one who never had to sweat for his dinner. Unlike her dad and oldest brother. Even if Matt Kido weren't completely off-limits, he would not be the kind of guy you could cuddle up and eat atrocious junk food with at the end of a long week juggling twenty cases. He was the kind of guy who attended galas and would expect any woman on his arm to know which fork to use.

Someone not at all like Bridget.

Despite knowing that Matt was the last man for her—even if she wasn't off men—sometimes she caught herself staring at the way his lips and throat moved as he talked. She wasn't in danger of asking to lick his dimple—the one that popped out when he was laughing about something with the other interns coming back from grabbing coffee from the cart outside—not at all.

Since she wasn't in danger of becoming obsessed with him in a way she hadn't been obsessed with anyone since the kiddie-pool incident when she was four, it couldn't hurt anything to ask him if he wanted to have a drink with her.

She absolutely wasn't palms-sweating nervous as she approached his desk and he was packing a notebook into his beat-up leather messenger bag.

"Do you have plans tonight?" She didn't mean to sound breathless, but she most definitely sounded breathless.

He looked up with wide eyes, and she almost walked it back. Or asked him to stay and file something. But his face changed and softened when he met her gaze. As though he saw her nervousness and responded to it. "Probably just going to get a pizza and drink a couple of beers on my patio."

It sounded so normal, like a summer evening she'd like to have with a man who definitely wasn't him. Someone who might be for her. She looked down at her hands, chickening out as the seconds ticked away.

"Did I miss some important bit of filing?" There was a hint of humor in his tone.

She shook her head and met his gaze again, careful not to tilt her head in a way that could be interpreted as flirting. *This* was why she needed to keep him at a distance. The last thing she needed was him running back to his parents and telling them that she was a dirty old lady hitting on her interns. Or for him to think that she thought she could flirt her way into the fellowship.

She needed to maintain professionalism. They could have a professional drink, where she would ask him professional questions. And she certainly wouldn't touch him unprofessionally—like the way she wanted to personally investigate whether his mouth tasted as good as it looked.

"No, I was just wondering if you had time for a drink." There went the breathy voice again.

For the first time that summer, his dimple popped in reaction to something she said. "I'd love to."

"I mean . . . I just think that since you're missing out on all the lunches and fun summer things at a big firm . . . the least I can offer you is a cheap beer at a dive bar." She needed to make sure that he didn't think she was asking him out on a date. That wouldn't do.

But he winked at her, and it definitely felt like sparks hit her skin when he did that. "I would love a beer at a dive bar."

AGAINST HER BETTER JUDGMENT, they went to Dooley's. Chances were that Chris would not be there. He was mostly likely at his office until the wee hours, doing very important work defending a big corporation doing awful big-corporation things, like dumping plutonium into schoolchildren's water.

But there wasn't a more authentic Irish dive bar in all of the South Side of Chicago. Patrick and Chris's great-grandfather had founded the place, and the dark mahogany bar, lovingly maintained booths, and stained-glass windows held a huge amount of history. Dooley's was basically her second home.

She'd spent summers during college slinging beers from behind the counter after spending the days doing admin work for her dad's contracting company. It had been convenient to work there, because she and Chris could always sneak off to the supply closet for a quickie if things were slow.

It was a bad idea to be here, but she didn't want to take Matt to some other dive bar. This place, where she had so much history with the only man she'd ever been in love with, would force her to behave. It would remind her of the connections and complications that she didn't want anymore.

Being here with a guy who very inappropriately made her heart race would remind her with every strain of Irish music from the ancient sound system that she couldn't let herself fall in love again. Or even in lust.

She definitely hadn't brought Matt here in hopes that Chris would find out that she'd moved on and might be a little less smug about his flavor of the week or month or whatever when she had to spend a whole weekend with him in Vegas in a couple of months.

Mr. Dooley had mostly retired. He came in every once in a while and hollered at the manager and bartenders his sons had hired after his second heart attack. But he was mostly at home, cussing at the housekeeper his sons had also hired after their mother passed.

To her surprise, Chris's older brother, Father-as-in-priest Patrick Dooley, was behind the bar. Despite the fact that she now hated his younger brother with the chill of a thousand dead suns, she couldn't help but smile seeing Patrick. As much of a fixture in her upbringing as Chris, he'd always felt like another big brother. Only, he was always nice to her, and patient. And he always listened when she had a problem. It helped that she hadn't wasted a dozen years of her life on him.

She loved him, and a small pang of grief that he'd never be her real family hit her.

"Patrick," she called out with a wave as she and Matt sidled up to the bar. The place was middling busy, but he wasn't filling any beers at that moment.

"Kiddo!" Patrick's face lit up, and he waved them over.

As they approached the bar, Patrick filled a pint glass with a dark lager, her usual. Matt surprised her by saying, "I'll have what she's having. Thank you."

"Good taste." Patrick had an inconvenient knack for seeing things that other people didn't want him to see. For years, she'd taken his "What are you doing with my idiot brother?" comments as a joke because they were so good-natured. Only after the breakup had she realized that Patrick was seriously befuddled about what she'd been doing with his idiot brother. So when Patrick said "good taste," Bridget knew that Patrick was complimenting more than Matt's taste in beer. He was complimenting him for being in here with her.

In retrospect, Bridget should have clarified that this wasn't a date, that she was just bringing her intern out for a casual beer. But as soon as he put down their drinks, Patrick disappeared to help other customers. Plus, if Chris found out that she'd been here with a guy as ridiculously good-looking as Matt, so be it.

"Who's that guy?" Matt's question, the tone of it, surprised her.

He sounded almost—*jealous*. She should not have enjoyed the fact that Matt was maybe, possibly, jealous of attention on her from another man. He was her *intern*. If only continually reminding herself of that actually worked.

Bridget let out a laugh. "*Father* Patrick Dooley. I've known him since I was a kid."

"Oh?" Matt looked relieved, and the secret part of her that knew she was lying to herself about not being attracted to him thrilled at the idea that he had in fact been jealous.

"I dated his brother for over a decade." She shouldn't have said it, shouldn't be sharing her dating history with Matt. "It's been over for a while now."

"And I assume we're at his family's bar?" One of Matt's brows quirked up. Shit, he was going to think that they were here to make Chris jealous.

"Yes. But he won't show up." She took a sip of her drink. "And it's the best dive in town. Promise that's why I brought you here."

Matt smiled at her. He didn't believe her. But before she could go on trying to reassure him, he waved at her face and said, "You have a little . . ."

She swiped at her upper lip. "Did I get it?"

He shook his head. Before she could swipe again, he reached out a thumb and ran it across her top lip. She could have sworn at that moment that her heart stopped. She'd been very careful not to touch him, and he'd just gone and *done it*.

Once she'd brushed against his shoulder as they made their way through a scrum in the courthouse. Her shoulder had felt as though it were on fire. She'd touched it on and off the whole day.

After that, no touching. Until now.

"Foam." It felt as though he was twinkling at her. Now that they weren't in the office together, something felt like it had twisted and loosened. Instead of her intern, it was so easy to see him as a man she would be hopelessly attracted to—if she allowed herself to do that kind of thing anymore.

She tried to remind herself where he came from—a whole different world. Tried to remind herself that his shoes probably cost more than her first car, and that he was going to tell his parents—the ones who held her financial future in the balance—if she did anything unprofessional.

She wiped the spot he had touched again, and he smirked. "I got it all."

"Um, thanks." Time to change the subject. "So . . . what made you decide to spend the summer with us?"

That got her a dimple, and she instantly regretted the question. "Is this a very belated job interview?"

She shook her head. "No, I'm just curious. You could have gone to a firm, worked on Capitol Hill. But you decided to come to Cook County. It's an odd choice."

"Can I tell you a secret?" Jesus, he made that sound like flirting, and flirting was the last thing she needed right now. His secrets were not for her.

Still, she nodded, hoping he would tell her that he secretly wanted to slip out of the bar and do all manner of filthy things to her. That would be delicious.

"I broke up with my girlfriend a few days before we were set to start at the same firm." He actually blushed, and she found it adorable. "And it had the bonus of irking my parents."

"So mature." She took another long gulp, needing to cool off and remember that he was definitely a dilettante—not her type. And he was off-limits at that. "So why special prosecutions?"

"You tell me." Turning things around on her. He was going to be a very good lawyer when he was older and not a punk kid trying to piss off his rich parents.

"*Law and Order: SVU* was my after-school babysitter for a while."

Matt laughed again, bigger this time. It sounded like music to her, and it did nothing to assuage her growing fascination with him.

"Why are you laughing?"

He sobered. "You knew it was nothing like that going in, right?"

"Of course. By the time I got to law school, I realized that every case wasn't going to be as satisfying as an episode. First of all, none of the detectives we work with are Olivia Benson. And second, a lot of the worst people have the most money and can buy their way out of getting prosecuted."

Matt looked pained. "That seems like a dig."

Bridget's face heated. She hadn't meant it that way and didn't want to hurt Matt's feelings. She was trying to reverse any damage she'd done by hazing him for the past few weeks. "It's not. I mean . . . at first when they told me who you were, I worried that you weren't going to take this seriously. I misjudged you."

He nodded and took a sip of his beer. She watched his throat work over the drink, and her face heated even more. This was the first and last time she'd hang out with him outside the office. Without the reminder of her desk and the antiseptic office smell, there was no way she could keep herself under control. She had to stop lying to herself about that.

"I mean, it's totally legit that you would think I was an asshole," he finally said. "I think I'm an asshole half the time."

"You're not an asshole." The oily, guilty feeling was back. He really didn't deserve all the shit she'd given him over the past couple of weeks.

"But you thought I was?" His voice held good humor, and he ran his tongue over his bottom lip. And he was kind of too much for her.

She'd never felt this way about a person before. Of course, she'd been attracted to people before. But never had she had this intense awareness of a person other than Chris. And at the end, that had faded into anger and resentment. Nothing like the way she was feeling now—as if there were sparklers on fire underneath her skin. Being around Matt made it hard for her to stay still.

It had never occurred to her that she might feel that way again.

She controlled everything, including herself. And she never imagined that her pledge to focus on her own life and priorities would end with her losing control and humping her intern because he smelled so good and his smile made her skin flush. Ironically, focusing on her career might be her downfall.

"I just—" Oh, for fuck's sake. Being this inarticulate was really off-brand. "You have no good reason to be here—your grandfather was a senator. Your parents are, like, legit captains of industry. I figured you either wanted to polish up your family's reputation or had done something warranting a summer of banishment."

"And you changed your mind?" He lifted his beer. "What did I do that made you think I'm all right?"

"I didn't say you were all right." She pointed a finger at him, unable to keep herself from flirting. "I just figured out that you weren't a total shithead."

"Not a total shithead. I'll take it." He tapped her beer with his own, and she couldn't keep the smile off her face.

"It's a high compliment coming from me."

"I guess you wouldn't say the same nice things about your ex."

Talking about Chris wouldn't get them anywhere. "I don't want to talk about him."

"So, it's over?" He sounded a little too happy about that, and she had to extinguish the strain of hope behind his words.

"It's over, and I'm done with dating."

"Seriously?" He looked her up and down, and she caught him. To his credit, he blushed at getting caught. "I mean . . . you're a catch. Why would you give up on dating?"

"I'm focused on my job." She shrugged. "You know what kind of hours I work. Like, I don't even have time to date. Or, given the kinds of cases I catch—like the one we interviewed that cop about today—why would I ever want to date? Right after Chris and I broke up, I did go out on a few dates, but I found myself casing the exits."

He looked down at his beer. "I hear you. But you could work any kind of case you want."

"Well, I don't want to work drug cases."

"You don't?" He looked surprised.

"I hated putting people away for stupid shit that only hurt them—like drug possession. Mostly, those defendants needed treatment. Before the new state's attorney came in, there wasn't a real diversion program. And there's no drug treatment in prison."

Matt raised his brows and gave her another long, assessing look. "Now you've surprised me."

"Really? How so?" As far as Bridget was concerned, she was incapable of surprising anyone. She lived by a routine and never diverted from it—this evening excluded; the last time she surprised anyone, it had spelled the end of her relationship with Chris. And that had just been a conversation over a surprise chicken dinner. In her book, surprises were dangerous.

"Well, I just figured you for a hard-core, tough-on-crime type."

"I can see why you'd think that because I'm a white girl from the South Side. It would track." It seemed that they had both misunderstood each other.

"Yeah, sort of." He paused. "I'm sorry I misjudged you."

"Apology accepted." An awkward silence stretched between them. "And I'm sorry, too."

"Listen," he surprised her by saying, and she jumped. "How about we start over?"

"How so?" She hoped he wasn't going to shift this into creep territory now that she'd softened up a little bit around him.

"I'd like to use this summer to learn from you. It might have started out with me trying to avoid my ex-girlfriend and buck my parents' keeping an eye on me at all hours, but I really admire what you do."

"I can probably trust you to do more than filing for the rest of the summer."

He then made a raise-the-roof gesture that was so deeply dorky she couldn't help but giggle. "Seriously, that calls for another round." He motioned Patrick over.

"Another?" Patrick looked entirely too pleased to see her giggling and ordering a drink with someone he thought was her date. But she'd straighten that out later.

"One for me, and one for the lady," Matt said. Patrick took their pint glasses and went to grab them fresh ones—only VIP treatment for her at Dooley's. "And what do you want? You're way too smart and talented to stay a staff attorney."

Looking back, she'd regret saying it, but Matt had gotten under her skin. "I want to pay off my student loans, and then I'll think about it."

"My family has a fellowship—"

"I know." She bit her lip. "I applied for it last year." She really didn't want to talk with him about this right now. It made her feel even more guilty about the way she'd treated him, and she didn't want it to seem like she was trying to get an edge.

"And you didn't get it?" He looked perplexed.

Bridget shrugged. "Lots of deserving applicants."

"I might be able to help with that," Matt said.

"I couldn't ask you to do that." She shook her head. "My boss saddled me with you as an inducement for a recommendation."

"And you like me now despite that?"

"Don't get a big head. I never said I like you." The smile on her face belied the fact that she was trying not to inflate his ego.

"So, you teach me some stuff, and I put a good word in with your boss and my parents." Matt leaned in, and she should have known the kind of trouble his next words would get her into. "And after the summer is over . . ."

"And after the summer is over, we stay friends." She couldn't give him any sort of hope. For one thing, she wasn't available for any other kind of relationship. And she wouldn't be right for Matt even if she wasn't done with love.

For another thing, the way Matt made her body feel out of control and shaky wasn't safe. She could never get involved with someone who made her feel that way. It was just way too big. Her more muted attraction to Chris had almost been soul destroying. Even a fling with someone as potent as Matt was to her senses would burn her life to the ground.

"I was thinking more along the lines of—"

"Pen pals?" She could keep the reaction she'd get to an e-mail from Matt under wraps. He would never know how she felt if he couldn't see her face-to-face. "I'd be good with pen pals."

"If my only options are pen pals or friends—"

"They are." She sounded much more firm on the issue than she felt.

"Then I guess we're going with friends." He held up his glass.

She clinked her fresh beer with his. "Friends."

When he reached over and wiped her second foam mustache of the evening—even before that—she knew it was lie. But a lie she would have to keep up for the rest of the summer.

CHAPTER FOUR

Two months later

JUDGE DICKERSON WAS AN asshole on the best of days, and this was not the best of days. It wasn't just that he tried to look down her top every time they had a sidebar during hearings; it was that he all but announced that he thought that most survivors of sexual assault were just making shit up before hearing every one of her cases. He was a cranky old misogynist, and Bridget wished that the pack of cigarettes he smoked every day would do him in before this case went to trial.

But unless that happened over the weekend—the weekend she was supposed to be spending in Las Vegas for her brother and Hannah's combined bachelor and bachelorette party—she was going to be standing here on Monday, hoping her complaining witness didn't decide that she couldn't face her rapist in open court.

And she really didn't want that to happen. Matt, the intern she definitely had not been lusting after for three months, would lose the only case they'd been able to get an indictment on. He was the most diligent—and frankly gifted—of the interns, and she really wanted him to have a positive experience in this office so that he would put in a good word on her fellowship, and maybe stay in touch after he went back to school.

Although, if she was being honest with herself, having to see him every day was excruciating. The way he wore a suit should be fucking outlawed. Multiple times, she'd nearly pulled a muscle in her neck trying to avoid checking him out—even after they'd agreed that they would just be friends. But she'd held fast to her professional image. Just to be safe, she hadn't asked him any personal questions. Not even a "How was your weekend?" since they'd had drinks. He probably thought she was kind of a bitch or had a personality transplant. But that was better than him thinking she was a pervy old lady.

"Now, if I just gave continuances out like lollipops, cases would never get tried." Judge Dickerson spoke, and her stomach dropped. "And the defendant deserves a speedy trial under the US Constitution. You are aware of the US Constitution, aren't you, Miss Nolan?"

She didn't know why it pissed her off so much that he used "Miss" instead of "Ms." But it was the punctuation on his condescension that almost loosed her temper. That and the fact that it was in front of Matt. Though she'd never be able to date him—or get naked with him like she'd been thinking about nonstop since they'd had drinks at the beginning of the summer—she wanted him to think highly of her. She craved his admiration as though it would stand in for any romantic feelings he might have had if she wasn't significantly older than him, and his boss for the summer.

"Yes, Your Honor. But I have a family event this weekend that I can't change. The state needs an additional three days to prepare its arguments." She knew the defendant's very expensive lawyers were rushing this trial because they knew the victim was wavering. Mary Louise had been employed by a commodities trading firm and had been working late when the CEO of that firm pushed her into a dark hallway and assaulted her.

Even though she'd done everything she could to preserve evidence and headed to the hospital for a kit right after the attack, her former boss had the most expensive firm in town doing everything they could to intimidate her.

And it just happened to be the firm that Chris worked for. So opposing counsel likely knew that she had plans that weekend because Chris had shared those plans. For all she knew, Chris had wanted them to oppose the continuance so that she would have to cancel and he wouldn't have to look at her while he got cozy with shot girls for three days.

"Is it a funeral, Miss Nolan?"

"No, Your Honor." She wasn't about to tell him that she'd been planning on going to Vegas for the weekend. That would leave the old lech with images of her in pasties, like a showgirl. Which would probably give him a heart attack, which would be a good thing. She shook her head slightly and shivered at the thought. Still not worth it.

"Then I'll see you bright and early on Monday." Judge Dickerson slammed the gavel down.

DURING HIS ENTIRE INTERNSHIP, Matt hadn't seen Bridget with so much as a hair out of place. So when she nearly growled when his dad's creepy golf buddy Mick Dickerson denied her continuance, he knew something was up. She'd been the consummate professional the entire time she'd been his boss. Except for that one time they'd had beers. He would never let on how often he thought about how soft her skin had been when he'd wiped that foam off her lip.

He'd thought that was the beginning of an actual friendship, and he'd invited her out for drinks the following week. Although they hadn't regressed to the point where she saddled him with copying and filing, she made it clear that they were more friendly work colleagues than actual friends.

Other than the fact that she had an ex-boyfriend—with whom things were definitely over with and that she didn't date—he didn't know anything about her outside of how hard she worked and what he'd been able to glean from scrolling through her sparse Instagram feed—that she had two brothers, liked to cook, and had a wide-open smile that she didn't show at work.

Oddly, the not knowing had made her even more compelling. When he'd first started working with her, trying to keep up with his cases had been like drinking water from a fire hose. He could stop thinking of her now and then.

But now that his internship and the work were winding down, it was harder to ignore the spark he felt whenever he was in the same room as her. She'd never given any indication that she felt the same way, so he knew he had to let it go. The less she gave of herself, the more he wanted to know. He'd never been that guy who liked the chase before, but the puzzle of Bridget Nolan had infected his brain. And he knew that leaving after the internship—which ended tomorrow—wasn't going to cure him.

That was why he'd decided to shoot his shot after his internship was over. He'd tell her how he felt about her—just laying it all on the table. Then he'd ask her out and politely accept her certain "no."

When they got out into the hallway, he struggled to keep up with her. Though he didn't know any facts about her life, he knew what she was like when she was frustrated. She'd never yelled at him; he'd been very careful not to give her any reason to. But when a judge did something that she felt was unfair or a cop was rude to one of her complaining witnesses, the anger seemed to snap off of her like a force field. She became an avenging angel when it came to doing the right thing by survivors, and it was about the hottest thing Matt had ever seen.

Not that he would ever say that. Not this week.

"Hey." He tried to keep his voice level, but it was hard because her being angry made him angry. The way Mick had talked to her made him angry. "What's wrong?"

She stopped in the middle of the hallway and turned to him. For the first time since they'd met, her eyes didn't look like the open sea on a cloudy day. They were soft and wet, and she appeared to be at her edge. He didn't know what to do with that, so he just stayed still.

After a deep breath, she said, "I'm supposed to go out of town this weekend for some wedding stuff for my brother."

"I'm sorry."

She waved her hand at him. "You didn't know."

"It's only Thursday afternoon." If they pushed it, they could have the opening and closing statements prepared and a plan for cross-examining the defense witnesses done by the end of the day tomorrow. She'd been doing this so long, it was like second nature.

"But we should be interviewing Mary Louise and prepping her all weekend." The complaining witness had been making noises about not wanting to go to trial during their last call, and they both knew she was wavering. Matt didn't blame her.

"We could do that tomorrow and stay in touch with each other over e-mail, so you can go to your—thing." Since Matt would never be her boyfriend, he could at least be the most helpful intern in the history of interns.

"It will probably mean an all-nighter tonight and maybe tomorrow." At least she sounded a little bit hopeful now.

"We can do that." In fact, getting to spend time alone with her sounded really great. He knew nothing would happen between them, but he still wanted to spend as much time looking at her as possible in the next week.

She sighed, clearly not as excited about the prospect of doing overnights with him as he was with her. "I have to stop at my dad's place before going back to the office." The idea of getting to see where she grew up excited him. "You don't have to come."

"No problem. I'll drive."

OUT OF THE CORNER of her eye, Bridget looked at Matt driving. She'd perfected the move over the months they'd spent together. There was a snap, crackle, pop of chemistry that filled the car, and she regretted agreeing to let him accompany her to her dad's place. She'd never brought a guy home, other than Chris. And that hadn't been bringing anyone home, but more of a shift in the dynamic with a guy who had practically lived between their houses. There'd never been another guy she'd even thought about bringing home.

She needed to break the news that she was probably going to miss the weekend trip, and she knew her dad would be more sympathetic to it than Hannah. In person seemed like the best idea. The last thing she needed was Hannah storming her office in response to a text saying she couldn't come. She'd gotten her work ethic from her dad. It had driven Chris crazy that she'd never been interested in playing hooky or lying around all weekend, but that just wasn't how Nolans operated. And out of the Nolans, her father was the most nose grinding. He would get it and tell everyone else to keep their fool mouths shut and leave her alone to get work done.

She felt a flash of embarrassment as Matt pulled into her neighborhood. Although she'd deliberately tried to ignore his background since deciding that he didn't totally suck, it was obvious that everything he wore was expensive. Bridget's family had been upper-middle-class for her whole life. Although her mother had a fancy job, it wasn't the kind that came with a lot of money. Her father and brother ran a contracting company, so their family wealth had seen drastic ups and downs over the decades.

Still, her father owned the house she directed Matt to, and Sean Nolan had made sure she graduated from law school with as few loans as possible—given that she'd gone to law school during an economic downturn and one of her dad's lean periods. She could mostly afford to live on a public servant's salary for the twenty-plus years that she'd spend paying them off. But she didn't come from forty-thousand-dollar-watch money.

She took off her seat belt. "You don't have to come in."

Matt smirked, and everything below her waist turned to jelly. "You embarrassed to be seen with me?"

More like the other way around. "No, but my family is a lot." And she hadn't brought a guy home—even a strictly platonic guy—

since Chris had dumped her. Even if Matt wasn't on-fire hot and obviously eligible, her family would make assumptions about him.

"I like a lot." He smiled again, and she was sure she wouldn't be able to get out of the car on her boneless legs.

"Your funeral."

"You could probably get a continuance that way."

She laughed at that.

CHAPTER FIVE

OH, HELL YES. MATT was finally going to get more information about Bridget. He might never get to touch her in the very non-platonic way that he wanted to touch her, but he just might get to know her. And that was almost as good. Although spending time with Bridget around other people was bound to be difficult. He had enough trouble training his face not to do a sappy puppy-dog thing whenever he looked at her. It would be all the more difficult if he knew more about her. Like where she grew up and how she interacted with her family. *Worth the risk.*

He liked the trimmed lawn and the neat brick house. It looked so *normal.* So far from what he'd grown up with. The back of his neck was damp with sweat as they approached the door to her childhood home, and not only from the August heat.

Before she fit her key into the door, she said, "My parents were divorced for like twenty years, and now they're back together. It's weird, and we don't talk about it because we're Irish. We don't talk about a lot of things—race, religion, politics, and sports now that we have a Notre Dame–Michigan rivalry in the house. We save it all up and yell at each other once a year over the holidays. And then we pretend that it's just about the food." The words came out in a rush, and Matt wanted to reach out and pat her on the back. Like always, he stopped himself. It wouldn't be appropriate. Why was she so nervous?

"It's okay." Maybe sharing something about his fucked-up family would make her feel better. "My parents are still married, but I've seen them kiss maybe twice."

"Count yourself lucky. Now that they're back together, we might be walking into some grossness."

"It'll only be gross for you. I don't know them at all."

She looked back over her shoulder, and her mouth twisted with a hint of humor. Just a little bit of her Instagram smile. His insides rioted with the need to touch her. The need to have her want him to kiss her. "Trust me, it will be just as gross for you."

They entered the house, which was brighter than he expected it to be. As much as he wanted to linger at the wall of photos, he followed Bridget toward the back of the house. When they got to the kitchen, an older couple were sitting at the dine-in table, next to each other.

When he looked at her mother, he saw where Bridget got the eyes and the cheekbones. The man, presumably Bridget's father, stood up and eyed Matt warily.

"Mom, Dad, this is Matt Kido." Both of them extended their hands for him to shake.

"Mrs. Nolan," he said as he shook the older woman's hand. "It's a pleasure to meet you."

"It's Molly, please. Mrs. Nolan was my mother-in-law." She

pulled a face, which endeared her to Matt. Like Bridget, there was something inherently genuine about Molly.

Bridget's father tried to crush all the bones in Matt's hand, and he barely kept a grimace off his face. "Mr. Nolan."

The other man grunted.

"Dad, he's my intern. Could you not break his hand?" Bridget sighed. "We have a lot to do this weekend."

"But you can't miss the party." Molly sounded as though it was a personal affront.

Bridget ignored her. "Can I get you a sparkling water, Matt?"

He nodded at Bridget. "Sure." Although he would have understood if she'd wanted to leave, he liked seeing how her family interacted. They were so different from his. When his family was all alone, they were normal. But because of who they were and the fact that people always wanted something from them, they had to be more careful in the presence of outsiders.

"Take a seat," Mr. Nolan grunted.

"Call him Sean," Molly said as he did so. "So, you're an intern with the state's attorney's office?" He felt the woman sizing him up. From his research—and after the first day at the office, he'd done research—he'd found out that she was a curator at the Museum of Contemporary Art. She probably knew his parents, but he wasn't about to make the connection for her. A connection with his family wouldn't do anything to further the cause of Molly continuing to like him. His parents were, technically, part of the problem, even though they were passable philanthropists—mostly for the tax write-offs.

"Yes." He cleared his throat. "I'm going into my third year at the University of Chicago."

"And you didn't want to go to a firm?" Sean Nolan asked.

Bridget put a glass of sparkling water with a slice of lime on the table and sat down next to him. "Matt's not a money-grubbing jackass like Chris."

He'd never heard her speak quite so harshly, and she'd let slip a bit of a South Side accent. He liked it. But he also realized that he knew even less about her than he'd thought. Everything about her at the office was a façade. And that made him sad at the same time that he wanted to get to know her after he was done being her intern.

The front door opened and loud voices drifted in—two men and one woman. All three walked into the kitchen, and Matt figured that now was as good a time as any to meet Bridget's entire family. She caught his gaze and rolled her eyes at him.

He stood up and shook hands with both her brothers as she introduced them. Luckily, neither of them seemed to be as irked by his existence as their father had been. And Bridget's future sister-in-law, Hannah, looked downright hopeful about his presence.

HANNAH NEEDED TO WIPE that fucking twinkle out of her eye. Bridget recognized and feared that twinkle. That twinkle meant trouble. Her future sister-in-law was like her Frenchie with a bone when she got a bright idea in her head that resulted in a twinkle in her eye.

"Matt's my intern." Bridget moved toward the door. "And we have to leave."

"You're not even going to stay for dinner? It'll be so nice that we're all together." Bridget's mother sounded pained, even though they hadn't had a family dinner for two decades before last year. All of a sudden they were a family again? "And your nice young man is certainly starving."

Bridget shot a look at Matt that hopefully said, *Let's get out of here before she just up and adopts you.* On the other hand, an evening with her family might leave him not caring about his parents who never kiss.

She nearly sang with relief when Matt looked everyone in the eye and said, "We really do have a long night ahead of us, and I'm good with takeout." In that moment, he was her knight in shining armor. Though he seemed weirdly excited to stay up all night working on the case, she wasn't in a position to question it right now.

"And you're sure you're going to skip the weekend?" Hannah asked, pouting at Bridget, which prompted another eye roll. She was going to sprain something if her family didn't cut it out.

Though her brothers might be okay with her missing Las Vegas—because they knew Bridget would spend the whole weekend trying to get them to take stupid drunken pictures—she knew Hannah wouldn't let her off the hook quite so easily. Before she could protest, Bridget said, "Yeah, we have to work on this sexual assault case. It's important to get justice for the victim."

Her future sister-in-law had to understand that.

Hannah opened her mouth, closed it, opened it, and said, "You'll be working all weekend? With Matt?" She didn't look upset at that idea at all. In fact, Bridget detected a subtle eyebrow waggle.

Bridget narrowed her gaze at her future sister-in-law, who apparently had a death wish. "Yes, because I know how to live."

Hannah just shrugged. Apparently, she thought that prepping for a sexual assault trial with an intern she supervised was a recipe for romance. Bridget shook her head while Hannah mouthed, "Call me."

Her family had already been insufferable. Growing up mostly with three men who had pictures next to the definition of "dude" was bad enough. Now her mother was back in the picture and ready to make up for the time she'd missed out on parenting teenage Bridget. And she had a matchmaking future sister-in-law.

Matt chose that moment to shoot another devastating smirk her way. "Gino's East?"

Fuck. Maybe Hannah had the right idea, and he really was perfect.

CHAPTER SIX

MATT HAD NEVER BEEN the kind of guy who partied so hard that he often woke up disoriented, not knowing where he was. It had happened maybe once or twice when he'd wanted to get in trouble with the proctors at boarding school so his parents would pay him a bit of attention during term breaks. But he hadn't pulled an all-nighter in years.

And he'd certainly never woken up on a couch as ratty as the one in Bridget's office, which had been there long before her tenure at the state's attorney's office. So waking up to her banging her office phone against the cradle over and over again, the sound like a crack of thunder in the tiny office, had him sitting straight up. Mindless of the crick in his neck, he stood up ready to fight someone. Her obvious distress made his chest ache in a way he couldn't examine right then.

She'd been up all night, her stamina lasting long past his. It was sort of edifying to see her normally sleek hair disheveled and the dark circles under her eyes. He'd previously been under the impression that she was totally unflappable. She had this distinct air of not needing anything from anyone, which he recognized right away, because he'd worn that attitude himself for a long time. When he still bought into his parents' bullshit worldview.

At the same time, concern rushed through him. He wasn't sure when it had happened, but seeing Bridget in distress—however subtle the signs of that distress might be—made him deeply uncomfortable. That need to try to swoop in and take all of her stress away wasn't very progressive, and he tried to tamp it down whenever it came up. He knew for a fact that she wouldn't appreciate it. She'd probably fire him if she thought he was too far up in her business.

It didn't even make sense. She wasn't his girlfriend, and she was never going to be his girlfriend.

The only thing that would be worse than watching Bridget lose her shit right now would be to be cast out of her orbit prematurely. His internship was over today. Without this case to work on, she would send him home, and she would never see him again. He had to drink in as much of her as possible because he was pretty sure she wouldn't give him the time of day if he wasn't somehow connected to work.

At that moment, she was still banging away with the phone. Knowing that she'd regret smashing it to pieces, he approached her and took it out of her hands, setting it on the cradle. Feeling particularly brazen, he took both of her hands in his and squatted in front of her. He ignored how touching her made him feel.

She met his gaze, and her eyes were glassy and wet. One tear escaped, and he wanted to wipe it away. He couldn't.

"What happened?"

"She . . . she decided not to testify." Her voice was smoky and ragged, and it turned him on, despite himself. "Someone must have gotten to her."

Matt's guts twisted. He wasn't sure that he wouldn't have thrown everything on the desk onto the floor if he was in Bridget's position. She might have this reputation in the office as an unstoppable badass, but it was only because of how deeply she cared about her cases and the complaining witnesses she worked with.

"Do you think talking to her would help?"

"No." Bridget's voice broke on a sob. "She hung up on me and said she was changing her number."

Matt rested his hip on the side of Bridget's desk, ignoring her raised eyebrows. Even ticking her off a little by casually occupying her space was better than the crying. He picked up her phone, and the dial tone was miraculously still online. Then he pressed redial and got a message that the number was no longer in service.

The complaining witness had worked fast. He met Bridget's gaze and he knew they were thinking the same thing.

"He got to her and paid her off." Bridget's words were flat and full of scorn. "Rich assholes always get away with this shit."

Matt tried not to flinch. He was a rich asshole born to a long line of rich assholes. Even though he was pretty sure that his crush on her was obvious, he hadn't been too much of a dick about his family money.

He wasn't stupid enough to hate being rich—not when it opened so many doors and gave him so many options. But he didn't like that the whole point of being wealthy, for his parents at least, had been to stay rich. He knew that his father's colleagues, if not his father himself, had probably paid off people wronged by their company in the way that Mary Louise had been paid off.

Maybe working here this summer—throwing himself into it—had been his attempt at penance. But it was paltry and inadequate. It had been stupid of him to even try when there was no way that he wouldn't become exactly the kind of guy that Bridget hated—a rich asshole whose only objective in life was staying rich.

"You did your best." He was pretty sure that wouldn't comfort her. "And, hey, now you can go to your family's bachelor-bachelorette thing in Vegas."

When he said that, Bridget rolled her eyes. And he couldn't help it, but that turned him on, too. The way her emotions flashed in her pretty gray-blue eyes drove him wild. *She* drove him wild.

And without this case, he was done working for her. There was nothing stopping him from telling her how he felt about her now. Nothing except for the fact that she'd given him no indication that she felt anything but mild annoyance for him.

Bridget ran her fingers through her hair with a sigh. "The thing is, I don't want to go."

"Why not?" Her family was perfectly lovely—so much more open and friendly than his parents that he hadn't wanted to leave their neat brick house the night before. "It seems like it will be fun."

Her lips pressed together, and for a long beat he was pretty sure she was going to tell him to buzz off.

He stood, even though it hurt to stay away from her. "You don't have to tell me. It's none of my business."

She waved a hand in front of her face. "It's not that." She paused again, and he stuffed his hands in his pockets so he wouldn't reach out and move the recalcitrant strand of hair off her face. "My ex will be there and this was going to be a good opportunity to miss out on seeing him."

A hot spike of jealousy ran through him at that. Jealousy that he had no right to feel. The proprietary interest he had in Bridget and whoever she'd dated in the past wouldn't be a good look even if she was into him and he hadn't spent the whole summer as her employee. She'd made it clear that she didn't see the potential for anything romantic between them even after the summer was over. So he trained his face to stay impassive.

Still, curiosity got the best of him. "What happened with the two of you?"

She grimaced. "It's a long story . . . like since-we-were-four-and-six long story."

Even if she wanted to date him, Matt couldn't compete with that kind of history. Not that it was a competition. *You're better than this, Kido. Without your trust fund, you wouldn't even be able to compete with the guy she's been in love with since she was four.*

To his surprise, she kept talking. "It's over. Really over." She sounded unequivocal about that. "I'm just really mad that this rich fuck is going to get away with this."

It was his turn to grimace. She'd just reminded him that even with the trust fund, he wouldn't be the guy for her. And after meeting her family the night before, he understood. She needed someone who would fit into her loud, boisterous family—not some poor little rich boy who didn't really fit in anywhere.

When had he started feeling so sorry for himself? Once school was back in session, he needed to get back on the dating horse, maybe someone not in law school.

The idea of dating anyone but Bridget didn't sit well, though. And he wished they had time to figure out why that was.

"Unless . . ." Bridget's words pulled him out of his sad-sack quagmire. "Do you have plans this weekend?"

THIS IS COLOSSALLY STUPID.

He'd met her family the night before and was probably terrified of them. She was, and she'd grown up in the midst of their mess. He probably had plans with some gorgeous girl his own age—maybe even one of the other interns. At that moment, she regretted boxing him out as effectively as she had.

If she'd learned more about him, perhaps her crush wouldn't be going strong three months later. She might have learned that he had some hideous political views or was the total fuckboy that his reputation said he was. Given her experience with Chris, neither of those things would have been enough to warn her away.

On the other hand, this might be a good idea. Spending the weekend with him could get rid of some of his mystique. When he'd asked about why she and Chris had broken up, she was tempted to tell him the real reason—the reason she hadn't even shared with her own family. Not because she was ashamed of her choices. She couldn't afford the shame. But they didn't need to know all the details. Chris was still for all practical purposes part of their family, and she wasn't about to blow that up just because they weren't together anymore.

The longer Matt waited to respond, the more Bridget wanted a hole to appear in the floor under her chair and swallow her completely. She made a nervous wiping motion with her hand. She said, "Never mind—" at the same time that he said, "I have plans now, with you."

"It was really stupid of me to ask." She stood up and crossed over to the coatrack in the corner of the room, anything not to have to face him.

"I want to go. With you."

She turned around, and he smiled at her. Tingles hit her from her hairline to her toes. "Why?"

He looked down and then and up under his way-long lashes. "You haven't figured it out?"

"Figured what out?" Yeah, she'd seen the way he looked at her, and she was flattered. But that didn't mean anything. She'd enjoyed the feeling that someone other than Chris could find her attractive for the whole summer, and she'd been prepared to leave it at that—for the sake of her professional reputation.

"I like you, Bridget."

Gah! She liked the way he said her name, the way it sounded like he rolled it around in his mouth first like expensive wine. But she didn't want him to think that her asking him would have any impact on the glowing recommendation that she planned to give him.

"Nothing has to happen."

He stuck his hands in his pockets and smirked at her. "What if I'm hoping that something will happen?"

"This has nothing to do with your internship."

"My internship that's over now?" He moved closer to her, and she shifted on her feet. "Now that I don't have any cases to work on." He'd gotten in her space a lot more that morning than he had in the past. Like now that the internship was well and truly over, the invisible tether holding them apart had snapped, that magnetic polarity that had them moving away from each other had suddenly reversed.

"This would just be a favor," she said.

He shook his head. "I think you and I both know that it's more than that."

She echoed his motion, shaking her head. Some strands of hair came loose from where they were piled on her head. He smoothed one behind her ear, and she fought with all she had not to lean into his touch. They needed ground rules—and no more touching than necessary needed to be one of those rules.

"I shouldn't . . ." Even though he no longer worked for her as of this morning—she grimaced thinking about how the case had ended—it wouldn't look good for them to run off and have a weekend of debauchery as soon as it wasn't technically against office policy to do so. "It could look bad."

He sighed. "The way I see it, we're both consenting adults. I no longer work for you. And I think you're attracted to me, too."

She couldn't deny it, and he wouldn't believe her if she did.

CHAPTER SEVEN

BY THE TIME SHE met Matt at the airport, Bridget had settled down. She'd had more than an hour and a half to reconsider her rash decision to ask Matt to be her date to the weekend's festivities. She'd chewed so long on the impulse to text him and tell him to stay that she arrived at the airport before working up the courage to send the text. But something about the flush that spread across her skin when he'd looked at her and told her that this was *not a favor* stopped her.

He was waiting right in front of the curbside check-in. She got out of the car, and he grabbed her suitcase from the driver before she had a chance to.

Their hands brushed as she went for the bag's handle, and some electricity that had always been there but that she'd successfully not acknowledged ran up her arm and heated parts of her that had been cold for way, way too long. Until this summer.

And then she *saw* him. He looked . . . different somehow. He wasn't dressed differently from how he'd dressed at the office. The collar of his crisp white shirt was open, and his sleeves were rolled up. But otherwise, nothing had changed about his outward appearance. He was still drop-dead handsome.

It was something about the gleam in his eye, the smirk that made his mouth look lush and sexy, like she wanted to bite his bottom lip while she finally got to touch the silky black strands of his hair. It was as though her body knew that there were no longer any ethical or professional obligations keeping her from doing all the things to him that she hadn't let herself think about while she was his boss.

"You don't have to get that for me." Him taking her bag made this feel too much like a date. She needed to make this *less* like a date before she did something crazy like climb him like a tree and kiss him until they both suffocated on lust.

She'd never been this way before. Not with Chris, and not with any of the guys she'd had crushes on while Chris was acting like a dingus. Because if she'd felt this kind of way about someone during the decade that Chris had taken a romantic evening to mean a steak house and half-hearted thrashing on top of her, perhaps she wouldn't have stayed with him so long. She might have given in.

And Matt didn't just take her bag; he handed it to another dude and gave him stern instructions about its handling.

"He's probably just going to give it to our baggage handler," Bridget explained, though she didn't know why she needed to. "I mean, once he tags it."

Matt turned to her and smiled again in a way that told her she wasn't the boss of him anymore—and she liked it. It didn't help the tree-climbing instinct *at all*. "He's bringing it to my plane." He shrugged. "Well, my family's plane. He is our baggage handler."

The fuck?

Matt didn't react at all to the way her jaw must be dragging on the floor. He just moved her purse to the top of her shoulder from where it had slipped down the crook of her elbow. And he took his time doing it. His lips parted and she could smell his minty breath as he caressed her arm through her clothes. Bridget had to lock her knees to keep from leaning into him.

She had to remind herself that this was a fake date. She had to be strong. And she could absolutely not, under any circumstances, lean into the nape of his neck and sniff him. Highly inappropriate would not be even close to the way to describe that.

"You ready?" He pulled back, and she could just tell that he knew she'd turned the corner from her carefully cultivated indifference of how handsome he was to something more. He took her elbow and ushered her into the airport, bypassing the long ticket lines, and through some sort of expedited security check. They shuttled to an area where Bridget had never been—the hangar where private jets stood by—and up to the tiniest jet she'd ever seen.

Fear seized her. Although it looked to be in good repair, it really wasn't that much bigger than a propeller plane. Like the prop planes that went down in fiery conflagrations in the middle of suburban neighborhoods all the flipping time.

"Ouch." Matt's word snapped her out of her imaginary scenario—the one where she and Matt's corpses decorated someone's trees in Nebraska. She looked to see that she'd made a white-knuckled grab for Matt's arm.

"Sorry." She grimaced. "I can't . . ."

"Get on the plane?" Matt guessed at her anxiety, though it wasn't a hard guess. God, he probably thought she was such a plebe. He'd probably never flown commercial, and here he was. He was fine, not a scatter of limbs across a cornfield somewhere. "Listen, if you want to fly commercial, we can. We'll just get there at the same time as your family if we fly this way."

"You did this for me?" It touched something in her that he would be so thoughtful. Chris had never been thoughtful, but she needed to stop comparing him to Chris or anyone else. Despite her dogged resistance to his charms, there was really no one like Matt.

That's what made him so dangerous. He was nothing but her intern—her former intern now—and she couldn't have a crush on him. She was too old for him, anyway. Given that he had a private plane at his disposal, models in Ibiza were probably more his thing.

Shame coated her as she recalled her late-night Google searches of Matt Kido. Although she was older than him by half a decade, he was definitely more experienced than her in the dating sphere. Models, actresses, American aristocrats, all numbered among his exes according to the Internet. Naomi Chapin, his childhood friend and law school classmate, had been only the most recent.

And even though it didn't seem like he'd dated anyone over the summer, now that he was free and going back to school, the merry-go-round of women who were more attractive, and probably much nicer than Bridget, would likely resume.

He was probably just being thoughtful in hopes that she'd write him a good recommendation to whichever circuit court judge he was going to clerk with after school. That's the one thing she had over the circles he usually ran with—a recommendation from her wouldn't be tainted with cronyism.

"Should we turn around and go back to the airport?" Matt bent his knees slightly so that they were eye to eye. "It's been a while since I've flown commercial, and it would probably be good for me to remember why I hate it."

Bridget shook her head. "No, I trust you."

To her chagrin, it was true. She trusted him when he said it was safe to fly with him. It wouldn't do very well for him to kill his boss.

MATT HAD MADE AN error in judgment. He'd been trying to impress Bridget when he arranged for the family's private jet to take them to Vegas instead of to meet his parents at their beach house in Martha's Vineyard for a holiday before heading back to school.

His mother had had questions about all of it. *Is this about a girl? When can we meet her? Who is her family? She's not another model, is she? Why won't you give Naomi a second chance?*

He could probably have avoided his mother's questions by saying that it was his boss at the state's attorney's office. Although he knew that his mother would love Bridget if she got to know her, his mother should think of her as a dowdy bureaucrat until Matt convinced Bridget to be his girlfriend and introduced them properly.

Still, he'd had to suffer through a good five minutes of lecturing about not doing anything that would look bad for the family while in Vegas. Matt shook his head.

"What? Is something wrong with the plane?" Bridget's voice came from behind him. She really was worried about riding in the small plane. He'd been flying private since he was in diapers, so it sort of rolled off him. And seeing Bridget afraid of something—anything—and being vulnerable endeared her to him even more. He'd seen her tough, angry, and disappointed. But afraid was something entirely new. He didn't like it, but it gave him more of her, and he was thirsty for every swallow of her she'd let him have.

"Nothing's wrong," Matt said, trying to keep his tone reassuring. They entered the plane and the flight attendant showed them to their seats. Matt took the seat facing the back of the plane because he thought that Bridget would appreciate facing forward. That's how she liked to face everything. "I was just thinking about what my mom said when I asked to use the plane."

"Was she mad?" Bridget sat down, and she really *must* be scared of flying because she let him buckle her in. She'd let him touch her more today than he had all summer. If this kept up, he wouldn't be able to stop. One of these times he grabbed her bag or made sure she was steady and safe—like a goddamned gentleman—he was going to forget himself and kiss her.

Since he still didn't know whether she would slap him or kiss him back, he needed to not let that happen.

"Nah, she was curious."

"About me?" Bridget's eyes got big.

Matt didn't answer but handed her a glass of champagne. "Drink up."

"I haven't had anything to eat. Fair warning, it will go straight to my head."

"Do you want water instead?" Matt wasn't trying to get her drunk, even though he assumed that was part of the agenda for the weekend because—Vegas.

He started to motion for the flight attendant, but Bridget said, "No. Champagne is good."

"And I asked them to get some food . . . just meat, cheese, and fruit for the flight."

Bridget took a sip, and a wry smirk twisted her lips. It made him want to kiss her. Well, everything made him want to kiss her. He would definitely get hard if she said something sarcastic right now. "You just think of everything, don't you?"

Yep, definitely hard. To hide it, he leaned forward so that he was in her space again. So he could smell a hint of the shampoo she'd used when she was all naked and soapy in the shower not that long ago. "It's about time you noticed."

She leaned forward to meet him, and their mouths were so close that he could taste her if he turned his head a little bit. They just stayed there for a long moment, and the chemistry that had been fucking with him for months settled over her. He could see it in the glassy quality of her gaze, feel it in the speed of the tufts of champagne-scented breath against his cheek.

But he couldn't do the last thing. She had to come to him. Despite the fact that she thought it was inappropriate, in that moment he knew she was as affected by him as he was by her. But he knew her well enough that crossing the professional boundary that she imagined between them had to be her decision. If he kissed her right now, the wall would go back up—even more fortified than it had been before.

So, he waited. And breathed in the scent of her—the one he'd only had hints of all summer. He wished for her mouth until the boundaries of propriety snapped and he had to pull back for fear of seeming like even more of a perv than he actually was.

He leaned back in his seat. "The flight attendant will be out with food after we're at altitude." He winked at her, trying to seem much cooler than he actually felt. He checked his watch. "By the way, my internship is *officially* officially over . . . right now."

SHE'D ALMOST KISSED HIM. And he totally would have kissed her back. Until today, she'd thought he'd been flirting with her so that he could look good for a clerkship or to rehabilitate his family's image or because he was just a really nice guy.

But he wanted her. Her mind flipped through the possible scenarios for this weekend. If they drank together—which they would—they were going to make out at the very least. God, she missed making out. It had always been high on her list of favorite things to do, even though Chris had always seemed to tolerate it in favor of getting to his favorite parts—the ones where he squirmed and grunted on top of her and she pretended to come more than half the time.

All while lying to herself that she was lucky that someone like him wanted to be with her. And to give herself some credit, being with Chris had made her feel safe and secure when everything in her life had fallen apart.

Chris had been safe, until he wasn't.

Matt Kido was anything but safe. He lived in a world of private jets with champagne that probably cost more than one of her car payments. He probably *owned* a tuxedo. Maybe he'd gone to boarding school, joined a secret society, and had all variety of indiscretions covered up.

She didn't know because part of her had always been too afraid to ask. She'd been too intrigued by him and hadn't wanted to scratch the surface for fear of figuring out that he really was too good for her.

That had been another advantage of her relationship with Chris—he'd been inside her heart from the start and had never put her life in danger. He fit inside everything she'd thought she'd wanted. Someone like Matt could change the whole game.

It wasn't like that, though, was it? He was doing her a solid because, for some reason unknown to her, he liked her. Maybe he had a thing for authority figures and wanted to sleep with her. And Vegas represented an opportunity to get that over with. She was probably an item on his summer checklist. That was all.

Still, it would be better to get everything on the table beforehand. "Why are you doing all this for me?"

While she'd been ruminating, he'd politely taken out his phone, leaving her to her thoughts. He looked up at her words. "All what?"

"Coming with me." She motioned around with the glass of liquid courage he'd so kindly provided. "The private jet, the champagne . . ." She hesitated. "That almost-kissing-me thing that you did just a second ago."

He smiled at her, and she was dumbstruck again. He had to stop doing that. His shit-eating grin with all those straight white teeth was going to be the death of her. "I didn't almost kiss you. You almost kissed me."

She would have scoffed at him if he hadn't been totally right. It wasn't like she couldn't have pulled back at any time. So she'd just ignore it and move on. "And everything else?"

His smile faded. "To repay you."

"For what?" She was too surprised to mince her words—not that she could ever do that around Matt. "Being a bitch to you all summer?"

"I think I was the one who was your bitch." Something in the way he looked her up and down told her that their previous power dynamic—her being the boss—was as over as his internship.

And now she had to find out if he'd liked that experience enough to want to hook up with her. "So none of this actually makes sense."

"You gave me a break from being a cog in my parents' respective machines."

None of this made sense. He was a golden boy; everything he could ever want could belong to him with nothing more than a few phone calls. Why would he need a break from that? "Explain."

He scrubbed a hand through his hair, sending a few strands every which way. She wanted to smooth them, but that wasn't going to happen. It looked so silky, though. She bit her lip and balled her free hand into a fist.

"I love my parents, okay?"

Bridget nodded. She certainly understood loving her parents but not wanting her whole life tied up in their bullshit.

"But they want me to live a certain way." He grimaced. "Being a part of my family comes with certain responsibilities."

That she understood less. Her parents might have been messed up, but they'd never expected her to be anyone but herself. "I get it."

"You can't. Not really." He took a deep breath, and she waited for him to talk. For some reason, knowing this man—even a little—was vitally important to her. "It's like this . . . Between the relatives on my dad's side that came over on the *Mayflower* and the ones who came here from Japan and had a lot of things to prove, I can't let down either side by being anything less than the best at anything. And until recently, I was doing okay. I was in law school, and one of my parents was going to groom me to take over one of their companies. I was practically engaged to Naomi."

A hum of anger filled Bridget's mind at the idea of Matt marrying Naomi—whom she knew of through Hannah, whose ex was married to Naomi's cousin, Madison. Or something like that. Thinking of her with Matt—and how good they looked together— made Bridget feel dowdy and inadequate.

But thinking of how everything in Matt's life was laid out . . . Bridget couldn't imagine the pressure. She was the best because that was who she'd pushed herself to be. All the pressure was internal, and the only person she would let down if she failed was herself. And the way she'd ridden Matt all summer, thinking he was some spoiled trust-fund asshole playing at charity, probably hadn't helped.

Regret bloomed in her gut. "I'm sorry."

"For what?"

"For being so mean to you."

The smile was back—the one she might do some very stupid things to see again. "I kind of liked it."

She had the feeling that he wasn't talking about just work. It didn't take crackerjack prosecutorial instincts to get that.

"So, you're doing all of this for me because you're grateful that I was a bitch to you all summer?"

"Not exactly." He looked at her from under his lashes. Mischief personified. "I liked that you treated me like any other grunt, that you didn't expect great things from me just because of who my parents are. Who my grandparents *were*."

Not wanting to be defined by her family was definitely something she could understand. But she wasn't ready to reveal all of her bullshit to him. Wasn't sure that she could give anyone that— especially someone she wouldn't really see after this weekend. Someone who didn't fit in her life.

CHAPTER EIGHT

MATT WASN'T SURE IT was a good idea to reveal any vulnerabilities to Bridget. She was way too savvy to just let that pass without exploiting any weaknesses he revealed. Although their relationship had changed—she was no longer in a position of authority over him—he'd come to Vegas with her in hopes of turning the tables.

He hadn't been entirely honest about why he'd wanted to bring her to Vegas in his family's plane. He'd definitely hoped to relieve some of the tension between them. Sure, all of that was wrapped up in wanting to spend more time with her salt-of-the-earth family and place whatever guy who'd had the audacity to discard a creature as glorious as Bridget in check.

And he hadn't lied. He really was grateful to Bridget for giving him shit all summer. No one at either of his parents' companies would have done that. They would have let him fuck everything up then quietly cleaned up after him. They'd done that his whole life, and he was frankly tired of it.

The flight was uneventful and—more importantly—Bridget

had loosened up enough that she seemed like she kind of enjoyed it. He liked her this way, bouncing in her seat like a kid when they passed over the Rockies. She'd lose it when he brought her to his family's place in Aspen.

Shit—when had he started thinking of doing things in the winter with Bridget? That wasn't what this was supposed to be at all. He was just doing her a favor by running interference with her douchebag ex for one weekend.

Then he would go back to school, and she would go back to working one hundred hours a week without having to supervise an idiot intern.

Still, when he put his hand on the small of her back at the bottom of the steps leading to the tarmac, it felt right to be next to her. He wasn't normally a possessive dude, but he liked being next to her and wanted everyone to know. He wanted her gaze to find his across a crowded room when she needed something.

Whatever she wanted, he wanted to give her. Not that she would accept it.

BRIDGET HAD NEVER SEEN anything like how Matt was treated when they got to the hotel-casino where her family was staying. Before they'd even gotten out of the car, their luggage was whisked away, and they didn't even have to stop at a reception desk. Instead, they had a private concierge who met them at a private elevator car and led them all the way up to the penthouse.

She didn't like to think that she was susceptible to this kind of thing. The Nolans were the sort of people impressed by nothing but hard work and smarts. Still, she was kind of dazzled by the whole thing. She wondered if she would feel the same way if she was being dazzled around anyone but Matt.

Probably not.

It was as though he'd shed some sort of skin that made him seem like a regular guy as soon as he stopped being her intern. It was as though she couldn't really see him before now. And she wasn't sure she could go back to not seeing him.

Especially when he turned to her and said, "Your family's going to come up and meet us for lunch."

"But how?" When had he had time to arrange that?

"While you were freaking out about the tiny plane." So, when she'd been freaking out about almost kissing him. "I sent some e-mails and upgraded their rooms."

"That was really nice of you. Not necessary—"

He waved a hand. "Not the Douche's, though." Matt leaned over and whispered to her, though it wasn't strictly necessary. It gave her goose bumps. "They put him next to the ice machine."

That was it. She wanted to keep him. More than the almost kiss, the private plane, the champagne, the lunch, or the fact that he'd generally saved her sanity over the summer—it was the fact that he'd gotten a little petty revenge on her behalf that made up her mind.

Maybe, just for the weekend, she could forget behaving appropriately. She could pretend—in her head—that Matt was actually her date. That he was actually her next chapter rather than a hopeful yet temporary epilogue to her failures with Chris.

"You're kind of wicked." She bit her lip and his gaze dipped to her mouth. Brazen, like he wanted her.

He winked. "You have no idea."

BRIDGET'S FAMILY WASN'T ANY less overwhelming in a suite that took up most of the top floor of a shiny new Vegas hotel than they were in their little house. Adding in her ex-douche and Hannah's bestie, Sasha, the cacophony might cause a noise complaint on a lower floor.

Good thing he knew from experience that the soundproofing in the penthouse was solid.

Matt hung back, following Bridget around the room, promising himself that he would only interfere if Bridget's ex-douche got too close. As it was, he didn't like the way that Chris was looking at her, with a mix of longing and irritation.

Bridget didn't pay her ex any attention, but Matt caught her looking at him quite a few times. It made it easy for Matt to keep his promise to avoid macho posturing. He knew that would piss Bridget off, and that was the last thing he wanted to do. His only objective for this weekend was to show her a good time. That didn't mean that he didn't want to posture a little.

After all, he was just the former intern who was doing her a favor. He had nothing on the decades of history Bridget shared with Chris Dooley.

For some reason, he'd expected the guy to at least be handsome. Chris was an associate at a law firm in the Loop—one that Matt's family had employed from time to time. He was shorter than Matt, with sandy blond hair and a dad bod. Not that it mattered, but Matt hoped that Bridget liked the way he looked more than she liked the way her ex looked.

Matt was careful to hold Chris's gaze for a second too long, just to make sure the other guy registered that Matt was on to him and his smarmy smile and the way his eyes raked over Bridget. Matt wanted to tell the other dude, *Too bad you lost her*, but he knew for a fact that Bridget wouldn't appreciate that.

Still, he hadn't been able to conceal a smirk when some sort of realization crossed over the other man's face. Matt didn't think it would be that easy, but after a summer of being a grunt, he kind of liked being that rich asshole who was going to steal Chris Dooley's girl at the moment.

Matt thought Chris was going to thank him for his hospitality, but that was not what he came over to do. He should have expected him to do what he did, which was say, "How'd you meet Bridget? From what I can tell, she never leaves the office."

"Good thing I met her at her office, then."

Chris gave a pointed look at Matt's watch. "You don't seem like the type to work some dumb civil service job."

He grew up in a nonviolent home. Aside from running the odd racist kid over, the Kidos limited themselves to verbal barbs. He hadn't even been allowed to try out for the football team, because it was too violent for his parents. He didn't know how to throw a punch, and he'd never had quite the urge to do so until Bridget's ex sneered at what she did for a living.

Although Matt didn't have any right to be jealous of Chris, or any reason to think that Bridget wanted her ex back, he hated anyone thinking that her job—this thing that meant more to her than anything other than her family—was something to sneer at.

His pulse rose, and he could feel his skin heat, and before he could tell Chris to shove it, the other man said something that pissed him off *almost* as much as insulting Bridget's job. "You're Jane Kido's kid, aren't you?"

He'd done nothing to distinguish himself from his family, but he still didn't like hearing that he was just his mother's son. Especially not from this guy. So all he said was, "Jane Kido is my mother."

"How'd you meet Bridget, then?"

Matt didn't want to answer the question, but he wasn't going to lie. He didn't have anything to be ashamed of, and maybe Chris would respond with something that would give him an excuse to punch him in the jaw. "I was her intern."

The short laugh almost got him that punch. "Why on earth would you intern there? You could get in everywhere."

Matt tried to look at it from Chris's perspective. He'd come from a less privileged background than Matt, and it might never to occur to him to not want a life where all he did was sit on a growing pile of money, just screwing people over to make it grow more. Matt hadn't started out his summer with pure intentions—merely hoping to get out of seeing Naomi every day and having a job that his parents would have a hard time arguing with. But that didn't mean he was going to stand by and let Chris disparage what Bridget had chosen to do with her career.

No wonder she thought she was done with relationships if this was the guy she'd been dating.

Matt stood up straighter and looked down his nose a little bit at Chris. He wasn't going to make a scene or put the guy in his place. He wasn't the person to do that. Bridget could do that her damn self.

So he smiled and said, "You really have no idea, do you?"

"I don't know what the fuck you're talking about, man." Chris looked confused, so Matt decided to illuminate things for him.

"You really have no idea what you're missing."

Chris just gave him a shitty grin and said, "You have no idea what you're in for."

CHAPTER NINE

DO YOU THINK THEY'RE going to fight?" Hannah's question surprised Bridget. She'd been busy staring at Matt and Chris and cataloguing all their differences. It wasn't just that she found Matt more appealing aesthetically; it was that he stood straighter than Chris. His confidence shone in a way that Chris's never had—maybe because Chris had relied on her for years to prop him up.

That was the thing she'd realized when they'd broken up—both of them had been each other's only real friends, each other's only emotional outlet. The relief she felt at not having to be the sole receptacle for someone's fears, anxieties, and grief had been almost overwhelming.

Right now, she could look at Chris objectively and say she was no longer attracted to him. It hadn't been familiarity alone that begat the contempt that she felt for him—it had been overuse. She'd loved him because he was like family, until she just didn't anymore.

Hannah waved her hand in front of Bridget's face. "Earth to Bridget Nolan."

"What?" She glanced over at her ex and her fake date again, and everything looked copacetic.

Hannah gave her a look that said, *Oh you sweet summer child*, that her future sister-in-law could only get away with because she'd become such a good friend. No one looked at Bridget that way. Bridget hadn't let anyone close enough to give her that look before.

Well, Chris had. But he was firmly in her past now. Looking at him interacting with Matt only confirmed that inside her head. She'd spent months wondering how she could put things back together again—wondering if she could make the kinds of compromises that she'd need to make to be with him—before it had really sunk in that she and Chris were not going to share the life they'd planned together. At times, she'd had to white-knuckle the remote so she wouldn't reach for the phone.

Part of it was that she'd never understood *why* he'd broken up with her. She'd been shocked, and it had come out of nowhere. Just a conversation over dinner that had gone terribly wrong and left her bereft.

"When we move in together—"

Bridget's fork froze in the air over the chicken thigh she'd carved off the roast chicken that had taken her all afternoon to cook. "What do you mean?"

"When we move in together, I think the cat should move in with your dad because of my allergies."

"But I love Licorice." Bridget was bewildered, and a squeeze of the fear she'd been trying to ignore grabbed her. They'd been floating along—everything was fine—for a while now. But she'd known that things would have to change eventually. She knew Chris was allergic to cats, but the reality of having to give up Licorice was a little much.

79

"But you love me more, right?" Chris's smile made her feel nauseous. She knew that wasn't good, but she'd been trying to deny it.

She couldn't meet his gaze, but he plowed on without noticing. "I have news."

That sounded ominous. "News."

He nodded happily. "Our down payment was accepted."

"Down payment?" She was definitely going to puke. "On a house?"

"Yeah." He said it like it was no big deal.

"A house I haven't seen?"

"Bridge—it was going to sell right away."

"So, you bought a house I haven't even seen, without even calling or texting?" Her voice rose on the last word, and she could detect that Chris's mistake was slowly dawning on him.

"I mean, the schools are great in Skokie."

Bridget stood up then. "I'm not fucking moving to Skokie!"

"Calm down." And then he went back to eating his chicken.

It took a lot for Bridget to lose her temper. It was the ultimate slow burn. But, when it boiled over, it took out everything in its path. And Chris was now in its path. Just eating his chicken after blowing up her life without asking her.

"Do you know how long it takes to get downtown—from Skokie?" She tried to keep her voice calm, but it wasn't working. She knew she sounded unhinged.

"C'mon. It was only a matter of time. We were always going to do this. Now we can get married and start having babies." He explained how he'd taken all her choices away as though he was explaining the rule against perpetuities in property class. But he was similarly incomprehensible.

The man she'd been in love with since she was four years old hadn't *been in the same relationship she'd been in for a long time. And she was angry—less at him and more at herself. For a woman known and feared for her smarts and killer instincts, she'd sure been really fucking stupid. Stupid enough to believe that he really knew her. Dumb enough to ignore the fact that he never really listened to her anymore.*

Her whole future flashed before her. They'd move to the suburbs and get pregnant right after they got married. She'd go back to work after the first baby, but he'd talk her out of it after the second. After all, her paycheck would barely cover day care for one kid. And she'd hate her three hours of commuting and spending about five minutes with her kid so much that she'd probably even think it was a great idea.

So, then she'd cart her kid to lessons and other stupid shit that kids had to do to get into the right preschool in the minivan that Chris also talked her into. She'd never get to wear real clothes. Just that stretchy athleisure shit. Probably in bright colors that clashed with her hair.

And she wouldn't complain.

Because Chris would be the one paying her student loans—actually all their bills. She'd get no say. He'd have all the power. And she'd be trapped out in the suburbs, until she died from pretending to be happy or she bugged out on everything—just like her mother had.

Maybe she'd be okay. Maybe it would be relaxing to sink into the comfortable suburban beige of chain restaurants and chain barre classes. Maybe she was the luckiest girl in the world. But her racing heart and sweaty upper lip told her that it wouldn't and she wasn't.

"*When were you going to show me the house where you expected me to start popping out your fatheaded babies?*"

He suddenly became very interested in his chicken thigh—the one she wanted to jam down his throat, bones and all. "*Seriously, calm down.*" *He took a bite.* "*Chicken's great.*"

"*I hope you enjoy it.*"

She must have sounded as stone-cold as she felt because he looked up at her then. She wasn't about to back down on this. And she wasn't going to cry in front of him. Not when that might let him see her weakness. Not when that might let him see that she wasn't completely sure that she was going to break up with him. That wouldn't do. She was going to make him break up with her, and she wasn't going to let him see her cry.

"*What's wrong?*" *Poor baby. He sounded confused now.*

"*You tell me, babe.*"

"*I don't understand why you're so upset about this.*" *He waved a hand.* "*We're getting too old to just date.*"

"*Says you. Try again.*" *Bridget was still standing up and wouldn't be finishing her dinner. She doubted that she'd be able to smell roast chicken after this without wanting to throw up. Why couldn't he have ruined one of the things she made him that she didn't like? She could live without smothered pork chops or chicken-fried steak.*

"*You don't want to move in with me? You don't want to get married? Have kids?*" *Chris tossed his fork on the plate.* "*Damn it, Bridge.*"

She had to suppress the urge roll her eyes. He was going to play this like an overdramatic baby man. That was his signature move whenever they got in a fight. Like the time he'd wanted to hike the Inca Trail over spring break when she'd just wanted to read books on the beach in Maui. He'd won that time. Or the time he'd shown up blasted, with an unexplained cut on his head, to her law school formal. They'd gone to the emergency room instead.

Instead of apologizing to her, he liked to deflect. Make it about her. And he was going to do that again in ten, nine, eight . . .

"I'm sorry, Bridge."

Wow, he'd managed to shock her. He hadn't apologized in years. "Sorry for what?"

"I thought you wanted this." He paused. "I'm in love with you."

"No, you're not." She seldom used the voice she used when cross-examining a witness with Chris. He hated it. But since he didn't care what she wanted, she couldn't give two shits right now. "You're only sorry that I'm not overjoyed that YOU BOUGHT A HOUSE WITH-OUT EVEN FUCKING ASKING ME."

That finally got him to meet her gaze. "You're so ungrateful, Bridget."

Bridget snorted. "That's rich."

"I just wanted a future for us."

The only future they had, the only one that wouldn't kill her slowly, was ending this right now. She took a deep inhale, ready to tell him it was over, when he beat her to the punch. "I guess I was wrong."

Bridget didn't think before saying, "Get the fuck out of my apart-ment, then."

"I can't even finish dinner?"

"Oh, you're finished." When he hesitated, she walked over to the entryway, where his shoes were carefully laid on her floor and his coat hung on her coat rack. She opened the door and threw all of those items down the stairs, to the building's foyer. "Get out."

The worst part was, six months later Licorice had died. "Fucker," Bridget mumbled under her breath.

"Language, Bridget Mary Nolan." Of course, now that her mother was pretending to parent again, she was policing Bridget's language.

"I cooked him the chicken, Mom." The chicken that used to be known as Ina Garten's Engagement Chicken. Of course, in her world, it was now known as the Relationship Ender.

"You cooked for Matt?" her mom asked.

She was similarly perplexed with her own behavior. Why the fuck would she cook Matt chicken? He is—was—her employee. And she could never date him for real now that he was going back to school.

"She's talking about the other one," Hannah said. Even though Chris had been Jack's best friend since they were in diapers, Hannah wouldn't even say his name out loud. She was polite to him, but only in a way that made it clear that he didn't exist to her after she found out about how the breakup with Bridget had gone down.

"Why are you even thinking about him anymore?" Her mother really didn't get her at all.

"We were together for over a decade." And she hadn't been thinking about him of late. The only guy she thought about these days was Matt.

Hannah looked between the two of them, and her eyes widened for a second before her event-planning instincts kicked in and she did the whistling thing with two fingers in her mouth to make it extra loud. "Okay." She clapped her hands like a kindergarten teacher for extra emphasis. "The official itinerary of debauchery is slightly behind schedule because of this lovely reception by Matt, but we have a schedule to keep. Dinner is in six hours and I have spa treatments booked for those who are interested. The rest of you will have to gamble and bathe in stripper glitter." She looked at Chris for the first time in maybe ever with that last part.

Bridget had always wanted a sister and really couldn't have asked for a more loyal one than Hannah.

"Wait, wait, wait! I have a toast!" Sasha clinked her glass with a pen to get everyone's attention. She spread a palm down the front of her dress and cleared her throat before speaking. "Since Father Patrick couldn't join us in the City of Sin to absolve us of our sins personally and simultaneously with us committing them . . ." She gave a meaningful look to Jack, who had his arm around Hannah's waist and his hand creeping ever closer to her boob. "I have taken it upon myself to set some ground rules."

"Jesus Christ," Bridget's dad muttered. Her mother slapped him on the shoulder playfully, and Bridget winced. She hated seeing her parents flirt. It was unnatural.

"First of all, please remember the cardinal rule—beer before liquor, never been sicker."

Chris raised his glass and said, "Who's wasting their time on beer?" Bridget resented the fact that he was drinking the very fine booze provided by her date. Matt for his part seemed totally relaxed, with one arm looped around her shoulders. It felt heavy in that moment, but in a way that kept her rooted to the ground and safe rather than burdened.

Sasha looked at Chris with a narrowed gaze and a wrinkled nose that reminded Bridget of Sister Antoninus in a very frightening way. "Also, let's avoid bringing in any strays to the group."

"You're no fun," Chris responded, and Bridget wanted to kick him in his face. He hadn't matured a single day since he pissed in her kiddie pool, and she didn't know how she hadn't realized that before now. Had she actually married him her life would have been terrible. He was not even half the man her father was. If they'd had a child together—well, it would have ended in a bigger disaster than her parents' marriage had. She shuddered at the thought.

Matt noticed, and he leaned down to whisper in her ear, "Are you cold? Did you bring a sweater?"

It was surprisingly arousing, and she definitely should have known that she was in grave danger of wanting far more than friendship with benefits with Matt Kido right then.

Instead, she focused on Sasha's impromptu speech. It was much safer that way. "And, since most of us are Catholic, I've called ahead and scheduled a private Mass at a church about thirty miles away. It starts at six thirty a.m. on Sunday, so we'll all need to be at the bus at five forty-five. I would advise that we lay off the booze on Saturday night."

Everyone was silent for a few long beats, as though they were waiting to see which one would tell Sasha she was going to be going to Mass alone—that or the first one to check to see whether she was a pod person and figure out what she'd done with the real Sasha.

Sasha broke before any of that was necessary and dissolved into giggles, nearly falling to the floor.

"That was not funny, Sash," Hannah said, shaking her head. "If you weren't my best friend, I would have kicked you out of the wedding."

Sasha sobered a little bit. "C'mon, it was a little bit funny." She pointed at Matt. "He laughed."

"Yeah, but he doesn't know that you're a heathen like the rest of us." Hannah grabbed a bottle of Dom away from Sasha when she reached to refill her glass. "You're cut off."

"You're so mean," Sasha complained.

"Yeah, but you love me anyway."

"For some reason."

Hannah shook her head, then clapped her hands. "Now, you know the actual plan. Let's get it done."

EVERYONE LEFT ONCE THEY had their orders from Bridget's impressively scary future sister-in-law. Bridget seemed surprised to see Matt standing there when she turned from putting all the empty champagne glasses on the bar.

"You don't have to do that," he said.

"What are you still doing here?"

"Don't we have to get ready to go to the spa?"

"I thought you'd be more into the gambling and showgirls."

He'd done plenty of gambling in Macau over spring break. And gambling and topless dancers didn't have Bridget. "I came here to hang out with you."

"But . . ." She seemed to be thinking of a way out of it but gave up after a few seconds. "Okay. Where's the bedroom?"

"You need a nap already?" He smiled at her when she looked at him like he'd grown a second head. When they'd been working together, he'd never dared to give her an iota of shit. And now that they were on an equal footing, she couldn't just dismiss him. Now that he'd brought her here on a private jet and arranged for a suite, she kind of had to be polite to him. It wasn't the most noble thing, but he liked it. And he had a whole summer of being noble to make up for. Maybe if he was a little bit of a shit like her ex-boyfriend, she would pay attention to him, as something more than just an employee or a convenient date to an event that she didn't particularly want to attend.

She motioned to her flight-rumpled clothes. "I need to shower."

Matt stifled a groan. She had no idea how attracted he was to her, and he wasn't about to disabuse her of the notion that he was just grateful for the experience she'd given him over the summer. Thinking about all that freckled skin getting pink under the heat of the rain shower wouldn't do anything to help his cause.

That would only tell her how much of a perv he was when it came to her.

After a few awkward years in adolescence, he'd never had to work to get a girl to like him. Being damn near irresistible without the hefty trust fund—plus the actual trust fund—usually meant that he kind of just had to exist.

Maybe part of the reason he was so sprung for Bridget Nolan was that she didn't give him the time of day when it came to anything but work. Except something had changed when they'd gotten on the plane that morning. The way she was looking at him now, flush high on her pale cheeks, biting her full bottom lip until it was more rose pink than petal—almost as though she was attracted to him.

The idea that she was into the money and everything that came with it crossed his mind, but that didn't seem like her. That hadn't mattered one whit to her during the whole summer. Maybe she'd been suppressing the same attraction that he had been over the past few months, and now that they were alone in a hotel room, she couldn't keep it in any longer?

That was what he hoped.

"You're going to come get manicures and pedicures with us?" She raised a quizzical brow.

"I have hands and feet." He held up the back of his hands to her, and she caught her breath. Was she into hands? Good thing he was into putting his hands all over her.

"Are you going to get waxed, too?" She smirked at him, and he wanted to kiss that sarcastic smile off her mouth. She was across the room, though. And she'd given very little indication that she wanted him to kiss her.

"I'll probably pass on that." He waxed his balls for no woman.

She must have been thinking about his balls, too, because her flush deepened. "I'm just going to go . . ."

He motioned toward the bedroom at one end of the suite, where the porter had placed her luggage. "By all means."

FIRST ORDER OF SHOWER business—stop thinking about licking Matt Kido's treasure trail and what a shame it would be if he waxed. Second order of shower business—stop thinking about having his really superlatively masculine and gorgeous hands all over her.

While she accomplished neither of those things, she did get clean and down to the spa in time for a massage. Matt was in another room, because the Lord was merciful and wasn't going to let her see him mostly naked.

"Relax," the masseuse told her as she dug her elbow into the rigid muscles between her shoulder blades.

"This is about as relaxed as it gets," Bridget mumbled.

From the table next to her, Hannah smiled with her eyes closed. She didn't even want to think about what Jack had done to put that smile there. "You should have availed yourself of a quickie with Matt. That would have relaxed you."

"It's not like that. This is a fake date to piss Chris off. Not a real date to get my rocks off."

"But it would be so convenient," Hannah said, loud enough that Bridget's mother would probably hear.

"Shhh." The last thing Bridget needed was her mother hearing about her nonexistent thing with Matt. "I'm never going to see him again after this weekend. He's going back to school, and it's not like he's going to come work for the office."

For some reason, that thought made her very sad. She'd gotten used to seeing Matt every day. And she could admit to herself that she thought about him more than she'd ever thought about any of her other interns. She thought about him more than her colleagues and her student loan payments combined.

"That's why it's perfect."

"How is it perfect?"

"A little one-night stand to get your mojo back."

"Who says 'mojo' anymore?" She had to get Hannah off this topic. If she didn't, she would start to think about how crisp and white Matt's shirts were and how gold his skin looked against the fabric. How he made Chris look schlubby by comparison. How, every time she saw Matt, she had to resist the urge to touch him. How she could fall for him. And how he'd forget all about her when he went back to school in a few days. "Besides, he's not even interested. This was just a favor because I gave him valuable experience this summer." Hannah didn't need to know about his declaration of interest and the almost kiss on the plane.

"The only valuable experience he's looking to get is—"

"Shut up, Hannah."

Hannah snorted. "Fine. It's probably better if I let you fill in the blanks."

"First time for everything."

"Hey!" Hannah got loud again. "I don't tell you half the things I could tell you about your precious big brother."

"Thank goodness for that."

"I want you to be happy." Hannah got quiet. "I know your parents and their messed-up failed divorce has all of you weird in the head about relationships. I just don't want you to give up after that loser Chris."

Hannah did have a point. She had given up on finding someone she could fit with after Chris. After all, if she couldn't make things work with someone whom she had decades of history with, who could she make things work with? If she couldn't make the necessary compromises for Chris, who had grown up the same way she had, what hope did she have with someone like Matt? Matt lived in a whole other stratosphere.

Matt made Chris look like a schlub, but he made her feel shiny and brand-new. That was why she'd treated him like gum on her shoe when he'd shown up a few months ago. She'd immediately sensed the danger. For the first time in years, he made her feel something other than sad. He didn't even have to do anything.

And every time he took a load of shit from her with nothing more than a twinkle in his eyes, he made her feel more feelings than she wanted to feel for him.

She hated it.

"I think the two of you are going to hook up this weekend." Hannah made it sound like a pronouncement more than a prediction. "I can feel it."

"Since when do you have a romantic bone in your body?"

"Since your brother's di—"

Bridget turned her head. "Nope. Don't want to hear it."

"Don't set yourself up like that, then." Hannah giggled. Bridget had the feeling that giggling was a new thing for her since meeting Jack. Too bad she was taking such joy in Bridget's current situation.

They were going to need a lot of champagne to get through the weekend.

CHAPTER TEN

MATT HAD A PLAN for the evening. He was going to stick to Bridget's side like glue, keep her douche ex-boyfriend from sidling up to her, and wait for her to come on to him. After that morning on the plane and in their suite, he had a feeling it was only a matter of time, and he also had a feeling that Bridget needed to be the one to make the first move.

Never mind the fact that he'd been making moves since weaseling his way into getting invited to come along. But that was just him being himself.

He'd mostly stayed quiet during manicures and pedicures with Bridget and her girls. Caught up on reading a book he'd had loaded on his phone and listened for sensitive intel. Unfortunately, Sasha, the maid of honor, had made a point of making him feel welcome, so he didn't hear anything good.

"I think it's so great that you're taking care of your hands." She'd looked off into the distance with a sigh. "Most men don't pay attention."

Hannah, the bride, had said, "Yeah, you wouldn't believe the kinds of claws I had to fend off from my lady bits." He'd wondered how much champagne she'd had to drink. "It's like . . . if you can't clean under your fingernails, I don't want your fingernails in my business."

For her part, Bridget had turned bright red and become deeply interested in a months-old *Entertainment Weekly*.

Bridget's mother had continued gulping down champagne like it was going out of style and stealing sidelong glances at her daughter. Later, when they were alone—God willing—he'd find out more about why Bridget and her mother seemed so distant. He'd spent the summer working in the state's attorney's office just so he could get a little acceptable distance from his mother, so he could identify with her.

He wondered when he'd gotten so interested in more than just something casual with Bridget. He really wanted to know her, and it would behoove him to pump the brakes on pondering her family shit and deep, dark secrets.

Especially since he was calling to thank his mom for making sure he could get the penthouse. He'd promised to check in, and he needed to lock down his feelings about Bridget before talking to her. She would know if he sounded too emotional, and he didn't want her prying about Bridget. He didn't want her interfering in another one of his relationships. It wasn't like he was this extravagant all the time, so it would definitely awaken her Spidey senses.

She picked up before the phone rang on his end. "Matthew." He knew by the tone of her voice that she'd been expecting the call much earlier.

"Mom." He'd wait her out to see if she was pissed. If it was minor, she would cut straight to the point and then probably get back to work and make more money in the next five minutes than he'd spent all summer.

"Vegas." The word dripped with disdain. She waited a single beat for him to explain, then continued. The call about the plane was not going to close the issue for her. "Is this about a girl, or do you have a gambling problem?"

"One time in Macau, and it was Dad who lost the most money."

"But he's not in Vegas right now."

"It's about a girl, Mom." He'd probably live to regret sharing this, but it was better than his mom locking down his credit card because she was afraid for the family fortune. "Her brother's getting married and she invited me to the bachelor/bachelorette party."

"Do I know her?"

He thought about the kind of woman his mother wanted him to marry. She'd never pushed him to date a Japanese American woman or even another woman from her business or social circles, but he couldn't imagine how she would react to someone as earthy as Bridget.

Although the two women were similar in a lot of ways— supersmart, no bullshit, and hard as nails—they couldn't come from more different backgrounds. It was clear that Bridget's family didn't hurt for money, but she hadn't been virtually raised in the halls of Congress the way his mother had. Hadn't had decorum and propriety stamped into her soul so hard that even her college rebellion— joining a punk band composed of fellow business students at Stanford—had played into her future success. It was a nice story she liked to trot out to show that she wasn't a total snob.

Everything about his mother was careful. At first, he'd thought that Bridget was the same. But now he knew that she had all this passion and fire that she kept locked up until she couldn't. He wanted nothing more than for her to let it loose all over him.

No, his mother didn't know Bridget Nolan. And he wasn't sure if they should ever meet. He definitely wanted to explore the chemistry that Bridget was on the verge of giving in to, but this might never turn into anything serious.

After all, they wouldn't see each other after this weekend.

"Nah, Mom." He paused. "Not that kind of girl. Bridget was my boss this summer, and this is strictly to help her out."

That's when he felt the topic of conversation's presence behind him.

STRICTLY TO HELP HER out. It didn't sound like this weekend was going to result in any orgasms she didn't produce herself after all.

Had it really been so long since she'd been in the dating game that she couldn't tell anymore whether a guy was into her? That's what she thought until Matt turned and winked at her, mouthing, "My mom."

Oh, so maybe he was actually into her but didn't want to tell his mom he was into her. So it was like that? He was thinking that this could be a weekend fling, too? Just a way to let off the steam that had built up over the summer. That's all this *could* be.

She knew she was assuming a lot based on very little. On an almost kiss and some looks. Perhaps they should be adults about things and have an actual conversation before anything happened between them. She could do that, right? Be an adult and tell another adult, who was not her intern anymore, that she wanted to get very naked and very sweaty with him while hopped up on champagne.

She hadn't had to have that conversation with anyone new for years. And whenever she'd asked for something sexual from Chris, he'd given her this look. A look that said, *C'mon, Bridge, you're a good girl. Why would you ask for that?*

Matt hung up after a few moments. His brow wrinkled when he looked at her. "What's wrong?" Like he really cared about what was going on with her.

"What are we doing here, Matt?"

"Going to dinner?" He seemed genuinely confused. "Hopefully having a good time."

"I mean . . . a few times you've looked at me like you want to kiss me." She hesitated. "And then on the plane . . ."

He looked down, and a smile played across his face. Then he did that thing where he looked up at her in this playful way that made all her insides melty. "Am I that obvious?"

"I wouldn't have noticed if I weren't looking for it."

"You were looking for it?" He bit his bottom lip the way she wanted to bite it. And then he stepped closer to her, close enough that she could feel the heat of his body through her little black dress. "Does that mean you want to kiss me, too?"

Of course she got shy then and couldn't hold his gaze. She was never this way with anyone else, and it should worry her. Being with Chris had made her feel small, until the only place she felt like herself was at work. That had been the only thing stopping her from kissing Matt before, to be honest. Because kissing him felt big. And she was afraid of big. But playing scared had gotten her a dozen years with Chris and a whole lot of no action. And she wanted action with Matt. She wanted him. And she wouldn't get him unless she took a leap into this thing that felt big. "I do want to kiss you."

A split second later, he wrapped his hand around the back of her neck, under her hair. The skin-to-skin contact seared her from the inside out. Her blood was pumping so hard and fast she swore she could hear it rushing through her veins. He smelled *delicious*— like amber and citrus and a light musk.

But he still hesitated. "Are you sure?"

"As sure as I've been of anything in years." That was a lie. She wasn't sure that the ground underneath her was still there or if she was floating off somewhere.

When his mouth touched hers, her heart jumped into her throat and she knew she was still earthbound. All the things that she'd liked about working with him—his attention to detail and complete focus—she extra liked when he kissed her. He left no part of her mouth unexplored when she let him in.

He wrapped his other arm around her and pulled her close, so she could feel the planes of his body and the press of him getting hard against her.

She ran her hands up his arms and pressed her fingertips into the short hair at the back of his neck. It was so silky and soft that she sighed into his mouth. Kissing him was a sensory feast, and she didn't even want to take a break to breathe.

But she had to if she wanted to live. And if she didn't want to get teased for months about being late for dinner because she couldn't keep her hands off her intern.

So, she did the seemingly impossible and pulled back. He bit his bottom lip, and that almost made her want to kiss him again. Instead she sighed and said, "We don't want to be late."

He winked at her again and nearly ruined her resolve. "Wouldn't want that."

CHAPTER ELEVEN

BRIDGET HAD ALWAYS HAD her father's temper—slow to boil, but then quick to boil over. When her mom had moved out of the house, on that last day before she left, she was packing up everything so that she wouldn't have to come back, she'd forgotten the cat's litter box. Because of course she was taking Bridget's cat.

All of a sudden, a hit of rage so strong flowed through her that she couldn't think straight. She no longer cared about what the neighbors thought or about being strong for her dad and brothers. She just wanted to hit out at something or someone.

She'd grabbed the litter box that held Stanley's litter and hauled it into the drive.

"You forgot something!" she'd yelled as her mother put the cat carrier into the back seat.

"Oh no, honey, I'll get fresh cat litter at my new place." Her mother hadn't realized how angry she was yet. That she was throwing away her whole family for something new. Her mother was leaving them behind like they were nothing more than dirty cat litter.

Not thinking about the fact that her mother wouldn't be around to clean it up, she poured the dirty litter out of the box all over the driveway. If she was going to leave them, she was going to have to see what she was leaving.

Her dad had not been pleased to have to hose cat litter off the driveway, but he'd given her the temper so he understood.

Bridget felt close to boiling over as soon as she set eyes on Chris at dinner with a strange woman in his lap—undoubtedly someone he'd met here after he realized that she wasn't alone. Bridget wasn't going to judge Thandie the winsome "redhead," but sitting on a virtual stranger's lap at a three-star Michelin restaurant in front of someone's parents was a little gauche to say the least.

Everyone seemed to be in good spirits, though—probably due to the fact that they were ignoring Chris.

Matt sat next to her at an appropriate distance, in between her and her mother. He struck up a conversation about his parents' recent donations to the MCA collection, which made her mother light up. Which meant that he must have done some research on Bridget and her family.

Bridget tried not to roll her eyes. She couldn't care less about her mom's career. To her, it was the thing that had taken her away. She didn't know why her mother had to up and leave—disappear for years—so she could find herself. Some women really didn't need to become mothers, and that was something that Bridget and ol' Molly had in common.

She tried to focus on Hannah and Sasha and their after-dinner plans—and eat some extremely delicious food. Crispy, crunchy fried pork tonkatsu made everything better. Her effort to ice out Chris was helped by Hannah repeatedly filling her sake glass from the carafe they shared.

It was all fine until her ex's gaze caught her hand on Matt's knee. She was just asking how his *nigiri* was and making sure that her mother wasn't being too annoying or trying to butter him up for donations.

But then all three of them were just looking at one another— Matt was looking at her, Chris was looking at her, and she was looking between them.

"What?" she asked Chris. They'd broken up two years ago. He was with another woman right *now*. Did he honestly expect her to be alone forever just because she hadn't wanted what he'd wanted to give her?

Chris's gaze was hazy, and he'd had plenty to drink before and over the course of dinner. But never in her whole life did she expect him to say, "Just wondering if you were going to kill his baby, too."

She froze.

Not that she had any shame about what happened a few weeks after they broke up. It hadn't been as though it was going to change anything. She hadn't been about to get back together with him. She didn't think she could have counted on him for child support without taking him to court. Chris wouldn't have helped with diapers and all that, because he could barely take care of himself. He wasn't about to be any help. She worked in public service, and six weeks of maternity leave was nowhere near enough. And she didn't know if she ever wanted a kid, but she knew she didn't want one on her own.

Besides, her parents had had three children in five years to try to save their marriage, and that hadn't turned out well.

No—her only regret about the whole thing was that she'd told Chris. He hadn't reacted at all at the time, but the scythe of this secret had been hanging over her head for two years. Of course he chose this moment to let it fall.

She didn't look down; she wasn't about to let Chris see her flinch. But she felt Matt grab her hand and squeeze it.

It was weird. They'd only ever kissed once, but it felt right to have him touch her right now when her very skin bristled over her muscles like an animal under attack.

How dare Chris do this now? How dare he do it ever?

"I didn't kill a baby, Christopher Thomas Dooley." She paused, taking a deep breath and not looking at either of her parents, her brothers, or her friends. "I had a few cells scraped out of my uterus so that I wouldn't be tied to you for the rest of my natural life."

Chris opened his mouth to say something, but her father stopped him with a fist on the table that made all the plates jump. "You ever talk to my daughter like that again, and I'll make you wish that you'd rolled down the crack of your sainted mother's ass."

Bridget looked around the table and realized everyone was looking concerned for her. They were on her side—although she had no shame or regret about her abortion; it was just something she had done. She'd had a problem, and she had solved it her damned self—just the way she'd done since she was a preteen.

She didn't look at Chris but saw him get up and leave with his date.

"I'm going to go to the bathroom." When Hannah looked like she was going to make this a group trip, Bridget stayed her with a hand. "Alone."

The restaurant was huge, and it seemed to take forever for her to make it into one of the several single stalls—never had she been so grateful for a single stall. She ran cool water over her wrists and refreshed her lipstick before a knock sounded at the door. To her surprise, her brother Jack's voice was attached to the knock. "Open the door, Bridge."

She opened the door with a pasted-on smile. "What? I'm fine."

Jack gave her a sidelong glance and pushed into the tiny room. "C'mon. You're better than that. Tell me what's going on."

Bridget had been very careful not to talk about her and Chris's breakup and the fallout with her older brothers. They were way too close with the Dooley boys for it not to be a mess. And if it became a mess, she just hadn't trusted that her brothers would have been on her side. And she wasn't going to make them choose between her and their best friends.

"You know what's going on now."

"Pull the other one, Bridge." Jack was way too smart for his own good. It made him a perceptive journalist, and it also made him a huge pain in the ass.

"We broke up because we realized that we didn't want the same life. A few weeks later, I found out through personal experience that the failure rate for the pull-out method is no joke." It might make her an asshole, but she enjoyed watching Jack flinch just then. "And then I took care of it."

"We would have helped you."

She knew that. Now. She did. But the time had not been right for her to have a kid. The other parent hadn't been right, either. So, she made the correct decision without bringing them into it. "I know that, but I meant what I said about not wanting to be tied to Chris."

Jack rubbed a hand over his face. He really looked like their dad when he did that, but she didn't think right now would be the right time to tell him that. "I always knew he was a dick, but I had no idea. I just can't believe he said that to you."

Bridget could only imagine what Hannah had to say about Chris. She'd never liked him and liked him even less as she'd become friends with Bridget. Hannah might have a temper almost as prodigious as Sean and Bridget Nolan's, but she was the most loyal person Bridget had ever met. She was perfect for her sweet softie of a brother. "Is Hannah plotting his untimely death?"

That got Jack to smile. "Yeah. He's definitely out of the fucking wedding."

"Thank goodness." Bridget lifted her hands to the sky and gave her brother a not-fake smile. "Can we leave the bathroom now?"

Jack opened the door and wrapped his arm around her shoulders. She let herself lean into him. "And can we get drunk after dinner? Like *real* drunk?"

"You got it, Bridge to Terabithia."

She hit him in the side because she hated that nickname. "You're buying the drinks."

CHAPTER TWELVE

WHAT DO YOU WANT to do first?" Matt asked.

Bridget was surprised that he didn't have more questions after what had transpired in the restaurant. "You don't want to talk about what happened in there?"

Matt shrugged. "I figure that you'll tell me what you want me to know."

"You really are a unicorn."

He gave her the lopsided smile that had made it really hard not to kiss him the whole summer. "Not a unicorn. I'm just not an asshole."

What a revelation.

Hannah and Jack walked out of the restaurant and onto the casino floor then. "After that, I think we should drink a lot," Hannah said.

"Jack and I had already agreed to that when he fetched me from the bathroom," Bridget said.

Hannah turned to her betrothed. "I knew there was a reason why I agreed to marry you."

Then her brother kissed his fiancée, and Bridget rolled her eyes. She caught her breath when Matt put his arm around her waist and put his lips against her ear. "Kind of cute, but kind of sickening, right?"

Her brother came up for air. "Just wait until it's you, little sister."

"You'll be waiting a long-ass time," Bridget said. "I'm not doing that anymore."

Jack gave her—with Matt's arm around her waist—a meaningful look. She wanted to deny that she was going to fall for Matt, but she sort of already had. She was in lust with him, and she really liked him despite all her efforts not to.

And it felt totally natural to walk around the casino with his arm around her waist. She liked the weight of it there. As soon as they'd kissed in the hotel room, a dam broke. She no longer wanted to be not touching him. She couldn't stop thinking about his lips.

Even with Chris making a scene, she'd only been partially distracted from the lust she felt for Matt Kido. And maybe that was why Chris had made a scene. Maybe he'd seen the energy between the two of them and it had made him feel like it was really over.

For Bridget, kissing Matt had been like closing a door on one thing—feeling alone—and opening a door on something new. Whatever it was with Matt wasn't going to last—he was way too young for her, and she wasn't even his type. But having him interested in her made her feel like maybe she could do a relationship again. Maybe she wanted someone's focused romantic attention on her.

She was way overthinking this as they wandered closer to the gaming tables. She was here to celebrate her brother and Hannah, not have fights with her ex and figure out her whole future—confused feelings and all.

It was sort of perfect when Hannah said, "I think it's time for some tequila shots."

ARE YOU SURE THAT we want to do shots?" Jack asked his fiancée in an indulgent tone of voice.

"It's not a proper bachelor/bachelorette party unless there are shots." Hannah looked at Jack as though he was new here.

"It's not a proper bachelor party at all. There are no strippers," Jack said.

Matt didn't know if he was witnessing a fight or a spirited discussion. All he knew was that it was highly amusing. Like, he didn't know if the betrotheds were going to tear each other's faces or clothes off. Their voices were completely sweet, but the snapping tension between the two reminded him more of his working relationship with Bridget than his previous romantic relationship with Naomi.

"I'm pretty sure the girl with Chris was a stripper," Bridget said. "And I vote for shots."

Bridget hadn't said much since the scene with her ex-douche, and he hated that. If it took shots to get her back into a good mood—or if she needed to forget the evening up until now with the help of an alcoholic anesthetic—he was going to be supportive.

He motioned for a cocktail server to come over and ordered shots for the four of them—everyone else had wandered off to gamble and drink on their own. It seemed that Jack wasn't going to let his little sister out of his sight for the time being, so there they were.

"Blackjack?" Matt suggested.

Bridget turned to him, a smile on her face for the first time in about an hour. "You really are the perfect date."

"I don't know about that." Matt could feel himself blushing. Something had changed after she'd kissed him. While he'd been working for her, he'd felt sort of awed and terrified the entire time. And now he felt like he was her knight in shining armor. He knew she didn't really need one, but he wanted to be that for her all the same. He wanted her to see him as an equal, even if it meant throwing some money at her problems tonight.

Because the shift in their relationship had happened so fast, the last thing he expected her to do was to kiss him on the mouth. But that's what she did. It was a quick thank-you, not the sultry kiss they'd shared upstairs, but they were in public and in front of her brother. He totally got why she wouldn't want to take it too far in front of Jack and Hannah.

He was just glad that she did it.

And he didn't have to worry about stealing a kiss in front of her big brother, because Jack and Hannah had taken a seat at a black-jack table near them. Matt wanted to focus on Bridget having a good time, so he didn't want to get wound up in playing the game, even though he liked that it required some skill in addition to luck. He'd gone to law school because he'd hated math, but he was good enough at it to count cards, even though that was frowned upon.

The server came back with shots for them and Matt motioned

for them to give the other ones to Jack and Hannah. Hannah winked at Matt when she looked over her shoulder, and Matt liked having the woman's approval. He didn't know her very well, but she seemed like the ultimate straight shooter. If she didn't like him for some reason, he could see Bridget taking her future sister-in-law's judgment to heart.

"Bottoms up," Bridget said, just before taking the shot. He was a few seconds behind her because he was looking at her with her head tilted back. She looked so different tonight than she normally did.

She wore a tiny sequined dress that barely covered anything at all. It had a low back, and he felt like he couldn't stop touching her soft skin. She had more makeup on than usual, and it made her eyes even more vivid than they usually were.

At work, she was an apex predator in prey's clothing— professional but with an almost-too-innocent face. Here, she looked the whole part, and he wanted to be devoured.

"What?" She was smiling, her cheeks pink and her lips plump and still wet from tequila.

He couldn't say all the things that he was thinking in that moment. She wouldn't be able to hear them without running flat out in the opposite direction. They didn't really know each other well enough for him to tell her all the possibilities they'd unlocked in his brain the second they kissed.

And he knew she wouldn't want to hear that he wanted to be her rebound guy and maybe more, because that sounded like it was jumping the gun—to him.

But something about standing there with her glittering eyes and shiny red-gold hair, and the lights of the casino making the sequins of her dress shimmer, made her look like a mirage in the desert to him.

Something in him made him want to reach out before she disappeared. He couldn't say any of that, so he took a shot and ordered another round.

CHAPTER THIRTEEN

MATT HAD WOKEN UP in a lot of hotels. He'd woken up with plenty of hangovers. But he'd rarely woken up not knowing if he was even in the right hotel room, with the night before wiped from his brain.

The last thing he remembered was walking out of the restaurant with Bridget, her brother, and his fiancée.

"Your ex is a Grade-A douchebag," was the only thing he'd said about the scene that Chris had made.

"I don't want to talk about him anymore," she'd replied, then held up the empty carafe of sake to signal the server. "We're going to need a whole lot more of these."

Matt had gone along with it and vaguely recalled committing to a modicum of sobriety to make sure Bridget was okay. At least until the bride-to-be ordered the third round of shots.

After that, everything got a little fuzzy. What a fuckup. He was pretty sure he could kiss any chance of a weekend fling with Bridget goodbye.

He looked over to the other side of bed. Whereas he was under the covers in his boxer briefs, Bridget was facedown in the little sequined dress that would haunt his dreams for years, her pert ass peaking out of the bottom and her face covered by her thick hair. If he could move at that moment, he would have brushed her hair away from her face and kissed her. But he didn't trust his stomach not to lose its contents if he tried for that.

He squeezed his eyes shut to keep out the searing pain and tried to make a plan. Bridget was probably hurting even more than him—or she would be when she finally woke up. If he couldn't remember the night before, he needed to make a plan.

First he'd order them both breakfast—the greasier and more bacon-rich the better. Then he'd take a shower—a cold one. Since they were on their own for most of the day, he'd try to convince Bridget to stay in the room and watch movies with him. Along with maybe a late ramen or pho lunch that might just have her feeling human enough to finish out the trip.

Bridget made a somewhat pathetic sound from the other side of the bed. Something between a moan and a wail. In an instant, she was upright, and he had to struggle not to laugh.

"Whaaat?" She looked at him, and then instantly looked a little sick until she looked down and saw that she was fully clothed. "Oh shit."

"If it will make you feel any better, I don't remember anything."

"That does not make me feel better." She flopped down on her back next to him and he took cold comfort in the fact that she didn't bolt for the bathroom or the privacy of her own room as soon as she woke up. "I was going to kiss you more last night."

"For all you know, you did that." He liked that she'd been thinking along the same lines but shared her disappointment. "We can always try again tonight."

"Chris always ruins everything."

"I got that impression." Relieved of the queasiness induced by worrying that he'd somehow fucked up with Bridget, he grabbed her hand. She seemed startled for a moment but then wove her fingers through his. "What do you remember?"

"After Jack came into the bathroom and we talked about the thing."

The thing. Matt wished he could say something to make her feel better about what had happened, but he didn't really know her well enough to know how she felt about it, and he wasn't about to mansplain her own abortion to her.

"You came out of the bathroom and ordered sake," he filled in.

"Then we went to gamble."

"And Jack ordered shots," he said. And they both paused to think about what happened next.

"Hannah won like five hundred dollars playing blackjack."

Memories started coming back to him as she talked. "And then she wanted to use the money to get bottle service at the club."

"We did that." Bridget slapped her hand over her mouth and laughed. "You are a terrible dancer."

"Don't rub it in." He wondered if he should tell her about the lessons that he'd had to take for years and how much he'd hated them. Maybe he'd save that for the second date—not that this weekend fit the traditional definition of a date. He was helping her out by bringing her here and irritating her ex—which seemed to be working. And kissing her. There was the kissing, too.

But it was probably not a date. He was going back to school in less than a week, and he knew Bridget would be waist-deep in work as soon as she returned to the office. He wondered if she'd worked that much while she was still with Chris. He couldn't ever imagine her half-assing her job, but it was possible that she'd used the breakup as an excuse to become even more of a workaholic.

"After that, I remember Elvis and purple flowers . . ." She trailed off.

He remembered Elvis, too. And laughing. Maybe they'd gone to see a show? Probably not. The lights had been too bright for a show.

"Oh shit." Bridget sat up again. This time he joined her in an upright position and immediately regretted it.

"What?"

"I think Jack and Hannah got married." She looked at him, and he wanted to smile. Her black eye makeup was smudged all over and her lipstick long gone. And her hair was a frizzy halo all around her freckled face. He wouldn't do it because his breath was likely classifiable as a lethal weapon, but he wanted to kiss her even more seeing her this mussed up.

And then he remembered obliterating her lipstick the night before.

Standing in front of Elvis.

In a wedding chapel.

Bridget in a veil . . .

"I don't think Hannah and Jack got married."

He pulled his hand from hers and looked at his left ring finger— the one bearing a probably fake gold wedding band.

Bridget saw it at the same time and her eyes got wide.

He nodded at her left hand, which she'd balled into a fist and shoved under the covers. "Let me see it."

She shook her head and blanched because her brain was probably sloshing around in the champagne he remembered drinking once they'd gotten back to the room—after their wedding.

"I can't," she said, sounding as though she was going to be very sick, very soon.

"I think we did." Part of him felt as sick as she did. This was a mess. Sure, he'd wanted to have sex with Bridget Nolan. He'd entertained thoughts of dating her once he was done with his internship. Maybe. But he'd never once thought about marrying her. He'd never really thought about marrying anyone, not even Naomi—much to his mother's chagrin.

Still, he was a little bit offended that Bridget looked as though she was going to throw up because they might have possibly, accidentally gotten married while drunk in Vegas.

As though something inside them had synched up when they said their vows in front of Elvis to the dulcet tones of another Elvis singing "Heartbreak Hotel," they both looked as she raised her left hand—the one that wore a definitely real, definitely large diamond solitaire.

"Oh shit," they both said simultaneously.

She mumbled something about an annulment, and he felt a hit of relief.

And then—he'd never seen a hungover person move so fast—she ran into the bathroom, slamming the door behind her.

OH SHIT. OH FUCK. What the hell have I done? was a continuous refrain in Bridget's mind as she vomited up the contents of her stomach.

Apparently, now that her heretofore most colossally stupid secret was out in the open in front of her family—not the abortion; the fact that she'd let one of Chris Dooley's players slip past the goalie—she'd decided to make an even bigger mistake.

She laid her face on the cold tile of the floor, and it felt so good that she teared up. She *never* did this kind of thing—had never gotten drunk enough to make life-altering mistakes. From the time her parents had gotten divorced, she'd taken the responsibility of being the lady of the Nolan house very seriously. Without being asked, she'd started making the grocery lists, cooking the meals. She'd stolen her father's credit card to hire a house cleaner—even she wasn't enough of a masochist to clean up after her two older brothers.

If someone had to pick one of the Nolan siblings to accidentally get knocked up or knock someone up and then get married to someone on a whim the same night everyone found out—it would definitely be Jack. Her poor, sweet sap of a brother had always fallen in love on a whim and been willing to change his whole life because of it.

Bridget had never fallen. She'd always been the kind of woman to airdrop herself precisely into the exact zone she wanted to be in. Until Chris had derailed her plans, she'd had everything mapped out. And she guessed this was as good a time as any to admit to herself at least that she'd been drifting ever since they broke up. Her only real goals after that had to do with her career—work at the state's attorney's office, pay off her student loans, figure out the rest of her life after that.

How could she have let this happen? How could she go from carefully contemplating a fling with Matt Kido to getting drunk-married in Vegas to Matt Kido? Thank goodness he wasn't the kind of well-known person who had paparazzi following him around. At least he was old-money-politics rich and not new-money-celebutante rich.

Christ, this was like a *Keeping Up with the Kardashians* subplot. She was sure that he was probably just as mad at himself, if not more so. Like, what would his parents think? What would her family think?

They would think she'd lost her mind. Maybe she had.

That thought got her up off the floor and had her turning on the shower. As she turned the knob to steaming hot, her gaze caught on the stunner of a diamond she wore on her hand. This time, it didn't make her sick. It filled her with a strange longing. Totally silly.

She took off her dress and underwear and stepped into the shower. As the hot water poured over her clammy skin, washing away the cigarette and booze smells, she let herself wonder what it would be like to be married to someone like Matt.

He came from an entirely different world than she did. She let herself wonder whether the kind of money his family had—that she hadn't really seen any evidence of him caring about—would make life with him easier or harder. If this was a real marriage and not one that he would probably demand to have annulled immediately, would she like being married to him?

Or would it be a kind of domestic drudgery in which she'd lose herself and eventually bug out from just like her mom?

Was marrying him in the first place evidence that she was just as impulsive and irresponsible as Molly? Because no matter how much she tried to be nothing like her mother, it sure as shit wasn't working on this trip.

She shampooed and conditioned the tangles out of her hair before getting out of the shower and pulling on Matt's robe. When she opened the door in between the part of the bathroom with the shower and the part of the bathroom with the vanity, she found her toothbrush and her pajamas.

It might have upset her that Matt went through her things, but they'd spent the whole summer in close proximity, and they were married now.

She shook her head. Maybe she should start looking on the bright side of things.

At least he wasn't her intern anymore.

CHAPTER FOURTEEN

SO, IS SEX IN a penthouse hotter than sex in a hotel room for plebeians?" The only thing that shocked Bridget about the question was that it came from Sasha instead of Hannah and that it didn't come right away. She almost didn't have the heart to tell her the truth. When she'd come out of the bathroom and into Matt's bedroom, he'd been gone.

At first she'd assumed that he was just taking a shower and/or throwing up in *her* bathroom. But the entire penthouse had been eerily quiet. On the one hand, she was tempted to go find him. She'd thought better of it when she realized she had no idea what to say to the guy she'd drunkenly married the night before.

Obviously, they would be getting an annulment. *Obviously.* And they could talk about that *after* several well-muscled young men gyrated their nuts in her face over Bloody Marys and massive amounts of bacon. She would be in a much better state of mind after that.

They'd been seated at the *Magic Mike XXL* live breakfast show venue for long enough to order drinks, and Bridget hadn't missed the looks between Sasha, Hannah, and their friend Kelly—who had flown in early that morning. Ah, this morning—the blessed time before Bridget woke up married to her former intern.

Bridget had elected to say nothing of her drunken nuptials to the other women in hopes that they didn't know or couldn't remember her getting married the evening before. The ragged edges of her mind didn't hold any snippets of anyone but Matt, her, and Elvis, and the fewer people who knew about the wedding, the better.

"Sex? What sex?" Answering a question with a question was how criminals answered questions, but the time that Bridget spent with them had to help her at some point. She even added a coy shrug. She was being honest about the no sex, but she was still hiding something.

Hannah just threw her head back and laughed. Kelly piped up. "Don't try to lie to the sex psychic here." She pointed her thumb at Sasha, whose steely gaze was still trained on Bridget's face so hard that she wanted to enlist her in interrogations. "She once guessed that I had received cunnilingus from the varsity coxswain at a party. And she wasn't wrong."

Bridget took a sip from her Bloody Mary, wishing she hadn't overimbibed the night before so she could have ordered extra vodka. "I don't want to talk about it."

"That bad?" Bridget was going to figure out an undetectable way to murder Hannah. She loved her future sister-in-law, but she had to die.

"I'm too Irish to have this conversation with you."

Sasha rolled her eyes. "It's written all over your face that it was good sex. Even your trapezius muscles are more relaxed than they were last night. Not that it would take much . . ." Sasha trailed off, realizing too late that Bridget wouldn't want to talk about the big abortion reveal from dinner earlier. However, now that it was out in the open, she was much happier to talk about that than the fact that she'd gotten married instead of getting laid.

"Not that you have to talk about it, unless you want to," Hannah said. Maybe she could live.

Still, Bridget felt better talking about her abortion than all the complicated pants and hearts feelings she was starting to have for Matt. Sleeping with him always would have been a mistake, but now it would be really bad because it would prevent them from getting an annulment.

And maybe she was more relaxed because she wasn't carrying a heavy secret around anymore—just a really stupid one. After the scene Chris had thrown at dinner, she knew she'd made the right decision terminating the pregnancy. He didn't want her, and he didn't want the baby they could have had. He just had a hard time knowing that she didn't want him, either. Sometimes she thought he'd never really intended to break up with her. He'd really just wanted her to settle for something less than what she'd thought they'd had together. He wanted to live the ordinary life that his parents had lived until his mother's death.

Where she'd thought their love story was epic because they'd known each other all their lives, he'd thought it was inevitable. He'd never even had to try to win her—she'd decided on him because he was there and constant, and he'd gone along with it. It was like the sweater from a great-grandparent at Christmas—two sizes too small because their memory didn't have room to account for growing children. Their relationship had been frozen in amber in high school, and it just took a while to realize it.

She could admit to herself now that—before the trip—she'd been harboring residual resentment for Chris. Somewhere, in the corner of her mind, she'd felt like he should have suffered more.

He'd made it clear that he'd been harboring a similar level of resentment. Even more.

"I mean, one in four women have abortions." Bridget knew she didn't need to justify herself to these women—hell, Sasha and Hannah had the local Planned Parenthood as a regular client on a reduced rate. But she still had a niggle of Catholic guilt about the whole thing. She could have been more careful.

"I've had one," Kelly said.

Sasha said, "I haven't, but I've had an IUD since sophomore year." She pointed at Hannah. "This one drove me to the clinic to get it."

"I didn't have sex for a couple of years there and have always been militant about condom usage," Hannah said.

Kelly snorted. "Hannah drove me to Chicago to the clinic for my appointment."

Hannah smiled. "As the only public school girl in our group, I was the only one who had comprehensive sex ed. Add that to my hippie mom, who sent a condom bowl for my freshman dorm room, and I took up the mantle of women's health."

Bridget knew they were just trying to make her feel better, and she wished she'd known Hannah back when she needed a friendly ride to the clinic. She had girlfriends, but her relationship with Chris had been the foundation of her social life for so long that she hadn't had anyone who didn't know both of them.

"I feel fine about it. Maybe not as callous as I might have seemed last night. But it wasn't the right time."

Hannah said, "That's good." She reached over Sasha's lap and grabbed Bridget's hand. "As long as you're okay."

That's what did it. The unconditional support and the fact that her mom had elected to skip out on the male strippers to spend the day with her dad was what made Bridget tell them. "Matt and I got married last night. By an Elvis. While drunk."

Never in a million years had she thought she could render Hannah speechless. Even when she was pissed off at Jack, she couldn't manage the silent treatment for too long. But all three women just gaped at her.

"We're going to get it annulled." As long as they avoided sleeping together—which she wasn't so sure they could do after last night. But she absolutely could not get a divorce. Something about that scarlet *D* on her record would make her too much like her mother. She should probably check on the legality of an annulment in Illinois after a marriage was consummated. Or she should check on getting a room where she wouldn't have to know how good he smelled or look at how good he looked.

"Can you get it annulled now that he did that thing that I'm guessing he did?" Sasha asked, with the closest thing to a shit-eating grin that the normally very staid woman could manage.

"Nothing happened." Her skin heated even though she was telling the truth. Nothing happened, but she wanted a lot to happen. But wanting wasn't doing.

"Listen, I don't know you very well." Kelly leaned in. "But it doesn't seem like something you would do based on how Hannah has described you."

"So, you think I'm boring?" Bridget wanted to deflect some of the attention and maybe blame someone else for how weird this whole situation was. "I mean, it's the craziest thing I've ever done, but I'm fun."

"It's very Britney Spears circa 2004." Except that time, Brit had married her high school flame. Bridget had married someone entirely new. Someone she didn't even know.

The lights started to go down, and Bridget sat back in her chair. "I really wish we could have gotten tickets to that show instead. I'm not really in the mood to have a sweaty dude grind on me in front of a bunch of people."

"Don't knock it until you try it," Kelly said.

"Brit's show was sold out," Sasha said.

"You can totally leave and go have a sweaty guy grind on you in the penthouse," Hannah said right before the music started.

MATT HAD ONLY AGREED to go see an early-in-the-day Cirque du Soleil show with Jack, Michael, and his friend Joey because Chris had been excommunicated from the bachelor party—and the wedding party. And because Matt felt that he was partially at fault for the dinner confrontation from the night before just because he'd shown up—he doubted Chris would have had his shit fit had he not been there—he agreed to use the ticket.

After, of course, he called his family's lawyer to figure out how big of a mess he'd gotten himself into.

As long as Jack didn't find out that Matt had drunkenly married his sister, everything would be fine. Perhaps the only people whom he dreaded finding out more than his parents were Bridget's big brothers.

They didn't seem like cavemen, but they treated Bridget like gold and had been plenty irked when it became apparent that their (former) friend had treated her as anything but. He valued his face too much to risk it by making her brothers think that he was any-where near as disrespectful as Bridget's ex-douche.

He didn't think that Bridget would want him to say anything to her family, but they hadn't spoken since she sprang out of his bed to go throw up. Of course, they'd be on the same page that their marriage was temporary, something that shouldn't have happened in the first place.

He still hoped that she wanted to do what they should have done last night—more kissing and maybe more than that. And he wanted to convince her that maybe they could date when they got back to Chicago.

But he could do all that without staying married to her. They could date—and just maybe forget that the whole Vegas wedding thing ever happened. It wasn't as though a marriage between the two of them could actually work. They were at completely different places in their lives, both coming off big, heavy relationships. Even though they had great chemistry, all they would ever be was a fling.

An annulment—a legal action making a marriage disappear as though it had never happened—was the right answer here.

His parents wouldn't have to know. Bridget's family wouldn't have to know. It could be a funny story that he and Bridget could share a knowing look over before they amicably parted ways in a few days.

Sitting in a darkened theater for an hour, watching human bodies doing things that human bodies were clearly not intended to do, was probably a good cover for all the thoughts roiling his normally pretty even-keeled psyche.

At least it was until Jack slapped the back of his head. "You *married* Bridget last night?!"

Oh shit. Bridget must have told Hannah. They definitely should have talked about this before leaving the room. "Uh . . ." He had no clue what was going to get him out of this situation alive and unmaimed.

"They got married?" Michael looked at Matt quizzically. Given the fact that his wife was currently divorcing him, he seemed confused as to why anyone would get married. "Fucking weird. I swear that I was switched at the hospital."

"Shut up, Mike," Jack said. "Just because you hate love doesn't mean the rest of us can't embrace it."

Before he could think better of it, Matt said, "Listen, it's not a love thing. I just . . . we just . . . had too much to drink and I think we thought it would be fun to get married by an Elvis."

He was trying to minimize it, but he knew how this would look to her family—profligate, poor little rich boy marries their sister for shits and giggles and drops her as soon as their dirty weekend is over. Given Bridget's previous taste in men, they'd be pretty justified in being skeptical of his intentions. Plus, there was the little detail that he'd worked for her until about twenty-four hours ago.

Not the most auspicious way to start a fling.

"You know, I've learned a lot about my sister in the past twenty-four hours," Jack said.

Matt braced himself to have Jack kick his ass. If he said anything shitty about the revelation from the night before, he would have to punch him in the face. But Jack surprised him. "She just keeps shit so locked down. I had no idea what a total prick Chris was because she never told anyone. I feel like such an asshole."

Michael grunted. "If I see him again before I leave Vegas, and I've had several more of these"—he held up his beer—"I will bare-knuckle box the stupid little prick."

Matt was relieved that they both seemed more pissed at Chris than him. "You guys aren't mad?"

Jack patted him on the back and grabbed his shoulder in a fraternal gesture. "You fuck with my sister, I'll let Hannah fuck you up. And you should really be more scared of her."

CHAPTER FIFTEEN

IT FIGURED THAT BRIDGET would run into the only person she wanted to see less than her new husband playing blackjack—her mother. She didn't want to see Matt because he hadn't been in the suite when she'd returned after the strip show. Fully over her hangover and having spent a few hours away from him, she didn't quite know what to say. Other than "Where do I sign?"

Seeing her mother alone at the blackjack table oddly reminded Bridget of when she was little and her parents had been together the first time; her mother had always gotten up earlier than anyone else. Not because she wanted to; Bridget had the impression that her mother would have liked to spend all day in bed with a novel if she didn't have three small children to look after and a man like Sean Nolan to keep house for.

As much as she loved and appreciated her father for everything he'd done—everything he'd sacrificed—for her, Sean Nolan was old-school. She was lucky that he didn't *expect* her to start cooking and cleaning after the divorce. Instead, he'd thanked her when she hired a housekeeper and made sure the grocery lists included plenty of food that could be made in a microwave.

But a housekeeper and microwave had never been up at six thirty humming in the kitchen and looking out over the backyard with a cup of English breakfast tea balanced in her fingers. Bridget had often come down and read quietly with her own cup of tea—mostly cream—not because she was naturally an early riser, but because she hungered for more time with her mother.

Michael and Jack were loud and boisterous—socialized the way that young boys had been for decades in America. As sort of a bookworm, Bridget had often felt lost in the shuffle.

But during those mornings with her mother, she'd felt a sort of peace. As though she belonged to a club with two members.

All of that had gone away, and she hadn't really gotten it back until Hannah had hooked up with Jack. Bridget had always had Chris, but she'd often felt alone in her own family.

Running into her mother, just as the hotel staff was putting out the lunch buffet, brought everything back—the feeling she'd had during those mornings and the loneliness after those mornings went away.

She was surprised to see that her mother seemed similarly haunted. They were both still for a second, and Bridget wondered if her mom was also thinking about fleeing.

"Join me for a game." Her mother's words weren't a question, and Bridget was tempted to refuse just because she was a grown-up now and she could. She could decide simply not to allow her mother back in her life. That decision would be complicated by the fact that her parents were back together. But she could make it work if she tried really hard.

Oddly, for a person who always tried hard, she didn't have it in her to do that now. "Fine."

They quietly waited together while the dealer laid down two cards each. And they were still silent as they both considered their options. The din of slot machines and drunken revelers filled the space.

"I heard you got married," her mother said. Bridget was going to kill Jack. She hadn't even decided whether she should hit or stay, but now she was going to have to defend her poor choices to a woman who probably had a PhD in making bad ones in addition to her degree in art history.

"It's not like that." Bridget struggled with how to explain herself without giving her mother any insight into who she was. Her petty bit of revenge since her mother had left was to show up when her mother wanted to see her but give her nothing of herself. Like, her body would be there when necessary, but her mother didn't get to *know* her. That was for people who had shown her she was worth the trouble. "We'd been drinking."

Her mother laughed but stopped when Bridget gave her a hard look.

"I'm not staying married to him." She sneered. "We're getting an annulment. I'll still be behind you and Michael on the divorce leaderboard."

Her mother gasped. Bridget was usually very careful to keep her disdain under wraps. She kept the hunger for love and affection from her mother, but she also kept her antipathy to herself. She'd always aimed for careful neutrality. But with a couple of cocktails on board, she just didn't have it in her to pretend that she respected her mother.

"Don't hurt my dad again, Molly." If she was going to speak the truth, she might as well speak all of it. "You broke him the last time, and there was nothing I could do about it. You hurt him again, and I won't even pretend that you're my parent anymore."

Her mother paled. Her gray-blue eyes got glassy. "I'm sorry."

"You think that's enough?" Bridget struggled not to yell. "My whole life is fucked up because of you!"

"Oh. Come. On," her mother said. "You are a fully employed adult and the only one of your siblings who does not rely on your father for money or employment."

"That doesn't mean my life isn't utterly fucked," Bridget said as she motioned for the dealer to hit. "And don't you dare lecture me about my language. You lost the right to do that the second you fucked off for grad school."

"I'm sorry." Her mother's voice was thin, less than the authoritative tone she usually used. "I'm trying to be better now, but I can't change the past.

"Do you remember how I used to make breakfast for the boys with you?" her mother asked. "I hated getting up early."

"I loved spending that time with you."

"We could have spent more time together, but I was always so busy trying to be the perfect mother—the perfect wife—I didn't have time or energy to really connect with anyone. Not myself. Not your father. None of you." Her mother took a deep breath. "I was a shitty mother, and I wish I could go back in time and take it all back ... Actually, no. I don't want to take back who I am. I just wish I could have done it without hurting you."

"So, you wish you'd never had kids." Bridget wasn't ready to give up her ire. Sean's temper in her belly wasn't about to let her back down. "Is that it?"

"Is that why you didn't want to have a baby with Chris?"

Bridget didn't have to answer to anyone about this, and she was really done talking about it. It happened, and it needed to happen. The whole truth was that she didn't know if she had it in her to be a mother or if she'd run off at the first opportunity. And Chris Dooley wasn't nearly the man that Sean Nolan was. Their kid would have been screwed. "Imagine Chris Dooley with an infant, getting up for midnight feedings and diaper changes."

Her mother shook her head. "I can't."

Her mother acknowledging that she'd probably made the right decision somehow dissipated the anger that had kept her going through the conversation. "I couldn't, either."

They played in silence for a few moments, but her mother wasn't going to let the whole thing pass in peace. "I like Matt."

"So what?" Bridget shrugged. "I like him, too. But I don't know him well enough to marry him."

"Maybe you don't know him well enough to know that you don't want to be married to him." Her mother narrowed her gaze at her. "And maybe if you tried, you'd see that it's not as easy as you seem to think it is."

"Oh, come on." She winced because she'd just lost another twenty dollars. "I'm not like you. I don't run off when things get tough."

"I'm not saying that, Bridget." Her mother held up her hands in surrender. "I'm just speaking from experience. Marriage is hard. You should give it a try before you accuse me of ruining your life by saving mine."

"You've always been so melodramatic." Bridget probably sounded sarcastic, but it was the truth. Her parents actually seemed to be happy together. Her dad seemed to *like* the melodrama now. And that was something she'd never seen growing up. That was the only reason that Bridget was even still trying a little bit with her mother— she seemed to make her father happy.

And making sure she wasn't a source of pain for her father wasn't something Bridget took lightly. It was the motivation behind her perfect test scores and perfect grades, the reason she hadn't gotten into trouble with boys until she was a full-grown adult, willing to take on the consequences. Because when Molly had left him, her father had been a broken man.

But he hadn't complained about the fact that he was a single parent to two feral boys and one moody preteen. He just did the job. And Bridget wanted to be like her father. She was. Take the pain; do the job. Rely on dark humor and hard work to get through.

"He's too young to be married. And he's, like, American royalty." She knew she was just making excuses for why it couldn't work. Deep down, she thought her mother was probably right. She'd sworn off long-term relationships after breaking up with Chris for precisely that reason—she wasn't cut out for it. But now, hearing her mother say it out loud made her want to make things work with Matt, just to prove a point.

"Oh, I know," her mother said. "His parents donated from their personal collection to replace the items that the Chapins had seized."

Bridget smirked. After Jack had broken a political corruption story last year, Senator Alexander Chapin had had his art collection, much of which was on loan to the Museum of Contemporary Art, seized. Her mother's consternation about that amused Bridget. It wasn't mature, but it was true.

"You want me to stay married to him to give you access," Bridget said.

Molly rolled her eyes and shook her head. "I want you to be happy, and he looks at you as though he wants to make you happy."

"Bullshit." Bridget pushed away from the table. "You want to prove a point and see me fail at this."

Her mother sighed. "You're just as stubborn as he is."

"I'd much rather be like Sean Nolan than like you."

She stood up and walked away, leaving her mother to lose money alone.

THE SOUND OF HIS ringtone wasn't more ominous than usual before he picked it up. He didn't know that shit was going to hit the fan, that something that should have been a story he told at cocktail parties when he really felt like scandalizing people was going to turn into a real issue that would fuck with his life.

He had three missed calls from Naomi, but the name on the display had him wishing it was her again.

"Matt," his father said on a sigh. His dad wasn't a big phone talker. He was busy, and text was easier to ignore.

"You got married?" Oh shit. His mom was on the phone, too? He took a beat, trying to come up with a way to respond that wouldn't give anyone an immediate heart attack. His mother took that opportunity to wind up the level of the conversation. "There are pictures online. You look drunk. Were you drunk?"

"First, how are there pictures?" Not that he would have been able to clock and avoid paparazzi, but they usually ignored his family. It wasn't like they were the Kardashians. Old money didn't have to court publicity like that. In fact, it was very much frowned upon. "Were you having me followed?"

"No. Some model you dated at some point was at the same club, and she was being followed." That was news to him. His mother sighed. "Your credit card also showed a charge at a wedding chapel."

"When you took the plane, we were a little worried," his father explained, as though monitoring his credit card charges was just a totally cool thing to do.

"You never take the plane," his mother added.

It was true that he was reticent to take advantage of his family's wealth. He hadn't done anything to earn it, and it made him look like an asshole. And it gave his parents the idea that they had sway over what he did with his life. "Trust me, I'm never taking the plane again. I can promise you that."

"But you got married to some redheaded floozy?"

"Mom, no one calls anyone a floozy, and Bridget is not a floozy."

"I'm assuming you didn't have a prenup drawn up while you were doing shots." His father was always straight to the point.

"You would guess right."

"That means that she can try to get half of your trust fund if you get divorced," his mother said, sounding concerned. He could hear her mind turning over the phone. Could almost see her chewing her thumbnail—something she only did when she was deeply stressed.

"Bridget would never—"

His mother cut him off. "You don't really know her, do you?"

"I know enough."

"Our lawyer has already drawn up annulment papers." Of course one of his father's buddies—one of the ones who probably wanted Matt to come work for them until he let himself get pulled into one of the family businesses—had already drawn up papers to get this little mistake behind him. "We're sending them over right now. All you have to do is sign them. Both of you."

"What makes you think that I want to get the marriage annulled?" He tried to let his parents' gasps of horror roll right over him. He didn't *really* want to stay married, but it was actually kind of delicious to ruffle his normally unflappable parents. To take a stand that they wouldn't be able to protect him from.

He liked his parents, respected them. But he didn't want to be them. They were woven into an establishment that he wasn't sure he believed in anymore. They saw things for him that he couldn't quite envision for himself. Wasn't sure he wanted to.

His parents would hate the fact that he was married to someone like Bridget—who didn't come from the right kind of family, hadn't gone to the right kind of schools, wouldn't do anything to enhance the family fortune.

They would sign the papers as soon as Bridget got back to the room. They weren't going to stay married. That would be nuts. His parents were right—they did barely know anything about each other. But he liked the idea of his parents freaking out for a few days. They could spy on him and demand he be accountable to them for all his choices, but he could make them suffer a little bit.

It wasn't mature or particularly kind, but he was in the mood to be a little bit of a shit.

Instead of telling them to shove it, he said, "We'll talk about this when I get back to Chicago."

CHAPTER SIXTEEN

LATER, BRIDGET WOULD BLAME the long ride up on the elevator for what happened when she walked into the hotel room and saw Matt with the top two buttons of his crisp, white shirt undone, and his hair mussed from running his hands through it.

If they'd been on a lower floor, she wouldn't have had the time to think about how Chris had insinuated that she was a coldhearted bitch, unsuited for relationships, which was really annoying because he was essentially just agreeing with the mean, shitty things she thought about herself.

And then she couldn't stop thinking about her mother, who wanted her to try things out with Matt because it would be good for the museum.

Both of those inputs—from people she wouldn't and couldn't trust—must have gummed up the gears in her brain pretty well.

That was the only explanation for what happened when the doors of the elevator to the penthouse opened up.

Later, she would tell herself that she'd gone temporarily insane—a defense that almost never worked in front of a jury, the elements of that affirmative defense were nigh on impossible to meet—when she grabbed her former intern and now husband by the placket of his shirt and pulled his mouth to hers before he even got out a word.

Nothing but a shocked sound and a groan before he pulled her by the hips flush with his body and set her on fire with his lips and tongue. And then she let go of his shirt and ran her fingers through his hair, scraping his scalp and the nape of his neck with her short fingernails. The sound he made into her mouth turning everything below her waist to Jell-O.

She didn't know if she was wife material, but she wasn't cold. Not with Matt.

And, like the unicorn that he was, he just rolled with it— grabbed her ass, picked her up, and lowered her to the floor as though he was a professional at seductions in a foyer.

For all she knew, he was. Maybe this was how one seduced multiple models in a weekend—unlimited funds and saving time by screwing on the floor at the entrance to a hotel room. But Bridget didn't want to think about other women right now. She wanted to think about Matt's sculpted body under the shirt he still wore. She wanted to think about his strong arms and the way his forearms flexed as he pulled off her shirt and levered her body up so he could divest her of her bra.

"What are we doing?" he asked. If she stopped long enough to think about what they were doing, this would all stop. And she didn't want it to stop. And she didn't have a good answer for him anyway.

"I just think we should stick with the original plan and have our weekend fling. But with the added bonus of it being blessed in the eyes of God and Elvis."

He leaned down so his mouth was really close to hers. He grunted in apparent surprise when she took his bottom lip between her teeth for a brief moment before wrapping her arms around his neck and kissing him.

And he dove in again and kissed her in a way that made it completely impossible to think or do anything but feel.

Apparently, her God-and-Elvis argument was a winner. Or maybe it just gave her the excuse.

This was good. At least if they had sex with each other, they would have a fond memory to look back on rather than a stupid mistake. That was the last logical thought she had before he pulled her head back by her hair and licked her neck. His hands found her ass and he rolled them over so that his back was against the marble floor.

She wanted all of his skin against hers. She wanted him to count every freckle on her body with his tongue. She wanted to taste every last inch of him and make him lose control and turn her inside out.

Instead, he stopped her. "Are you sure you want to do this?"

"I think we're both sure, Matt." She rolled her hips against his groin. "Are you sure?"

"I've been sure for a while, Muffin."

She smiled and said, "Don't call me that," before kissing him again. This time, he took her face between his hands and controlled the kiss. She knew he was methodical, but at work he was also fast. This wasn't a fast kiss. It was extremely slow and thorough and made all of the tension melt out of her body. She loved every second of it.

Without warning, he put his hands behind her thighs and stood up from the floor with her in his arms. Aside from the one time that Chris had to fireman carry her several city blocks after the St. Patrick's Day parade, she'd never been picked up by a dude.

She didn't like that she liked it, but she was going to set it aside. They were alone in this hotel room, and no one had to know that she liked a little bit of consensual caveman shit. He carried her back to his bedroom and tossed her on the bed.

He looked down at her with a grin on his face and an expression that said he very much liked what he saw. Then he did that thing where he grabbed the back of his mostly unbuttoned shirt and dragged it off over his head.

She hadn't taken time to really look at him before getting sick in his bathroom that morning, and he was a revelation. All smooth skin and abs—he was perfect. The little shit knew it, too, because he just stood there letting her inspect him.

"Are you just going to stand there looking like that?" she said in her most accusatory tone.

"You seem to like what you see." God, she loved his cocky smirk. She wanted to poke at him just to see more of it, but there was a different kind of poking that she also had an immediate interest in.

To that end, she shimmied out of her pants and pulled off her panties. That wiped any bit of a smirk off of his face. He looked at her with something that approached wonder. It was a heady thing, especially since she'd grown accustomed to being looked at as though she was a piece of the furniture.

He dropped his pants and crawled over her on the bed before she could properly admire his thighs. But while he trailed kisses over her neck and other bits of skin that his mouth wanted to explore, she got to touch him all over.

He smiled up at her. "I feel like I'm living out a very-hot-for-teacher fantasy right now."

"You need to shut up and keep kissing if you don't want all this to stop and for all of my clothes to go back on."

"Of course, Muffin."

She shook her head and kissed him again, urging him to put more of his weight on her. And then she sighed in relief when he did. She didn't know she could feel so much lust and get so much comfort at the same time. It might be dangerous to feel too much for her soon-to-be ex-husband, but she couldn't stop herself from wanting more and more of him in the moment.

Eventually, she wanted his underwear gone, too. He must have sensed her getting anxious because he paused. "What do you want?"

Everything. For this to be the actual start of something and not the end of it. "I want you to fuck me, Matt. And here I thought you were a genius."

"As you wish, Buttercup."

"That's not any better, Matt."

Matt's hands shook as he pulled a condom out of his pants pocket and rolled it on, betraying his nervousness. It made it all the more endearing that he was nervous about this, too. He must have brought them out of hope that this would happen. Maybe not the wedding, but definitely this.

That word "wife" rang out in her head right before he was inside her. In the dim room, his dark eyes were glossy and shining at her like a beacon. She didn't want this to be the last time as well as the first time.

It felt right in a way that she didn't want to examine too much at the moment.

She pushed those thoughts away when he finally sank down inside her. She wrapped her legs around his hips and her arms around his neck.

"More." Now that they were doing this after what felt like an eon of waiting, she wanted more.

"Always demanding," he said.

"You love it."

He laughed but didn't respond. Which she totally understood. Right then, all she could do was feel him inside her, revel in being wrapped in the smell of his freshly showered skin, penthouse-fine sheets scrubbing against her back as they moved together. She felt like she was floating and falling all at once. She felt like she wanted to cry, but she wouldn't allow herself to do that.

"I need you to get there."

She snaked her hand between them to touch herself, and he moved in and out of her. After that, they didn't need words. They just moved together for what could have been seconds or minutes or hours.

When she came around him, her teeth digging into the tendon between his shoulder and neck, he moaned and let himself come. After it was over and they lay together like a sweaty mess, she knew that she was changed.

She would never be the same.

SHIT. HE'D HAD THE concierge print out the annulment papers so that they could sign them before they left Vegas together. He'd been ready to gently, kindly ask her to sign them when she'd walked into the hotel room and kissed him so hard that he forgot his own name, much less that they weren't supposed to consummate their marriage.

He supposed they could file the papers anyway, but that would be a lie. And Bridget couldn't lie to the court—any court—while she was an officer of the court. It could get her disbarred.

So he couldn't ask her to sign the annulment papers now.

He rolled away from her flushed, sweaty, perfect body and looked at her. She was still breathing heavily, and her eyes were still closed. He hated to do this, but now was as good a time as any. "So, I guess we can't get an annulment."

Her eyes snapped open. "That's what you have to say right now?"

He knew then that he'd said precisely the wrong thing. He'd brought them back to reality.

But it wasn't like they could escape reality and pretend they hadn't gotten married—before God and Elvis and all that.

And it wasn't like they could *stay* married. That would be crazy, and that wasn't what she wanted. Was it?

"We could see if we can get a drive-through divorce on the way out of town." He turned over so he could look at her. Her eyes were closed again, a bad sign. Or maybe he'd fucked her into uncon- sciousness, which he would take as a compliment.

"Those exist?" Her voice was flat now. God, he wished he knew what she was thinking.

"I saw it in a movie once."

"Really reliable precedent, Counselor." She sounded sarcastic, which he was pretty sure was a good thing. "What if we don't get divorced?" And the sarcasm disappeared, which was a bad thing.

He liked Bridget. A lot. And he wanted to do what they just did over and over and over again. But they hadn't even been on a real date. And she'd been his boss until yesterday. She was already established in her career, and he had no idea what he was doing in his life. He'd never heard of such a precarious beginning to a marriage.

They'd be setting themselves up to fail. Not to mention that his parents would lose their minds over the whole prenup thing.

"Listen—"

She cut him off. "I know it sounds crazy, but I promised myself that I would only do this once."

"This barely counts, Honey Bun."

"That one is also terrible." She paused. "If we get divorced—"

"This doesn't mean that we can't date." At least he hoped it didn't mean that they couldn't see each other. Or hang out. Or, like, Netflix and chill.

"So, we'll be divorced with benefits?" She didn't sound pleased, but he wasn't sure what would please her. She couldn't possibly just want to stay married to him. Until the last few days, he'd thought that she'd thought he was just a nuisance. And now she seemed to be arguing that they shouldn't get a divorce and shouldn't keep dating.

"What do you see happening?" He hadn't meant to raise his voice, but she was being totally ridiculous. "We're at different places in our lives right now. You have a whole-ass career, and I'm still in law school. As much as I like how this is fucking with my parents—"

"I'm still naked, Matt." Like that meant anything. They'd been going to get an annulment when all their clothes were on. And now that they'd done dirty naked stuff, they were going to put their clothes back on and get a fucking divorce. Like *civilized* people who had gotten drunk-married in Vegas.

"I don't see what that has to do with anything."

Then she sat up, and he knew he'd really screwed the pooch. She even covered her really great naked bits with a sheet. "I just don't want to talk about getting a divorce until my orgasm fades, but that ship has sailed."

"So we're going to get a divorce?" He really hoped she was talking sense.

Bridget sighed, and it was wistful. And it almost made him want to take everything back. Because he could totally see himself with her. If the circumstances were different, and they had the same origin story that he and Naomi did—not that she was rich, just that they were closer in age and stuff—he could totally see himself marrying her.

But the way they'd started, a fling made sense. Getting married did not.

"You know a divorce in Illinois is not instantaneous?" she asked. "It will take at least a month, even though I want nothing of yours, and you obviously want nothing of mine."

"Yeah, which was why I suggested the drive-through." It had seemed like a sensible idea at the time.

"We should do it back home so that no one questions the legality," she said, finally sounding totally sensible.

"That makes perfect sense."

"But—"

Oh shit. "But what?"

"I guess, if we're getting divorced, we don't have to end our fling right now."

"You have a point." He pretended to think on it for a few beats. "I had planned to show you around rich-people Vegas." She pulled a face. "You don't like that idea? What do you want to do?"

"I was sort of thinking . . ." He was surprised when she reached out for him and said, "More sex?"

He had no problem with that idea. Anything to keep his mind off the fact that he'd gotten Vegas-married and then bungled his annulment.

CHAPTER SEVENTEEN

OH, FOR FUCK'S SAKE," she muttered to herself when the doorbell rang. And then she almost said the same thing out loud when Chris came to the door. Instead she asked, "What the hell are you doing here?"

"I'm sorry," he said. For years, she let him get away with an *I'm sorry*, but she didn't want to right now.

"What else is new?"

"I didn't mean what I said the other night." He looked down at his hands and up again through his long lashes. Ordinarily, this was the point where she would forgive him. That was how it had always gone. And maybe she would forgive him but for the fact that she'd spent the weekend married to Matt. Now that she felt the electric heat of attraction to someone else, Chris wasn't looking so good. "You made the right choice . . . I wasn't ready, and neither were you. Can I come in?"

"If you must, but we're checking out, and I have a plane to catch." The only thing that forced her to let him in was the immense history between them and the sense that he truly was feeling contrite about his behavior.

"You can't give me five minutes?" That was the thing about Chris Dooley—no matter how much she ever gave him, he always wanted more, and he gave her nothing in return.

"I gave you twelve years." More like twenty, if she counted all the time she spent simply pining for him.

"I know, Bridge," he said as he made himself comfortable in her spot on the couch. All of a sudden, she really wanted him to leave. There was something about having him in this space that she'd shared with Matt that made her antsy, and she didn't want to know what it was. She wasn't ready for a sudden pivot in her feelings.

For more than a decade, she'd felt everything for this man—all her lust and hope and pleasure were tied up in him. And now he looked pale and tired in comparison to what she could maybe have with Matt. The part of her that always dug in and stayed stubborn wasn't ready to deal with that.

She operated on the premise that she always knew what was best, and the only thing that could ruin her plans were the foibles of the other people in her life—her parents, her brothers, Chris, and stupid misogynist judges.

"I'm sorry." Chris said it again, as though if he repeated it he could erase the fact that he'd mortified her in public over something that he shouldn't mortify her about.

She was angry with him, and she was done pretending not to be. Maybe because she was the one who got to dole out the forgiveness in that relationship. The way of the world that made sense to her when Chris fucking up and her forgiving him was beyond over.

"I get that you're sorry, but I don't know what that has to do with me." She had to stay strong or this would just be another time she forgave him and took him back.

"I want you back."

She rolled her eyes at him. "No, you don't. You saw someone else with the toy that you used to like but no longer like to play with and decided you had to have it back. You don't really want the toy. You want to know you can have the toy."

Chris stood up and walked toward her. "It's not like that, Bridget. I love you."

Now he says it? When she was finally ready to move on for real. After she finally got herself to sleep with someone else. The nerve of this man. "Well, you're too late."

"What do you mean, Bridge? It can't be too late—"

"Matt and I got married." She wasn't going to tell him the part about how Matt didn't want to be married to her and how they were going to get divorced once they got back to Illinois.

That stopped Chris in his tracks. He paused for only a second and then put his sarcastic jackass face on. It was the face he usually wore whenever she said that she wanted something that he didn't want to give her. "You didn't."

"Yeah, I fucking did." Part of her delighted in knocking Chris off-balance. Her whole adult life, he had been the one with the power to knock her off her game. Now the tables were turned, and it felt really good.

"I knew he was into you the other night." Chris sank back down onto the sofa, making himself a little too at home. "But I didn't realize he was going to swoop in and steal you right out from under me."

"He didn't steal anything," Bridget nearly screeched. "I'm not a fucking possession, and we were never going to get back together. Never."

She wasn't going to tell Chris that she had never intended to get involved with anyone else after their disaster of a relationship. And maybe part of her knew that Matt was a danger to that assumption as soon as she'd met him. On some level, she'd always known that Matt would blow up both her new life plan and her old life plan. And that's why he'd had to stay safe in the employee zone and then in the friend zone. Clearly, the friend zone had a much less stable infrastructure, given that he'd broken out of it so easily.

"So you got married, like, all drunk and shit?"

Chris wasn't as stupid as he looked, but she wasn't going to tell him the truth right now. That her marriage was a sham and would be over very soon. If he got Jack to forgive him, she'd have to see him a lot leading up to the wedding in a month. And Bridget would try to get Jack to forgive him. Just because he sucked as a boyfriend didn't mean he didn't need his lifelong friends.

But she didn't want him doing whatever this was. There was no way that they could get back together. Never ever.

And now she had the perfect thing to keep him away from her. Surely he'd respect the institution that he was so reticent about entering into. "I'm married to Matt now, and all this is moot."

She crossed her arms over her chest.

"You're giving me the lawyer face again."

"I don't know what you're talking about." Still, she looked away from him.

Chris stood up again, studied her face closely. "You're in love with this guy, aren't you?"

"Why else would I have married him?" She wasn't in love with

Matt, but he was the kind of guy she could fall in love with if she allowed herself to. She wasn't ready for how Matt could change her life. Given his family's wealth, he was from a different planet than her. They had virtually nothing in common, and he definitely wasn't in love with her. Lust, they had established. But she would fall for him hard and fast if they kept fooling around.

"I don't know, to make me jealous?" Chris certainly had a high opinion of himself, but she hadn't given him any reason to doubt her. Ever. Not even when they'd been broken up for more than two years.

At that moment, she was struck by how pathetic that was. There was nothing special about Chris. He was just a guy. And he'd never been in love with her. But she'd just had to force things, hold things together, through sheer will for years.

With the distance provided by her sham marriage to Matt, she could see how messed up that was. And it made her question whether she had ever been in love with Chris or if she'd just imprinted on him because he was there.

But she knew she wouldn't figure it out with Chris trying to get back into her life. So she needed Matt for the time being. And she wouldn't figure herself out if she let herself fall for Matt. So she needed to keep as much distance as this situation allowed.

So she would stay married to Matt until Jack and Hannah's wedding—or at least she would try to convince Matt to not tell anyone that they'd gotten divorced. But she and Matt wouldn't actually be involved. They'd just go back to being friends.

The perfect plan, right?

"I have to go, Chris."

He dragged his feet leaving the room. Before she closed the door on him, he turned and got close, way too close. "Just remember what we had together."

She rolled her eyes and shut the door.

THEY FLEW COMMERCIAL BACK to Chicago. Bridget didn't ask questions, and she was kind of grateful for the din of the airport—still some people wanting to play one more round of slots before returning to the real world. She didn't want to talk to Matt. Who knew that getting married could make things more awkward?

Well, technically, she did. You were supposed to marry your best friend, but that hadn't so much worked out for her. And the only other marriage she'd seen up close, her parents', had been super-awkward. Still, she should say something while they sat in the first-class lounge, sipping on drinks.

But Matt also looked reticent, his brow wrinkled like it did when the copier at the office didn't work. And she had the feeling that whatever problem he was working out in his head was bigger than a paper jam.

"Are you okay?" She figured that was what a supportive wife would say. Hannah would probably tell Jack that he needed to look cheerier while drinking champagne. But Matt wasn't like her brother. Jack would tell Hannah that he had plenty of problems to deal with being engaged to her. Matt wouldn't strike back like that. Partially because she'd been his boss for much longer than she'd been his wife. Partially because he didn't have the years of training in sarcasm and its power that she did in having siblings.

He looked at her then with an almost steely look in his eyes. "Nothing's wrong."

"I'm sorry I kind of disappeared after we—"

"You didn't do anything wrong." He turned his body so it was facing her. "I just—I don't want it to end."

"You don't want what to end?"

He motioned between them. "Us. I want there to be an us."

"So, you think we should date during *and after* our divorce?" She didn't mean for that to come out as loud as it did. "But I thought we were in different places in our lives. You're still in law school." She parroted his reasons for wanting to end things back to him.

"For, like, eight more months." He smiled.

"Why do you want to date me? What's the point if we're not going anywhere?" She had to talk some sense into him. They were getting divorced, and that was not an auspicious beginning to a relationship. "I was a kind of straight-up bitch to you when you were my intern."

"I acted like a cocky little shit the first day." He shrugged. "I deserved it."

"So, you don't want to be married to me, but you want to date me—possibly long-term. What, precisely, is the point of that?" Bridget had to conduct this like a cross-examination. She needed to treat this like she did every other problem that did not make sense— take it apart on the stand.

He gave her a long, slow look that told her he liked at least one thing about her, and heat rushed to her cheeks. "I think I made the point very clear on the floor of the penthouse. And then in the bedroom. All night."

That look and that memory made her feel hot all over, but she forced herself to roll her eyes at him. "Not worth the trouble."

"Says who?" He leaned in and she got a whiff of his demon sex pheromones again. "We don't have to be married to have some fun. Honestly, the kind of trouble we could get up to not being married sounds like a whole lot more fun than staying married."

He had her there. She wasn't exactly an expert. All of the marriages in her family had ended in disaster so far. She had hope for Jack and Hannah, but they were a special case of two good people.

Given how her relationship with Chris had ended, she was either so much like her father that she'd bore him to tears after a few years, or so much like her mother that she'd bug out as soon as things got tedious or overwhelming. And when you were dealing with living a life with another person, things always got overwhelming.

And all the marriages she dealt with at work ended even worse than the rather quotidian explosions of the ones in her personal life. She didn't think that Matt was like one of those monsters, but stranger things had happened.

"It will end badly." She knew it was a weak sort of defense, but entering into some sort of amorphous, undefined affair with her former intern, ex-husband, and possible financial benefactor was all kinds of messy. It would probably be better to stay married and see where things went. Get divorced later. But she knew that Matt would never agree to that. He would never know for sure that she wasn't after his trust fund.

"Being divorced with benefits seems to be working out for your parents."

"See now? That was exactly the wrong thing to say." She didn't want to follow in her parents' footsteps in anything involving their romantic relationships.

Their quick divorce was going to be too difficult to explain as things were. She was already dreading Chris finding out that it wasn't true love and forever the way she'd implied it was. And her mother's insinuation that she *couldn't* make a marriage work amped up all of Bridget's competitive drives. She ached to show her mother that not only could she make a marriage work; she could be the best wife on the planet, because she was nothing like Molly Simpson.

She was going to have to chow down on all her petty desire and shame when word got out that she and Matt had gotten divorced. The last thing she needed was having to explain that she and Matt weren't married but they were still seeing each other. Or talking. Or hanging out. Whatever the kids called it these days.

She turned in her seat, ready to tell him all of that, and that was a mistake. He had his head back on the seat, his eyes almost closed. His perfectly pressed white button-down was slightly open at the collar and she could see every tiny shift in the tendons of his neck as he breathed.

How had she not noticed how really perfect he looked during the months they worked together? Sure, there had been sexual tension that she hadn't wanted to deal with, but it felt like something had unfurled in her over the weekend. This deep, achy need to touch him, to curl into his body and keep him next to her always. The way he looked and smelled and just *was* made her greedy for him, and that greed felt dangerous. Right now, until they filed divorce papers and got a final decree, which would take at least a month, he belonged to her. She had a claim on him.

That idea curled through her, and she kind of understood why people got married, outside of it just being easier than breaking up. Having someone like Matt be tied to her—forever—was more appealing than she wanted to admit to herself. But she was admitting her pettiness in wanting to prove to Chris that she wasn't cold and broken, prove to her mother that she was better than her, and prove to herself that she wasn't destined to be alone.

Shame over her pettiness and the greed she felt for more of Matt—not his money, but the man himself—tinged everything, but an idea began to form.

Maybe, if they had a month, she could prove to herself, her ex, and her mother that she could be a wife. But it would require Matt's cooperation; it would require him to lie for her.

He looked at her then with a quirk to his lips, as though he knew she was thinking about doing something foolhardy and petty and he might just be on board. "What are you thinking?"

"Our divorce is going to take like a month, right?"

Matt nodded slowly, as though he was afraid of what she would say next. "Well, the quickie annulment is out of the question. Since we consummated the marriage pretty hard, and it's our only option."

Bridget hated offering plea bargains. It was part of her job, but if she was sure someone was guilty, she wanted to take them to trial and make sure they weren't able to harm anyone else for a good long time. And she hated having to sell opposing counsel on a plea deal. But she did it superlatively, just the way she did everything. And she had to put her selling hat on right now, make Matt see that this was the best option for them.

"We'll still be married at my brother's wedding, then."

"Yeah . . ." Matt still sounded hesitant.

"And you kind of like how this is messing with your parents, don't you?"

He squinted. She was losing him. "I don't see how that has anything to do with—"

"I think we should not tell anyone that we're getting a divorce." He opened his mouth, but she plowed right through. "After all, it's going to be super simple. We'll each go in with what we came out with." She'd probably lose out on the fellowship no matter what happened if his parents were truly furious, but she'd have to worry about that later. At this point, her needing to prove that she wasn't a defective woman because she couldn't stay married overrode her worries about her financial future.

"You want to help me mess with my parents for a month?" He looked away as though he was actually mulling over the idea.

"And it will mess with Chris, and with my mom." She was willing to give him that much honesty.

"It will also keep Naomi at bay so that I can concentrate on school." A sliver of victory twinkled at her from the distance when he said that. She could taste it.

That's when she went in and dangled what he really wanted. They could have their no-strings fling but—to the world—they'd be newlyweds. "And no one will ask questions about why we're hanging out if we're married."

"So, we can hang out"—he waggled his brows—"until the wedding."

"I'll file papers tomorrow, so we'll technically be married." The gate agent called for the first-class cabin to board. She took a deep breath and picked up her bag. "Until the wedding."

"How are you going to explain the divorce?" That was the rub. No matter how she explained it, she was going to look bad having the divorce. It would have to be her initiative. She could tell everyone that he was too immature to be married. Maybe he wanted to travel for a year after law school, and she couldn't very well do that. Maybe they would prove to be too different to make it work. But as long as it was amicable, she would be able to prove her point—that she could be married but didn't want to be.

She felt like telling Matt all that would be a bridge too far. He might think she'd lost it and find a way to push the divorce through fast or embarrass her with it. She didn't think he would, had no reason to think he would. But she'd never thought that Chris would set out to publicly humiliate her, either.

Instead, she just told Matt what he wanted to hear. "The bottom line is that we'll keep getting to consummate the marriage, and you'll get a no-muss divorce with your whole-ass trust fund intact. Plus, you'll get to annoy your parents for a month and keep Naomi off your back."

"And you'll get to stick it to Chris?"

"Exactly." She showed her ticket to the gate agent and walked down the Jetway. "And we'll be friends with benefits."

He trailed after her. "But—to the rest of the world—we're married until then?"

"Look at it this way—it will be good for both of us," she said.

Her offer hung over them as they made their way to their seats. He stowed both of their bags and waited for her to sit down. Her nerves were frayed by the time he looked at her and smiled. "You really are kind of an evil genius. Let's do it."

CHAPTER EIGHTEEN

WHILE SHE WAS STILL with Chris, Bridget had read in a women's magazine that happily married couples had sex an average of seven times a month. She'd had a good laugh, because she and Chris had dropped off that particular cliff sometime during law school. It was one of the most ironic and unfair things about her ending up pregnant. The nuns hadn't been kidding when they'd said it only takes one time.

In that same issue of the magazine—it must have been a June wedding issue—they'd also reprinted a bunch of old advice from a 1950s home economics textbook. At the time, it had reminded her of her mother before she'd left them—when she'd let almost everyone believe that everything in the Nolan house was perfectly smooth sailing. The old textbook had basically advised young women—because of course all domestic peace and tranquility and their opposites emanated from the wives—to make sure that everything was perfect when their husbands got home from work. They were to make sure the house was clean, dinner was ready, the children were seen and not heard, and that they also looked perfect. Most important, young wives were admonished never to complain if their husband was late or surly.

Basically, wives were told that they needed to be hot, their house needed to be perfectly clean, their children needed to shut the fuck up, and good wives never nagged.

Bridget hadn't been able to keep this outdated advice out of her head. It came to mind whenever she thought about getting married. Part of the reason she and Chris would never have worked was that she could totally see herself becoming some sort of 1950s home economics textbook of a person. Not even a person. Just a shell.

She could recognize it as the patriarchy, but something in her psyche couldn't grasp that she didn't have to be that in order to be a partner with a man.

As she drove over to Matt's condo after work, she kept thinking about all the ways she'd already failed to meet that standard with him. From the first day of his internship, she'd bossed him around. That probably made her a nag.

They didn't have children, but she couldn't even get her ex-boyfriend to shut up around Matt. Chris was essentially a child, so she'd already failed on that count.

And Matt had already seen her at her worst—in her father's immortal phrasing, she'd looked "rode hard and put up wet" the morning after her wedding.

So, she wasn't going to be the kind of wife that her mother had tried to be. She was already a failure at that. But she wondered what kind of woman she would need to be to keep someone like Matt married to her. She racked her brain for anything she could come up with to make him hesitate to sign the divorce decree.

Everything about their situation was strange. She had filed their petition for divorce in family court that afternoon.

Irreconcilable differences.

And she was carrying around her father's wedding ring in her pocket, so he could wear it and they could lie to the rest of the world for the next month or so. If their differences were so irreconcilable, then why did everything feel so right when they kissed? How could she forget everything but the feel of his hands on her body when they'd been in bed together?

She'd never felt that way about someone before, never craved them like a drug. In that moment, she could kick herself for choosing Chris at such a young age. Would she be so mixed up by Matt if she'd dated other people?

Probably not.

But just because she probably wouldn't feel this way about Matt but for her bad choices, it didn't feel any less imperative for him to want to stay married to her. Maybe it all came down to the fact that she hated losing.

She could already feel the hot bands of humiliation squeezing her chest, thinking about the look on Chris's face when he found out that she didn't stay married to Matt. He would feel like he'd been right about her—that she was a coldhearted bitch who deserved to be alone.

It didn't make sense that she wanted Matt to want to keep her. But, in that moment, she felt like she was in the midst of a very long temper tantrum. Whereas before, she'd come to her senses not long after the kitty litter dust settled in the driveway, a part of her wanted Matt to want to stay married to her. It was odd.

But she couldn't be the perfect wife, and they hadn't dated in a normal way before getting married. And the only things she really knew about dating were admonishments from Sasha to "always make them hungry for more," which usually got eye rolls and vulgar gestures from Hannah.

As she pulled up to the valet stand outside Matt's apartment, part of a really dumb idea occurred to her. The only time he'd ever seemed to be out of control was when they were having sex. Although, to be fair, she'd been pretty out of control then, too.

And the only way she'd ever been able to manipulate Chris was through his dick. Matt seemed to be more complex, but he was also ostensibly just as susceptible to her feminine wiles.

Feminine wiles born out of more than a decade of sexual frustration held more power than she'd thought.

She gave her name to the doorman at the desk, and he directed her to go up. Of course Matt lived in the penthouse.

The long elevator ride gave her time to come up with another truly terrible idea.

MATT DIDN'T REALLY KNOW what it took to be a good husband. Let alone a good fake husband. His father kind of had it down pat—let his mother do and have anything she wanted, and everything would turn out just fine. Matt figured that he would go with that model and let things unfold.

They'd agreed on Monday night to meet at Matt's apartment to discuss their current predicament and how they'd go about pretending that this was a real marriage for the next month. Matt had no idea what to expect. He'd never been married to anyone he was only trying to date before. He'd never been trying to seduce a woman he was also divorcing.

And his nervousness was amplified by the fact that his mother was likely losing her mind over the fact that he'd done something this impulsive. He would be lucky if she didn't have him kidnapped at this point.

When his doorman rang up to let him know that Bridget had arrived, he ran around his apartment to make sure that that there wasn't any stray mess lying around that Bridget would judge him for. Her office was always pristine, and he assumed that her house was the same.

He didn't really know why he was doing it. It wasn't as though he needed to impress her as his soon-to-be ex-wife. Maybe he was just in the habit because of being her employee for three months.

Jesus, he'd never been this nervous. And now he felt as though he was going to pull his hair out over his wife.

His wife.

Even three days later, it felt weird. But oddly, even though they were most definitely still getting a divorce, not bad.

He let the weirdness soak him until he heard a knock at the door. He couldn't help running to open it up. "Hi." Hi? She was going to think he was daft. "Come in."

She did seem as awkward and stilted as he was. After all, she'd married him having never been in his home. There was so much they didn't know about each other. All he had was the fact that she was brutally competent and funny and had a complicated family.

One thing he absolutely knew about Bridget Nolan was that she wasn't the kind of woman who would marry him for his family's money and social status. She would have played being his boss totally different than she had. She would have flirted and simpered—or made his work life easier at the very least.

After spending the weekend with her, he knew that even more. Even when the messy aspects of her life came out at that dinner the first night, she hadn't tried to hide who she was or how she lived.

Part of why he knew he needed to get the divorce was that he was afraid that she was the kind of woman he could really fall in love with.

She stared at him for a second too long, until he remembered his manners. "Can I get you something to drink?"

"Something very alcoholic."

"Wine?"

"Perfect."

He moved to the kitchen but watched her taking in his space out of the corner of his eye. Sitting across from him at his kitchen island. He'd never felt embarrassed about his family's money and what that meant before he met Bridget. Sure, he'd tried to downplay it in order to avoid freeloaders and gold diggers—not that it worked for Naomi—but spending time with Bridget and working with her all summer made him confront the very real privilege he took for granted.

Bridget didn't say anything, didn't even look at him like he was a shithead. Not the way she'd looked at him that first day in the office. She took her wine and took a long gulp.

"Thank you for doing this." She sounded grateful, when he was the one getting a pretty good deal. He got to hang out with a gorgeous redhead, piss his parents off, and keep Naomi off his jock for a month.

"It's not a big deal." He took a drink of his own wine, but really wanted to taste her mouth. Ever since the day after their wedding, he'd been thinking about her mouth. Would never forget her taste. But it was the kind of memory that would make him an addict. He would never get enough of her, and he would be ruined. She was the end of him.

"It's totally a big deal." She put her hand over his across the marble island that took up entirely too much space between them. "You're really covering my ass."

"I like to be the only thing covering your ass." He wasn't going to tell her that he was getting as much out of this arrangement as she was. He had an ex to make jealous, and he and Bridget hadn't gotten close to covering the sex territory that he wanted to cover with her. "It's fine. Only a month."

Which suddenly didn't seem like enough time.

"Yeah, but there's a rehearsal dinner. And, shit, Jack asked you to be in the wedding?" She stood up and turned around. He made the mistake of following her hands when she stuffed them in her back pockets. Shit. He was going to lose it if he couldn't touch her again soon. It was as though having been with her just made everything worse. He'd never get the sound of her coming out of his brain, never be able to erase the sight of all that dark red hair messy and slipping through his fingers like water.

They should have met on neutral territory. Someplace he wouldn't be tempted to boost her up on the kitchen island and just ruin her mouth until it was swollen and her silver-blue eyes went molten.

"I think we should set some ground rules."

"There are ground rules for what we're doing?" This probably wasn't the time to be telling her that he was really turned on when she talked about ground rules.

Her expression was completely sincere—no hint of sarcasm. And that turned him on, too. "Yeah, like how many times a week are we going to have sex?"

His mouth twitched and he seriously wondered if he was going to be able to keep himself from bursting out laughing. She wanted to set a *sex schedule* with her friend with benefits. He kept it to a grin that he hoped she read as wry. "Is it going to be that much of a chore for you?"

Her face flushed, and he moved closer to her. She stepped back, and he stopped. "That's not what I mean."

"What do you mean, then?" He really wanted to get through this conversation so that they could schedule some sex for tonight.

"He was my first . . ." She paused. "I feel like I don't know what I'm doing with you."

"But *you* had fun, right?" he asked. She nodded and bit her lip. It was so endearing and fist-bitingly hot that he could barely stand it. He could also barely stand for her to think she didn't know what she was doing. The way she touched him—it was going to burn him alive if he wasn't careful. And he also wanted to rip her ex-douche apart. Letting Bridget Nolan think she wasn't the hottest lay in the history of hot lays should be criminal. "Here's the only ground rule I'm interested in—if you're having fun, then I'm having fun."

"Really?" she said. He hated that she seemed surprised.

"The first is never the best." He wished he was the kind of guy who would play dirty, who would remind her of the fact that, even though they didn't have the history she had with her ex-douche, they had something worth exploring.

She looked away from him. "You don't understand what it is to have that kind of history with someone."

"I certainly understand what it's like to have a shitty kind of history with someone," he said.

Bridget tilted her head. "I always thought that what Chris and I had was as good as it got."

"Yeah, I'll bet that it was just a whole barrel of laughs." He'd also bet that Chris Dooley couldn't find a clit with a flashlight, but he didn't think it would help get him laid to tell Bridget that out loud. He'd save it for the rehearsal dinner, if the ex-douche was even invited.

"Still, we need some more ground rules."

Matt took a big swallow of wine and motioned for her to go on. "Like what?"

"A sex schedule." Why was she still on that? "I want to make sure that I'm keeping up my end of the bargain and that you stay satisfied."

She was making this whole deal seem like a lot less fun than it had when she'd originally proposed that they stay publicly married for a month. He wondered what other fun-killing ground rules she would come up with.

"And what are we going to tell people about living in two different apartments?" he asked. Having her here with him would give them some flexibility with her stupid sex schedule ground rule.

"Don't you have a lease?"

Matt smirked. "My parents own the place."

"And my dad owns my place."

"Which means that there's no reason that we can't move in together."

Bridget shook her head. "No one will know that we don't live together if we don't tell them."

He was going to have to be more explicit about why he wanted her to move in with him for a month.

He stepped closer to her, and this time she didn't step back, although she took another fortifying swallow of wine. "I just think that we should live together if we're going to come to terms about the kind of sex schedule that makes sense."

"And that requires living together?" She kind of squeaked, and that sound coming from his usually unflappable former boss set him afire.

"You just don't get it." He ran his thumb across her lower lip. "You don't get how much I want you."

She tried to look away, but he gripped her chin. What he'd gotten out of this conversation so far was that she usually felt like sex was a chore to be scheduled with a chart or a reward to be doled out. He wanted to make her see that it was for her—that in any fling with him, she would enjoy everything they did as much as he did. Hell, he wanted her to have more fun than him because she'd apparently been missing out on so much for so long.

He held her gaze for a long moment. Her eyes glittered, and he wondered if she was pissed at him or if she was thinking along the same lines as he was. "What can I do to make this so much fun that we have to schedule two-a-days?"

Bridget started, and he expected her to pull away and eviscerate him with some scathing remark. The last thing he expected was for her to say, "Kiss me."

He'd never moved so quickly in all his life. He pulled her close and took her mouth. Her smell wrapped him up tight, and her soft lips yielded to him in a way that made his knees weak. Her warm curves somehow held him up, though, seeming to press against him as he ran his hands along her sides, pulling her hips close and inflicting exquisite torture on his poor dick.

He wanted to lay her out on his sheets and find every freckle on her gorgeous body with his mouth. He wanted to trace and map her and see the morning sunlight reflecting on her hair.

Most of all, he never wanted her to doubt that sex with him was so good that they'd blow any sex schedule or quota out of the water.

He had plans to do all of it—to tell her without words that she was a siren underneath her tailored suits and prissy demeanor. He meant to get started tonight, but unfortunately, his phone rang.

Bridget pulled away. "You should get that. It could be your parents."

He groaned. "It would be better if I didn't answer. It would help me piss them off more."

"I think you've done that enough by getting married to me in the first place. This is more to help me with my ex and you with yours at this point."

She had a point, so he pulled away and answered the phone. "Mom?"

WHILE MATT WAS ON the phone, Bridget remembered what she had to give him and reached in her pocket. She wondered what he would do if she told him it was her father's wedding band. It didn't matter that the marriage that ring had sanctified hadn't lasted, because this one wouldn't, either.

He sounded irritated on the phone but hung up quickly. When

he did, he looked as though he was ready to pick up where they'd left off. She wasn't so sure. Having sex with him in Vegas had been part of the whole impulsive thing. Sleeping with him now, when they were back in real life, would somehow mean more. Even if it wasn't supposed to.

That's why she'd wanted it to be on a schedule. So she could mentally prepare, do it in her role as the perfect wife. So she wouldn't really have to show herself to him and put herself at risk of real feelings.

The best way to avoid jumping his bones, right here, right now, was probably to remind him that they were currently married. She handed him the ring. "It isn't much, but this should be enough to convince your ex that you're a married man now."

The tips of his fingers singed her palm when he took the ring. He didn't say anything for a beat too long, just enough for doubts to creep in. "If you want to buy something more expensive, I guess I can't stop you."

"This is perfect," Matt said. She looked up to see him slip the ring over the knuckle on his left ring finger. It fit. She'd been a little worried that it wouldn't. Sean Nolan had a workingman's hands, bruised and battered and permanently swollen from the work he'd done all her life.

Even though she knew better—that Matt was bright and hard-working despite the fact that he didn't have to be—she couldn't help but compare his very elegant hands with the hands of the kinds of guys she grew up with.

And once she thought about his fingers, she couldn't stop thinking about how his hands had felt all over her body. Even though she'd kept everything compartmentalized for most of the day, she felt her body heat. She wanted to rub her thighs together, but he would notice because he was looking at her.

"What?"

"This is your dad's ring." He knew, and it meant something to him even though it shouldn't mean anything to him. They were both each other's means to an end.

"It is." They might be lying to everyone else, but she wasn't going to lie to him. "It doesn't mean anything. My parents are divorced."

"They're back together now." He smirked at her. "So, the inability to change one's mind is not a family trait?" He was trying to goad her. It was an obnoxious habit that he'd picked up somewhere along the line when he'd stopped being afraid of her. But he didn't look like he would eat her alive anymore; he seemed to sense that the mood had shifted.

"No." She didn't want to elaborate because every time she gave him a little bit of herself, she felt more intimacy with him. It made it harder to keep him in the friends-only compartment in her mind. Because every time she let him know what she was thinking or feeling, she wanted him to be feeling her in a more carnal sense.

This wouldn't do at all.

"Why Chris?"

He really wasn't going to let her get away with being evasive, was he?

"You know that we've known each other since we were little kids?"

"Yeah." He poured her some more wine. "I fail to see that as a reason to stick with someone forever."

"It just felt like it was meant to be. When it ended, it felt like I'd missed out on my one chance."

"What? You think it's fate or something?"

"Some might argue that my parents are fated to be together." She took a sip of wine. "I mean, they should have been able to stay far apart."

For some reason, she thought she'd have a harder time staying away from Matt once they were divorced than she'd had staying away from Chris, even though he was practically family.

CHAPTER NINETEEN

NAOMI WAS WAITING FOR him when he got to campus. Her glossy blond hair was almost blinding in the summer sun. And she was dressed to kill—a swingy little skirt and a top that showed just a little bit of midriff. And she knew he saw her because she looked at him over the top of her designer sunglasses as soon as he got out of his car.

Matt looked down at his wedding ring and moved it around his ring finger, still unused to the weight on his hand. But somehow, it was kind of comforting.

Even though he and Bridget had only ended up talking last night, and even though the ring was a lie, he liked what it symbolized. He liked the feeling of belonging with Bridget and her strange, loud family. He liked the feeling that he didn't have to pretend to be someone he was not.

He really didn't want to deal with Naomi today. Since he hadn't taken any of her calls over the summer, one would think that she'd gotten the hint that he was done with her. They'd never be able to avoid each other—not with their families so close. But if she had enough gumption to publicly declare that she was only with him for his family name and family money, he would have thought that she would give up the ghost.

He was wrong.

As he neared the building where his advanced tax law seminar was being held, she approached, and he braced himself. The first thing he noticed was that she didn't smell anything like Bridget.

The second thing he noticed was that he'd never noticed how annoying her voice was—probably because he'd been in love with her. "Matty, I've missed you." She threw her arms around his neck and hung there, choking him.

He was stunned for a second, until he noticed that there were plenty of their classmates in the courtyard, making their way to class. "What are you doing, Naomi?"

She must have sensed the censure in his tone because she pulled back and made her lower lip pouty. "You haven't forgiven me, have you?"

"Forgiven you for what, Naomi?" He was definitely going to make her say it, or at least think about what she'd done.

"The things I did . . . you know." She grimaced.

"For cheating on me and then telling all your friends that you were only with me because our parents forced us together? Or telling everyone that I was bad in bed?" Matt was over being embarrassed by that. Naomi had never had any reason to complain, and the petty, toxically masculine part of him was tempted to say it out loud.

Only he wasn't an actual sociopath, unlike Naomi.

"Matt, it wasn't like that." She put her hand on his chest but removed it when he flinched. "We were just joking around. You know I liked it."

"Listen, lots has changed." He started to walk away, but she hooked her arm through his.

"And I want to hear all about it."

He stopped and turned. "There is one thing I've been dying to tell you." He raised his brows and slowly lifted his left hand so she could see. "I'm married. To someone who likes the way I fuck her."

He left her standing in the courtyard, looking stunned. He'd never been so excited on the way to tax class.

JACK LOOKED AT HIS bride-to-be and quaked before her might and power. Chris Dooley was screwed if he thought he was going to be able to move Hannah off her no-Chris-at-any-wedding-of-mine stance. It was just the truth.

They were meeting on neutral territory. Jack had advised that Chris try not to breach the perimeter of their condo. Hannah would probably throw him out the window. She had very little patience for male fuckery, so defenestration was totally on the table. Since Jack gave her very little fuckery to worry about, she had a lot of pent-up justice to mete out.

And since Hannah and Bridget had grown very close over the past year and a half, Hannah was more than prepared to dish out a can of ass-whupping on Bridget's behalf.

As they waited in a booth at the back of Dooley's for Chris to show up, his fiancée's glee was almost palpable. It made Jack glad that he'd been able to win her over. Had he failed he was pretty sure that buzzards would have picked over his bones in the desert some months ago.

He was almost concerned for Chris but shrugged it off. When Chris had apologized for his behavior at their pickup basketball game, Jack had warned him that Hannah's forgiveness was hard to earn. And Chris wasn't allowed to earn it with sexual favors, so it was definitely not guaranteed.

"You're not allowed to maim him," he said, wanting to be sure the ground rules were clear.

Hannah took a drink of her beer. "C'mon! You never let me maim anyone anymore."

"I was running out of bail money," he said with a smile. "Seriously, what's the plan? Are you just going to make him beg or are you going to let him back in on the wedding?"

"It depends on what he brings to the table." She wrinkled her nose in this ridiculously cute way that made him want to leave and take her straight to bed. "If he promises to leave Bridget the fuck alone, I might let him back in the wedding. But I don't trust him. What he did in Vegas was beyond gross."

Jack tended to agree, but their family's history with the Dooleys made it nearly impossible to excommunicate Chris completely from their lives. His older brother was saying their wedding Mass, for Christ's sake. "I get that, but you don't have the history with him that Bridget does."

"Yeah, I wanted to punch his dumb face the night I met him."

That was the same night that they'd met. "But I talked you down."

"You bribed me with food."

"I kissed you." He didn't need to remind her, because he could tell by the look in her eye that she was remembering.

Still, she protested. "That was because of the tacos. Not because you're charming or anything."

God, he loved the way she busted his balls. He loved almost everything about her. If she wiped the sink after brushing her teeth, she'd be perfect. And then he really wouldn't deserve her.

Chris walked in then, which meant the chance to sneak off to the supply closet with the woman who would be his wife in a little less than a month was gone. Too bad, but he'd rather take things slow when they got home a bit later.

His lifelong best friend looked sweaty, disheveled, like he hadn't slept in a week. "Thanks for meeting me."

When Chris moved to sit down, Hannah gave him a look. "I didn't say you could sit."

"Oh," was all he said. Then he stayed standing. Smart man.

"Sit the fuck down, Dooley," Jack said. His friend sat, while Hannah looked at him like she was going over medieval torture methods in her head.

They sat there and stared at each other for way too long, until Jack checked his watch. He wanted to listen to Chris grovel while he finished his beer, let Hannah make him sweat, and then get home in time for sex. They needed to get on with this.

"Say what you have to say, man."

Chris looked at him and Jack saw an honest-to-God droplet of sweat make its way down his face before Chris looked at Hannah. "I'm sorry. I fucked up."

"You're going to need to be more specific," Hannah said, probably enjoying this far too much.

Chris buried his head in hands. "I'm sorry for what I said in Vegas. I was an asshole."

"Oh, I think you were an asshole before that," Hannah said in order to prompt his further contrition.

"I'm sorry I messed things up with Bridget before that happened. I took her for granted, and I didn't realize what I had lost until she was gone. And then I saw her with that other guy—"

Hannah smiled at him with fake beneficence. "You mean her rich, hot young husband?" Hannah winked at Jack, and he was a little relieved. For a second there, her enthusiasm for Matt Kido sounded a little too real.

"Yeah. That guy." Chris actually sounded a little pissed. "I promise I'll behave at the wedding."

"You won't interfere with Bridget and her new man?" Hannah raised her eyebrows in peak skepticism. "Because that's the only way I'm letting you back in the wedding. I need you to suffer for what you did to Bridget. You stole over a decade of my friend's—my new sister's—life. And the best thing I can think of to punish you is to make you watch her being happy."

"I promise I won't do anything." Chris sounded a little bit too relieved.

Hannah leaned over the table and met Chris's gaze. Somehow, he got even paler. "You'd better not." And then she added, "Now, leave. I want to finish my beer in peace."

Chris looked for a moment as though he was about to say something about this being his family's bar but thought better of it and walked out with a wave to the bartender. "Comp their drinks, please."

Hannah looked at Jack, smiling as though she hadn't just made a grown man nearly piss his pants in fear. She raised her glass. "Cheers."

Jack smiled back at her. "You're really something, you know that?"

She shrugged at him and threw in a fake pout. "What? How am I supposed to stay sharp given that you only let me punish you every other Thursday?"

"Fair point, Duchess."

CHAPTER TWENTY

BRIDGET WAS IRRITATED. SHE'D never hauled Chris around to run errands, and she didn't know why Matt insisted on coming along. Didn't having a wife mean that he didn't have to run his own errands anymore? He'd muttered something about fitting into her schedule, so it was probably a sex thing. She needed to get fitted for her bridesmaid's dress, pick out a gift, and grab her groceries. He was just making everything take longer. "I don't know why you need to be here for this."

His face was fake innocent, faux-nocent. "I'm in the wedding now, and I should help pick out the gift."

Bridget rolled her eyes and walked away through the crowds at the Michigan Avenue Bloomingdale's. "They have a registry. It's not that hard. I pick the thing that I can afford that makes me look the least cheap." Given how many of her friends were getting married, and how big her student loans were, she had to think about that.

"I didn't take Hannah for a girl with a registry," Matt said as he picked up a vase that probably cost more than a month's rent.

She loved but kind of hated how perceptive he was. She liked that he had an idea of what Hannah was like after spending not that much time with her. But it also meant that she had to keep her guard up lest she mess up and really opened up to Matt—she was just afraid that she would do something terribly stupid like falling in love with her husband. "The woman is pretty nontraditional in most things, but her lust for kitchen appliances can't be denied."

"I bet she also liked running around with the little scanner guns they give you."

Bridget giggled, and it surprised her. She laughed fairly easily, but giggling really wasn't her thing. She had to keep a lid on how easy it was to be around Matt. "She really did. It was a little bit frightening."

"I like your family," he said apropos of nothing. "They're really good people."

She wasn't sure what to say about that. She'd made assumptions about his family when she'd first met him. And maybe those assumptions were accurate, but Matt turned out to be a decent guy despite his family. They weren't married for real, and it wasn't any of her business why his eyebrow furrow made him look like he was doing a point-by-point comparison of their families.

"What's your family like?"

Curiosity killed the cat, and it would probably murder her pledge to keep Matt away from her pussy. But she couldn't help wanting to know more about him. The more she knew, the more she liked, and the more she wanted.

"They're pretty normal, despite the abnormal circumstances," he said. He picked up a wineglass as though he wished it was full. "I mean, I went to boarding school. I had nannies—my parents were really too busy to be too involved. But when they're there, they're there.

"And there are expectations. My dad's mom's family has been here since before America was a country. His dad survived the war in Japan and moved here thinking he'd married a pretty Red Cross nurse only to realize that he'd married this Boston Brahmin princess."

"That sounds like a lot." It sounded kind of like what she was going through with Matt. Only, she'd known who he was and hadn't consciously decided to get married. "And your mom? She runs a hedge fund, right?"

"She's actually much more chill than I made her sound." Matt gave her a grimace. "I'm just her only baby, so she's really over-involved in my life choices."

"I get that." She didn't, not given the fact that her mother had been conspicuously uninvolved in her life. But she wanted him to keep talking. Maybe it was the rush of shoppers around them, the fact that they weren't alone, but the sexual tension was thus lessened—at least for her.

"She used to be in a punk band. At Stanford." He laughed, prob-ably remembering a picture of his mom in ripped jeans and a shag haircut. You know, his mom having an age-appropriate moment of rebellion. As opposed to up and leaving after she'd had three kids.

"That sounds cool."

"It was. Made my grandmother so worried." Matt startled her by grabbing her hand and leaning over to whisper in her ear. "Always so concerned about what people would think."

"I mean, your grandfather *was* a senator." She tried to focus on the original topic of their conversation and not the fact that he was touching her or the fact that he didn't show any signs of stopping.

"Yeah, but he was a war hero. Everyone loved him, even his staff."

"Is that how you know the Chapins?" Maybe it would be useful to remind him that he was staying publically married to her to get his ex off his back. His ex who was also related to American royalty. Even if they were tarnished, they were still in the same social sphere. What was between Bridget and Matt wasn't real. Couldn't be real.

"Yeah, but I don't want to talk about Naomi or her corrupt fucking uncle." He tugged on her arm and stopped them both in the flow of people.

Time stood still in a crowded department store. She should tug her hand loose and get on with it. But she didn't want to. It was ten on a Saturday morning, and she wanted to do Saturday night things to Matt Kido in the middle of the same Bloomingdale's she'd bought her first training bra from. All she managed was a not-nearly-indignant-enough, "What are you doing? We're getting in the way."

He just smirked at her. "I found it."

"Found what?" All of her weaknesses, the way to get her all horned up while running errands, or something useful?

"The present." He pointed over at the KitchenAid mixer that Hannah coveted more than anything.

"I can't afford that," Bridget said. Not without eating ramen for a month. "You know how much I make."

"Relax, I got it."

But that didn't feel right. She was a bridesmaid, and it was her gift. They were only pretending to be married, and neither of them could afford to forget that. "I can't let you do this."

He said nothing, just continued to block traffic in the busy store.

"Seriously, it's way too much," she protested.

That's when it must have dawned on him why she was refusing. "We're still married. Technically, it's your money for another couple of weeks."

"But I don't want you to think I'm with you because of that—"

"No, of course not. You're in it for the sex. The scheduled sex."

She shushed him and then let him buy the mixer.

CHAPTER TWENTY-ONE

MATT'S SATURDAY HANGOUT WITH Bridget was going beautifully. He had her all to himself, and he was going to get to see the finished bridesmaid's dress. It was really the perfect date, and he didn't know why more people didn't run errands together as a way of getting to know each other.

First of all, there was none of the awkward eye contact required during a dinner date. Second, there wasn't the constant, distracting possibility of sex that went along with a more relaxed at-home dinner. While shopping, they could chitchat about everything and nothing. And Bridget's guard was down.

Once he'd convinced her to let him pay for all but a hundred dollars' worth of the mixer—since the gift would be from both of them—they'd moved on to tuxes. He had one, but he decided he needed a new one for the wedding because he liked the idea of Bridget picking out his clothes for him. It seemed like the kind of domestic thing she would do if she was really his wife.

He didn't even mind her watching as the tailor in his favorite bespoke suit shop was touching him in his bathing suit areas. He wanted that from Bridget, too. But that was far from all he wanted from her.

That should have been his first clue that he wasn't just in like or lust with her, that he was in real danger of falling in the kind of love with her that hurt when it ended. He wanted to spend as much non-naked time with her as he wanted to spend naked time.

He wanted more with her. And they'd definitely rushed into marriage, but that didn't feel as bad as it would have with Naomi. He was absolutely certain that Bridget would only be with him because she loved him. If they could step things back to dating, maybe he could convince her that this fling shouldn't be a fling. Maybe it should be a full-fledged relationship.

Even though he'd admired her tenacity while working under her, he wished she would give it a rest while he was working to get under her—and over her and to the side.

He was gratified by the fact that he'd caught her staring at him while his shirt was off. He didn't say anything because he didn't want her to stop staring.

Still, she blushed when their gazes met. "What?"

He raised a brow at her and buttoned the cotton and silk shirt that went with the tux he was supposed to wear for the wedding. He interpreted the fact that she went back to looking at her phone to mean that she was disappointed at no longer being able to ogle his chest. He lived ever in hope with Bridget.

"How much longer is this going to take?" And just as she gave hope, she took it away.

"It's a Saturday." He shrugged as the tailor put a few more pins at the hem of his pants and he perused cuff links. "We have all day. Relax."

Bridget stood up and walked toward him as he realized his mistake. "Really? You think it's a good idea to tell me to relax?"

"I'm sorry." He tried his best to look contrite, though he liked seeing Bridget get a little agitated and irritated. It was like playing with matches as a kid—dangerous but thrilling. "I know I can't have *those* kinds of benefits—since it's not on the schedule—but I figured I'd milk our marriage for the kind of benefits that get me more time with you."

Just like that, all the anger disappeared from her expression. Her shoulders dropped. She seemed soft and young and he'd never wanted to kiss her more. "You want to spend time with me outside of the schedule?"

The extremely discreet tailor moved away without a word.

"Of course," he said as he leaned down to brush his lips across her cheek. "We're friends."

"Good friends," she said, sounding dazed. He hoped her cheeks were burning because of the little bit of contact that she'd allowed. He wanted them blazing and flushed from a lot more contact than that. But he'd settle for this.

"The best." Before she could respond to that, he said, "Let's go get your dress fitted."

MATT WAS DEFINITELY GOING to send Hannah a fruit basket or a subscription to a wine-of-the-month club in addition to the commercial-grade mixer. Any woman who picked out a bridesmaid's dress that made Bridget look like an actual Celtic goddess rising from a lake to lead men to their dooms deserved much more than a simple kitchen appliance.

Not to mention the fact that, if he squinted, he could see Bridget's nipples.

"Thoughts?" She swished the skirt around her legs playfully, and he grew inexorably, painfully hard. If there wasn't an entire bridal party oohing and aahing over their newly engaged friend on the other side of the salon, Matt would be seriously thinking of begging Bridget to let him have her over the back of the couch he currently occupied.

She was gorgeous. The lilac-colored fabric kissed her figure and made her pale skin actually glow. Instead of saying that, or anything that would make her realize that he was more than halfway in love with her, he said, "Nice dress."

She squinted at him as she approached. "Nice dress?" He hoped she wouldn't look down at his lap and realize what a filthy, perverted liar he was. He was spared when she grabbed his glass of champagne.

"You look strange." She squinted at him, and he shifted on the couch. "Do you really like it?" she asked before tipping up his glass and emptying it. And then the little minx winked at him as she handed it back. "They're definitely going to have to do something about the nipple situation."

Matt coughed to cover up his reaction when she pointed out the "nipple situation."

Perhaps she'd been doing this on purpose the whole time, teasing him and enchanting him like a witch, because she smiled then. "You need to stop looking at me like that."

"Like what?" He'd really tried to look at her like a friend would look at his knockout of a friend and former colleague whom he happened to be married to.

"You need to stop looking at me like you are enjoying looking at me too much."

Impossible. "I'm trying."

She walked back toward the dressing room and said, "Try harder."

His trying wasn't the only thing that was going to get harder before the end of their sham marriage.

CHAPTER TWENTY-TWO

THIS IS NOT PART of the deal," Bridget said as Matt walked into her apartment that night. "I don't need your help babysitting a dog."

Her irritation at having him tag along for her shopping trip had faded. He seemed so intent on foiling her plans of being the perfect wife. His determination to spend all this low-key time with her—flirting and teasing—felt easier than trying to impress him and keep him at a safe distance. He was so charming and easy to be with. It felt utterly unlike her relationship with Chris. So much trying happened there.

She almost felt like she could do marriage with Matt, and she should be really afraid of it. He was going to leave her bereft in a way that Chris hadn't, because Matt actually made her feel less lonely rather than more. He made her feel more wanted than tolerated.

And the little shit he did to show her that he cared broke down her resistance to just being in the moment and enjoying hanging out with him. She should really hate it, but she didn't.

After he'd chipped in for the mixer, allowed her to ogle him without comment, and given her ego quite a boost at the bridal store, she'd been a little sad at thinking about him leaving her alone that evening.

But then Jack had texted and asked her if she would watch their dog, Gus, for the night. Apparently, wedding planning for her own wedding was more stressful for Hannah than planning other people's weddings—especially given that her own mother was very much against the entire institution. Jack had decided that they needed to have a pre-wedding honeymoon in addition to their post-wedding honeymoon. Hannah just called it was what it was—a dirty hotel-fuck weekend.

Although Bridget didn't need to know the details about her brother's dirty weekends, she was happy that he was having them.

Really, she was happy that he was happy. The pangs she'd experienced when Hannah and Jack had first gotten engaged had pretty much disappeared. And she wasn't going to think about how that might be connected to the man currently getting sloppy kisses of greeting from her brother's French bulldog.

"Be careful, he—" Bridget winced as Gus started humping Matt's arm. That probably wasn't the sort of humping that he'd been hoping for when he came back here with her. But Gus was really covering a lot of ground with this interlude.

When Matt figured out what was happening, she realized that she probably let it go on for longer than it should. "Um, is he humping me?"

She was having trouble suppressing her laughter. Should definitely not be laughing at this. If the dog was a person, she would have enough to indict him. "I prefer to think of it as an enthusiastic hug."

For a moment, she thought Matt was going to get mad. Had he done that, she might as well have kicked him out of her apartment like she had Chris. But he didn't.

He struggled up to standing—which was harder than it would seem given Gus's size—and started laughing. "I probably shouldn't give him a treat for that." He pointed at the dog, who sat on the floor, smiling up at his new boyfriend. "And he should definitely buy me dinner now."

At the mention of dinner, her stomach growled. Shopping was hungry work, especially when one spent a significant amount of energy pretending not to want to rip one's husband's clothes off. "You can stay for dinner."

For a few split seconds, she thought about cooking for Matt, how nice it would be to have a cozy meal at home with a man in her space again. She thought about how easy it would be to pretend that this was all real and they were going to give it a go as a married couple.

If their accidental marriage was intentional, the thought wouldn't have taken her breath away. And it wasn't even the image of her bustling around the small kitchen while Matt sat at her island with a glass of wine and watched her ass as she bent to get pans out of cabinets. It was the idea of how easy it would be, and how much she wanted it.

She'd always thought she wanted it with Chris, but she'd been lying to herself. With him, she'd been performing the role of the perfect girlfriend. With Matt, she wanted to actually be perfect. She wanted to be about a hundred times less stubborn.

Everything about him called her to soften into him. And it wasn't because he was any less of a guy-guy than Chris. The way he went back in to roughhouse with Gus, having found one of his rope toys, was all guy. The way he opened doors and held bags and rushed in to rescue her with the one-percenter-style trip to Vegas was chivalrous in the extreme. And she didn't want to like it.

It didn't feel right to her because that's not the way she lived and had never been what she valued. But she couldn't help but feel cherished by the things he did without thinking. It made her want to cook him dinner—every night.

That was exactly why she said something the perfect wife or the perfect girlfriend wouldn't say. "I'm going to order Postmates."

"Sounds perfect." He looked up at her, not knowing that she'd lived a whole lifetime with him in a few moments.

MATT LOOKED OVER THE dog's prone, farting body at Bridget. Her face was lit only by the glow of the television. And she was starkly beautiful that way even though he couldn't trace all of her freckles with his gaze.

She must have felt him looking because she glanced at him and rolled her eyes. "What?"

"I was just wondering what kind of dog you would get for yourself." Sorry excuse, but it was something he actually wanted to know. If things worked out with them, they'd be sharing this dog.

After thinking for a long moment, she said, "I'd like one as lazy as Gus who doesn't fart as much."

"I think the farting comes along with the lazy."

She smiled slightly, and it felt as though he'd won something. "You may have a point."

"And he sure didn't feel very lazy during our earlier interlude . . ."

Then she turned away from the TV and covered the pup's considerably large ears. "You're talking about my nephew, and his feelings are very sensitive."

"I didn't say it wasn't consensual," Matt said. His gaze dipped down to where her T-shirt had gaped open and he licked his bottom lip. He was such a lech when it came to her. "I know how he felt. I've been wanting to do that to you all day."

"Who knew that home goods were so arousing?" she asked. Her voice hitched on the word "arousing," as though she was thinking about doing it with him again. "You're hot. You're rich. You're good at it. You'd think you'd be more blasé about it by now. Why are you so horny for me?"

"Because you're my wife." And he didn't even want to think about fucking another woman. Funny how that worked when he fell for a girl. He wasn't quite done lying to himself—maybe he could fall for her without her ruining him. But doubts about that were starting to creep in.

"In name only." She looked at him under her eyelashes. "Tonight's not on the schedule."

He shrugged. "I just think we'll be more believable at the wedding if we have the sex glow of newlyweds who are fucking like bunnies."

"You're really grasping at straws, Counselor."

"Is it working?" He waggled his brows so she would know that he wasn't pressed about this. Truth was that he wanted Bridget more than anything, but he'd only go there if the feeling was mutual. He wasn't convinced that she wasn't attracted to him, but he was going to listen to her words.

"I'm not . . ."

"You're everything, Bridget. Sexy, funny, smart—and your heart's so good that I can't stand it."

"I never felt like I was good enough." She sounded so lost that he wanted to leave and kill that motherfucker Chris. Tear him limb from limb. But not as much as he wanted to make it clear to this woman what she meant to him. Even if he didn't have the words yet.

Bridget Nolan was dazzling. He couldn't stop looking at her, thinking about her, needing just a crumb of her approval. But it was starting to feel impossible to make her see that. After the day they'd had, he would have thought that she would relax with her ground rules and stop trying to push him away with the façade she'd put on as soon as they'd gotten married.

He'd never had to work this hard for anything, and he couldn't stand the antsy feeling under his skin that he wouldn't win her.

"What about you?"

She finally looked away. "What about me?"

He wished he could put into words how he felt about her in a way that wouldn't scare her off. But she'd offered him a deal. Friendship with benefits in exchange for a fake marriage for a month. That was it. And he'd seen—time and time again—how she never sweetened a deal after she offered it. Not at work. Not in life.

Still, he had to ask. "Don't you want—more?"

"More than what?" She looked guileless, but she wasn't fooling him.

She was the most cussedly stubborn woman he'd ever met—aside from his own mother.

He wasn't getting any more from her, and it seemed pointless to stay. Yeah, he was being petty and immature, but this was about more than the sex. He wanted her to let him in, but she wouldn't do that as long as she was still up in her head about not being enough for her ex-douche.

Defeated, he stood up and looked for his shoes and the garment bag that held his tuxedo. "I'd better go."

He was most definitely imagining the wounded look on her face when she looked up at him. "But the show's not over."

"I have Netflix at home." But he didn't have Bridget, who definitely didn't wince when he said that. That would be nothing but wishful thinking.

"Do you need me to walk you out?"

He gave her a weak smile. "Nah, wouldn't want to disturb my new paramour. I think I tired him out."

"Okay." She bit her lip. "Bye."

He didn't respond. Just waved right before the door shut.

ONE MINUTE HE'S TRYING to seduce me, and then he's walking out the door with barely a word," Bridget said to Sasha, who was sitting in the adjacent pedicure chair the next afternoon.

She'd never gotten to do a lot of girly stuff with her mom, and she'd been kind of a loner in school. As a teen, she'd spent a lot more time reading a book on the bleachers at Jack's Little League games than she had doing things like getting her nails done.

And then she'd had Chris.

Having girlfriends she could talk about boys with was a relatively new experience, and she was grateful that Hannah and Sasha had welcomed her into their coven. They hadn't balked that she'd been the kind of girl who didn't have a lot of women friends until relatively recently, even though Bridget was slightly shamed by it.

Bridget wondered if she'd been reticent to let other women get too close because the pain of having her mother drop out of her life had scarred her there. So she'd clung to the men in her life and kept herself aloof for years. After all, she had Chris—he really had been her everything.

"Wait a second. Why would he have to seduce you? You're married to him." Sasha really didn't keep her voice low enough, and now the whole salon knew she wasn't fucking her husband. "Why on earth not engage in some state-encouraged nookie at every opportunity?"

Because she didn't want to lose her heart. She had to keep it on lockdown. She couldn't let Matt get close because he would inevitably see all the pieces she was missing.

"I can't believe you called it nookie." The only option was to deflect.

"Don't do that." Sasha pointed over at Hannah, who was being led to the waxing room because her *hoo-ha was starting to look like a cottage a cursed hag might emerge from*. "She does that all the time."

Bridget tried to look innocent. "Do what?"

"Deflecting instead of telling me why you're not *fucking* your husband."

"Because it's a weird situation." Bridget looked away lest Sasha see any hint of whimsy on her face. "I mean, we're married and might not last. I don't want to get too attached. I think I married him just to make Chris feel like a douche."

Bridget looked at the nail techs, who were very professionally ignoring their conversation, for which she would probably tip forty percent.

"Chris already feels like a douche."

"So much of a douche he had to act like a petulant child in Vegas."

"That's because he saw how Matt was looking at you, and he was threatened."

"Matt looks at me like he wants to do it."

"True story." Sasha smiled dreamily. "It's vaguely worshipful, and I would jump on that train . . . again . . . if I were you."

"It's not that—"

"Was he bad in bed?"

"No!" If anything, he was almost too good. "I just don't want to get too attached. So, I sort of put it on a schedule."

"Is this because he *used to* work for you?"

She'd been friends with Sasha for long enough to tell her the real reason that she couldn't let herself fall in love with Matt. It wasn't because she didn't want to. The other night, she'd been close to breaking before he stood up and left.

"You know, I only had sex with him in the first place to prove a point." She shook her head. "I wanted to prove to myself that Chris was wrong, that someone like Matt would want me."

Sasha wrinkled her brow and was silent for a few moments. Bridget thought she might let the subject drop until she said, "And he does want you?"

"Yeah, I think so." Bridget then confronted the infrequent phenomenon of searching for words. "It's just—he never says he wants more than a fling. And this all feels so—dangerous."

"Danger can be good." Strange words coming from Sasha, who carried mace that looked like a lipstick in her bag. "What makes you think that he wants more?"

"Well, we were watching Gus last night."

"That is so *adorable*." Sasha clapped her hands together.

"And we were flirting."

"All very promising." She made a motion for Bridget to continue.

"We'd spent the whole day together, and it was so much fun. It felt really—intimate. And I was thinking about how it would feel like we were *really* together if we started making out on my couch. He was looking at me like that was going to happen." She paused. "And then he just got up and left." Bridget was still confused about it. She'd been this close to jumping into his lap and kissing him. Sasha just nodded.

"What?"

"I think you broke him."

Bridget almost laughed. He wasn't the one who would break if they weren't very careful. "I don't think so."

"Think about it." Sasha grabbed her arm. "This is a man that I am very familiar with. Not this specific man, but this type of guy, who has everything—including sex—handed to him on a silver platter."

"Sex on a silver platter sounds very unsafe. Someone could slide right off."

Sasha ignored her and continued. "But you put him on a *schedule*. And you might be telling me that it's because you don't want to get attached, but he doesn't know that. He probably thinks that you resent having sex with him, but then you're flirting with him. And it's driving him insane. Like, his brain is actually broken."

"He doesn't think that I resent it." At least he shouldn't. She didn't resent it. "He's not that simple."

Seemingly assured that she had the situation handled, Sasha went back to scrolling through Twitter on her phone. "Trust me, they're all that simple."

CHAPTER TWENTY-THREE

BRIDGET HADN'T FELT GUILTY about lying to Chris about her marriage because that was just about being petty. But for some reason, she felt guilty about lying to Matt's parents. And that guilt was compounded by the fact that she was still up for a fellowship from their family foundation.

A week after Matt had rushed out of her apartment, saving her from jumping his bones and falling halfway into love with him, she was going to have dinner with his parents. She was going to have to lie to their faces.

Not about being enamored with their son. She was hanging on by her fingernails to infatuated instead of butt-ass-crazy in love. It wouldn't be putting on a show to pretend to have all the newlywed feels.

But pretending that this thing between them was forever might be a problem. If she did that, she'd want to believe it. If she believed it, she would never heal from the aftermath.

That made her stop in her tracks on the way up their semi-circular driveway. Jesus, she was such a fraud. She didn't belong here at all, and definitely not under false pretenses. Matt was American royalty, and she was just a girl from the South Side.

Both of them were privileged, to be sure, but they didn't belong in the same circles.

"Are you sure you want me here?" She tugged on Matt's arm when he waited patiently for her. Damn, she liked that about him. She'd come to realize that Sasha—as usual—had probably been right about the other night. He was trying to respect the fact that she'd laid out ground rules about them having sex.

But those rules hadn't kept her heart safe. The only way she could have done that would have been to cut things off. Maybe never take him for that first happy hour. Never take him up on his offer to fly her to Vegas. She never should have kissed him that first night in the hotel room. Never should have gotten drunk-married by an Elvis. And she absolutely never should have come back to Chicago still married to him. They should have gotten a drive-through divorce before heading to the airport.

Still, Matt looked at her as though she'd lost it, squeezed her hand, and said, "Of course I want you here."

"But is your mom going to hate me?" Bridget had no idea how to be with moms. Chris's mom had died while they were in college, and she'd been more like an aunt than an in-law before that. Her own mother didn't like her all that much. And Matt's mom traveled in the same circles as hers.

Matt laughed. "My mom is going to be fine." He tugged on her hand, and she let him lead her into the house.

"How do you know that?"

Even though Matt was a step ahead of her, she could see the side of his face crinkle a bit. "Because you're just alike."

"Oh great," Bridget said, imagining his mother as even more terrifying now, given how she'd treated Matt when they'd first met. His mother probably already had a dossier on her and was clicking her fingernails against a table, waiting to tell her that she was trash.

Matt must have sensed her upset, because he turned and said, "You're both wonderful."

BRIDGET FOLLOWED HIS LEAD and took her shoes off when they entered the house. Sometimes it felt like his parents identified more as rich than Japanese American, but they'd preserved the no-shoes-in-the-house rule from their parents' homes. And doing it reminded Matt that he was bringing a girl to his parents' home who felt like more than a fling. He was way more nervous than he'd let on when she'd frozen up before entering the house.

He'd never had to really introduce his mom to a woman before. All the other girls he'd dated seriously hadn't been girls he would introduce to his mom or they'd been girls he'd grown up around. Rich people really were quasi-incestuous that way.

And if his mom didn't like her, this whole dinner could be a nightmare. He didn't want that for Bridget, given her fraught relationship with her own mother. It wasn't like she'd said anything, but he felt as though his mother freezing her out could be more painful for her than it would be for someone else. His father was easy and admired tough women—that's why his parents' marriage worked. And his father would see how Matt felt about Bridget because he was perceptive, and he would immediately accept her.

His mother didn't just accept things because they were. She changed things through her iron will. And he didn't have any idea of how his parents would react to this, now that they were past the stage where they could get an annulment. Changing his plans for the summer had been the first time that he'd done anything to really defy their expectations and ambitions for him. They might blame Bridget for that. Or they might see the fact that he was in love with someone emotionally sturdy like Bridget as a sign that he was maturing.

They'd accepted Naomi because she was a Chapin, but he'd never gotten the sense that she was really their favorite person to have around.

So, yeah, he was nervous and almost hypervigilant when they entered the formal living room where his mother served cocktails.

And then he stopped in his tracks. Naomi was here with her parents. He'd thought it was just a family dinner, and he felt ambushed. His hand tightened around Bridget's.

"What is it?" she asked quietly, looking up at him with concern.

"Naomi." Bridget's eyes widened at that one word.

"Well, shit." Bridget verbalized Matt's thoughts perfectly, and that gave him a measure of courage. It was nice to feel like he had someone on his team. He'd never felt that way before.

That was when his mother noticed them and approached. He tried to see her as Bridget would. Jane was tiny, about five one, but completely formidable. Her skin was smooth and poreless. The only sign that she was north of thirty-five were the three strands of gray hair in her blunt-cut bangs. When they'd grown in, she'd told him that it was considered a sign of wisdom in Japanese culture. So she'd decided to let them stay.

She didn't hug Bridget in welcome, but he didn't expect her to. She tilted her head slightly to the side in welcome, and Bridget extended her hand. His mother didn't rudely stare at it, which was a good sign. Instead she enveloped Bridget's hand in both of hers—a power play. "You must be Bridget. Matt has told me all about you."

Bridget gave a nervous laugh. "All good things, I hope."

"Well, he married you after knowing you for less than three months, so I would hope he hasn't discovered the bad things about you yet."

"Oh, he has," Bridget said, more mettle in her voice this time. "He just has the good judgment to ignore my bad qualities or use them to his advantage."

His mother looked at him with a twinkle in her eye that he did not trust one bit. It didn't tell him that she liked his new wife. It said that she believed Bridget was beneath him.

"I'm going to introduce you to my father now," Matt said. "I promise it will feel less like an inquisition."

Bridget smiled up at him, but she looked strained. He hated to see it.

MATT'S FATHER, BRIAN, WAS a treat. He had the same nice smile that Matt had. Though she knew he was a formidable businessman, he had a soft voice and an easy manner. Bridget couldn't help but see how Matt was formed out of the best qualities of his parents. He was kind and friendly like his dad, but he also had his mother's sharp mind.

She hadn't minded when his mother kind of inspected her as they'd first come in. If she had a son who'd gone off and married his summer-job boss on a wild weekend in Vegas, Bridget would certainly have concerns.

And when she thought about having a son, she couldn't help but wonder how any kids she'd have with Matt would be. She hoped they were more like him than her—kind, friendly, flexible. And she couldn't imagine ever wanting to leave them. So maybe she wasn't a flake like her mother after all.

Everyone sat down to dinner before Matt got to show her around his parents' beautiful contemporary home. Dinner was catered and delicious, but the whole production made her feel as though she was a guest star on a futuristic version of *Downton Abbey*.

After the appetizer was served—tuna tartare with dashi ladled over it—she leaned over to Matt and said, "You have butlers."

He smiled at her and she caught a whiff of his smell. "My parents have butlers."

"Whatever." He'd grown up with butlers.

"There's a difference, Snookums."

Bridget scrunched up her face. "I don't like that one, either."

"I guess I'll have to keep trying."

"Matthew, it's rude to have a side conversation," his mother said. Bridget felt that chastisement in her belly and took a long drink of her white wine to quell it. But then Matt's mother gave her a look that said she was worried about her drinking, and Bridget just wanted to melt into the floor.

Of course, Naomi—whom she'd been surprised to meet during the cocktail hour—chose that moment to focus on her.

Bridget had never really competed for a guy. She'd never had to mark her territory over Chris. Everyone in the neighborhood simply knew that he was hers. She'd never had to enforce it. With Naomi's cold gaze on her, Bridget felt jealousy for maybe the first time in her life. And she realized that she'd been feeling stabs of it since Matt had first mentioned Naomi and their breakup.

But she didn't have time to dwell on how she was really unable to deny that she had some very big feelings for the man sitting next to her. She had to focus on how to make this dinner much less mortifying than the dinner they'd had in Vegas that had caused this whole clusterfuck of a sham marriage that just happened to turn convenient.

Naomi looked at her, and Bridget could only describe her gaze as dead. She had the same blasé look about her that a lot of the cops who should have retired five years ago had. Bridget wondered what tack Naomi was going to take in trying to diminish her in front of Matt's family. Because that's what she was going to do.

"So your brother was the one who wrote the story that got my uncle arrested."

Interesting. She was going with the family angle. Probably to paint her as a working-class interloper who just didn't understand how things functioned among the obscenely wealthy. "I'm very proud of Jack. He won a Pulitzer for that story."

Naomi didn't miss a beat. "And you're a line prosecutor for Cook County? Didn't get a job offer from the US attorney's office?"

Now she was going for Bridget more directly, insinuating that Bridget wasn't smart enough to be with Matt. Bridget also noticed that she'd done this during a lull in the conversation. Matt looked ready to say something, but Bridget put her hand on his forearm. She could have gone for the thigh, but she was thinking about saving his thighs for later. And she wanted the whole table to see that she didn't need him to speak up for her.

"Well, after my Seventh Circuit clerkship, I had offers to join the US attorneys' offices in the Southern District of New York, the Eastern District of New York, the Northern District of Illinois, and . . ." She paused for effect. "Oh, the solicitor general's office in DC."

"And you turned those down?" This came from Matt's mom, whom she'd clearly not won over to her side.

Bridget wasn't about to tell her the real reason she hadn't taken any of the very good offers she'd received after her clerkship—Chris hadn't received any of the same kind of offers, and she hadn't wanted to outshine him because she was just going to get married, have kids, and drop out anyway. She had the feeling that wouldn't get Jane to like her any more. So she said, "I can make more of a difference at the local level. It's much more rewarding to put a rapist in jail than it is to futilely go after white-collar criminals."

She looked at Naomi when she said that last part—given her close relation to certain white-collar criminals.

CHAPTER TWENTY-FOUR

BRIDGET WAS QUIET IN the car on the way back to her place after dinner. As they'd left, Matt apologized for Naomi's presence and his mom's prickliness. She didn't think he needed to apologize about either thing, and they weren't why she was quiet anyway.

No, she was thinking about the crooked smile he'd given her when she put Naomi in her place. The way he'd slung an arm around her shoulders even though that wasn't the kind of thing one probably did at dinner at his parents' house. She thought of the way he'd pointedly looked at his mother, with a silent *Enough*. And she thought about the way that made her feel safe and cared for—and how she hadn't realized how much she craved that until Matt gave it to her.

And she was thinking about how she wanted to ask him for more when the car pulled up outside her condo. Her hands were clammy, and her heart was beating fast, but she knew that she'd regret it if she didn't say what was on her mind.

"I think we should revise our schedule."

He stared at her, and she was about to take it back when he said, "Really?"

"I think—um—a newlywed sex glow would be nice. I'd like to add it to my skin-care routine." She was grasping at straws here. After she'd rejected him the other night because she couldn't get out of her own head, she knew that he wasn't going to be the one to instigate. Conscious of the driver in the front, the one who definitely wanted them to get out of his car so that he could pick someone else up, she said, "Do you want to come up?"

"Are you sure?" Matt asked. One of the many things she appreciated about him. He didn't ask in a patronizing way, as though she didn't know her own mind. He asked because he wanted to be sure that she was choosing him. He was so remarkably open and vulnerable. Meeting his parents tonight, she'd wondered how he'd gotten that way.

"Positive."

After that, he couldn't get out of the car fast enough. Her hands shook as she tried to retrieve her keys from her purse. To her relief, Matt took the keys and got them in the lock. She might have fumbled for an hour and lost her courage.

The time in Vegas was different. It was impulsive and friendly and fun. It had given them both something that they needed in a strange moment and an unfamiliar place. It had seemed right to fuck Matt in a Vegas penthouse and have the fond memory of the time she'd done something wild and out of character.

He'd still been careful to make sure she was on board, but he'd overwhelmed her senses and caught her off her guard. It had been so much that it had almost reinforced her walls in a way.

This was a choice.

And there were feelings now. Big feelings that she couldn't label "love" if she wanted to actually go through with this. And she also couldn't *not* go through with this.

She had no idea how he'd walked out of her place the week before if he had anywhere near the attraction to her that she had to him. But she was grateful that he did. Back then, a week ago, she would have been overwhelmed by how much she liked spending time with him in combination with how much she wanted to jump him.

She'd never had that. Her relationship with Chris had been destiny, an inevitability, and a responsibility.

This was a choice.

She was choosing to give him a part of herself that no one had ever seen. Just like he'd chosen to show his family in a not-so-subtle way that he was on her team. When they got into her darkened living room, she stopped short and his body pressed up against hers. His hands came around her waist and he lingered. He was hard and part of her wanted him to take her on the floor right where they stood.

Her passion for him was sort of shocking, really. She'd never thought herself capable of honest-to-God yearning for another person. Had always read romance novels with a hint of skepticism over her mind. Maybe flakes like her mother could really lose themselves in another person, but Bridget wasn't that weak.

But, standing in her living room—with a guy she didn't know if she could get rid of touching her, waiting for him to do more—she wasn't so sure she knew who she was anymore.

His mouth was level with her ear. When he spoke, his breath brushed against her skin and sent a shiver down her spine. "What made you change your mind?"

She wasn't quite sure what to say to that. "Do you care?" That came out sharper than she wanted it to, but it was out of need. She didn't want him to make her think about this any more than she already had. She was at that perfect point of knowing that she was probably making a mistake but knowing that she needed to make the mistake. It didn't make sense, and if wanting him was a crime, she wouldn't have any defense. "Do you really want to know?"

"I need to know, Bridget." No stupid endearment. He was deadly serious. How had she not really seen him until that weekend in Vegas? Her mind had probably protected her from noticing how his fingers might feel as they trailed up her rib cage to rub the bottom of her breasts through her dress and bra. Just like it had protected her from his smile having a direct dial-in line to her libido.

She'd been smart enough to be blind to his charms while they were still working together, but her brain wasn't going to let her protect her heart from him permanently.

This was a choice.

By changing the rules, she was allowing herself to give in to the greedy need for another person that she'd thought she'd been able to bury.

"You're not in love with her anymore, are you?"

His hands stopped roaming, and he turned her in his arms. "Why are we talking about Naomi?" He found the light switch and she squinted against the overhead light. Kind of a mood killer, but it was her fault for bringing it up.

"Because I need to know. This feels like it could be a thing, and I need to know."

"Is that what the sex schedule was about?" He looked confused. "You didn't want this to feel real?"

"You caught me off guard," she said, acknowledging that this— right here, right now—was a choice for both of them.

"Same goes. But why now?" He seemed to insist on knowing the answer before they commenced with filthy fun times, so she looked up at him with a smile that she hoped looked wry instead of like she wanted to crawl inside him and never leave.

"You're a good man. And I like being with you. And I want to get naked with you and have orgasms. Why do we need to make it any more complicated than that? I was making it more complicated than that, and I don't want to anymore."

It didn't even take a full second before his mouth was on hers. And a cocktail of relief and lust flowed through her faster than an IV drip. She was so caught up that she dropped her purse on the floor. He broke contact with her mouth to pull her dress up over her head. She was tempted for a second to rip the buttons on his shirt open until she remembered that the shirt was probably terribly expensive, so she fumbled with the buttons as he backed her up to the couch.

"Ooof," she said, as he lifted her by the hips and put her body where he wanted it. "That was smooth," she said when he relented to give her some air.

"Are you besmirching my prowess?" he asked with a wink.

She nipped his bottom lip. "I like it. I like everything you did the other time."

He finished undoing the buttons of his shirt and pulled it off. She didn't even try to stop or hold back from running her hands over his chest. And he rewarded her with a soft growl of approval as he looked down at her with a lascivious hooded gaze.

"I want to do everything you want," he said. "Tell me everything

213

you've wanted to do but never got the chance." He left the part about "with Chris" unsaid.

Although she tried to let her mind run free, all she could think about was wanting him all around her, holding her, inside her. She wanted him to never stop looking at her the way he was looking at her right now.

"I think naked would be a good start." She bit her lip as she took off her bra. She expected him to go for the fastening on his pants, but he just stared. In that moment, when she felt fumbling and awkward, too anxious that taking too long would make him change his mind, the way he looked at her shifted something inside her brain. With him staring down at her with his thighs straddling her legs like a titan straddling the earth, she believed every little bit of gossip that she'd read on the Internet about him being an international playboy. In that moment, she wished that he was her impossibly sexy husband for real.

Goodness gracious, it was sexy to have all of his attention on her almost-naked body. She'd never felt wanted like this, and it was heady and intoxicating. She wanted to bottle it up and keep it close for when this all ended in a couple of weeks. After the wedding.

"Are you just going to look?"

"I like looking," he teased, but then he undid his pants and moved off the couch to pull them down. He lifted his chin at her and said, "Panties," which sent her scrambling as though it was a serious order.

He crawled back over her body, on her couch, with the overhead light highlighting every freckle and fold, and he looked enchanted.

He kissed the freckles on her shoulders, and she shivered. Almost purred in pleasure.

"Turn around." She jolted a little bit at that. "I want to pull your hair and see this . . ." He grabbed a handful of her ass.

What he wanted wasn't kinky in the slightest, but he could make anything they did together seem like the height of decadence. So she arranged herself facing away from him, supporting herself on the back of the couch while she grabbed a condom from his pants— glad he'd been prepared even after the weirdness of the other night. She didn't care because she'd been lying to herself about not wanting him. Maybe he'd never told himself the same lie, and that was probably why she was falling for him.

"Anyone ever tell you that you have a really cute butt?"

She looked at him over her shoulder and answered honestly, "Nope." Chris had never even told her she looked pretty, but she pushed that thought away.

"That's a damn shame," he said as he pushed inside her and gathered her hair in his hand, cupping her skull.

Damn, he really was smooth.

After that, she couldn't think, didn't want to, just wanted to feel him inside her, breath in the scent of his sweat, and touch herself until she came. And then he came.

And, after that, she absolutely could not be bothered to get off the couch while he cleaned up. So he carried her over the threshold to her bedroom. And she tried not to think of it as the beginning of something because she knew it was definitely the beginning of the end.

MATT KIDO WAS FALLING desperately in love with Bridget Nolan, and that was before he spent the night in her bed. This was a huge problem given the fact that she couldn't seem to meet his gaze when he brought her coffee the next morning.

"Did I do something wrong?" he asked.

"No." Bridget shook her head, and it just made her hair cover her face. He liked how messy she looked right now because it was such a contrast to how put together she usually was. Then she winced. "Did I do something wrong?"

Matt wanted to laugh. The idea that she could have done something wrong the night before was so out of the realm of things he expected to hear. She could have told him that the sky was brown, and he would have been more likely to believe her. But he didn't laugh. "I think I should be the one worried about that."

She looked up at him. "You have nothing to worry about. I've just . . . I've only been with one guy my whole life. And Vegas was kind of a blip."

Oh shit. He should have known. This was sort of a big deal to her. It had been a big deal to him because he loved her, but it was a big deal to her because he was new dick. And she hadn't had any new dick.

He sat on the edge of the bed and kissed her nose. Her forehead. The freckle right next to the corner of her mouth. "You're pretty perfect."

"You don't have to say that."

"I know, and I wouldn't dare lie to you." He tried to coax a smile out of her. "You can spot a liar a mile away."

That got her to smile. "Do you have to go?"

Her question hit him in his chest. He *did* have to go. At that moment, he hated himself for signing up for a seminar that required him to work on a group project in his third year. If he had his way, he would stay here with Bridget, all day. He'd make sure she knew that she was beyond perfect for him. He'd kiss every inch of her body again and again.

Hell, he was tempted to be a shithead and claim he wasn't feeling well and beg off the group project. His stomach certainly ached at the idea of leaving Bridget. That was the last thing he wanted. He wanted to spend all his time with her. Drink her in. Having her would make failing out of law school worth it.

But that would mean that Bridget had been right about him the first day of his internship—that he was only a useless rich kid, getting by on his family money and family name.

"I have to go." He hated saying it, and punctuated it with a deep, long kiss that couldn't be mistaken for an attempt to placate her. It was a kiss that would lead to things that he couldn't follow through on in that moment. "But I want to come back."

"I want you to come back."

"When?" He knew he had to pin her down when she was feeling good about them, before she closed up again on him.

"I'm making dinner for Hannah and Jack . . . and Patrick tomorrow night."

So dinner with the family priest, the one who happened to be her ex's brother? This was a big fucking deal. "Is this in service of the ruse, or because you want me here?"

"I want you here. For real."

Matt got dressed and left her place before he let loose with any of the fist-pumping enthusiasm for a dinner party at his wife's house.

CHAPTER TWENTY-FIVE

STUDY GROUPS IN HIS constitutional law seminar were assigned randomly, but Matt had the feeling that Naomi had pulled some strings to be assigned to his group after he'd revealed that he'd gotten married to someone who wasn't her. Sort of like she'd invited herself to dinner at his parents' place the night before. He'd been hoping to end up with some of the friends he hadn't spoken to for most of the summer out of embarrassment. Instead, he had to be here with his ex.

She hadn't wanted him before, when he was readily available to her. But now that he'd found someone else, she had to try to get him back. It was sad really, and he didn't want to feel sorry for her.

But he did. She wanted something that wasn't any good. What they'd had together was like the bargain-basement version of what he had with Bridget. There was nothing wrong with it if you didn't know any better, but now he did know better.

Ironically, falling for Bridget had made him feel much more charitable toward Naomi. That was probably why he hadn't told his parents about exactly why they'd broken up. He didn't want to cause a rift in the family-friends fold, and he didn't want to embarrass her.

But as he sat in a conference room at the law library, feeling her gaze on his face while he was trying to work, his patience was waning. She hadn't contributed anything, and spending time with her after his night with Bridget felt like wearing a hair shirt.

Thankfully, the rest of the group was engaged, and they kept their meeting to two hours. He hit the head before leaving for his car, and thought he'd made his escape. But Naomi was waiting for him outside the bathroom.

"Heading back to wifey?" He hated the sound of her voice in that moment, and he was deeply grateful that they'd broken up at the beginning of the summer. If she hadn't pulled the trigger, he'd be hating the sound of her voice from inside their relationship. He'd never have bailed on the firm, and he never would have met Bridget. She'd done him a favor.

He tried to remember that gratitude before responding, but a shitty part of him won out.

Matt looked to the heavens and took a deep breath. "What do you want, Naomi?"

"What I've always wanted." She stepped closer to him, but he stepped back. "You."

He put a hand up. "You don't get to have me anymore."

"It was just the one time."

He stepped around her to head to his car. He was not going to have this conversation. He was going to go home and work out and not think about this anymore. He was going to focus on a future— one that finally excited him.

But Naomi grabbed his arm, her nails digging in. "Why won't you listen to me?"

"Because I've moved on." He turned and looked at her, trying to summon up any dregs of empathy he could strain from the antipathy she was fostering at the moment.

"Seriously? With her?"

"Don't do this, Naomi."

"Do what?" She stuck out her bottom lip in a way that used to make him want to bite it, not that she would be into that. "Keep you from ruining your life?"

"No, ruining my life is what would have happened if we'd stayed together."

"She's only with you because of your family's money."

Matt saw red. The only woman he'd ever been with who'd been all about his family name and the money was standing right in front of him. And she hadn't even had the courtesy to keep her cheating private like people of their ilk were expected to do. "You're certainly not one to lecture me on gold diggers."

She balked at that, but it didn't satisfy him. He just wanted this to be over. "Even if I wasn't married to Bridget now, we would be over."

She slid back into her seductive nymphet persona so smoothly that he barely noticed the seams. It was really quite impressive. "You don't mean that, Matty."

"I do. We're done." He moved around her again. This time she let him. "And don't call me 'Matty.' I really hate it."

As he walked to the car, she said, "I'm not giving up."

"Wouldn't expect you to." He hung his head, feeling defeated, even though being married to Bridget and not being with Naomi anymore was winning.

BRIDGET HADN'T BEEN TO church since her cousin Shannon's wedding a year and a half ago. Despite twelve years of parochial school, she wasn't really religious and wasn't sure whether she believed in God at all. Still, it was comforting to sit in the hard wooden pew at the back of St. Bartholomew's, mumble the words, hum the songs, and go through the ritual of standing and kneeling and sitting.

And Patrick really was a good priest. Unlike a lot of the old dudes, it didn't seem like he was phoning it in. During the homily, he made eye contact with almost everyone in the mostly empty church. And his sermon wasn't what she'd call traditional. It was more about generosity and kindness rather than what to do with body parts.

It made her think about Matt and how she hadn't been generous with him when they'd first met—how she'd made shitty assumptions about him because of who his parents were. And it shamed her as much as an old-fashioned no-sex-before-marriage lecture.

She wasn't actually here to reflect on her own actions; she was here to check in with Patrick to see what he knew about the trip to Vegas—and everything that Chris had said. Even though she didn't care if the church condemned her, she didn't want Patrick to be mad at her. He was sort of like the spare older brother she'd never really wanted, but she still needed him in her life.

Losing Chris had been painful—even though she could now admit it had been a long time coming. Losing Patrick would be like adding insult to injury. He was the one of their crew who had always tried to make sure she was included. Good people like him didn't happen every day. He needed to be cool with how things had gone down. Or at least accepting.

She lingered after the recessional outside of the sanctuary, waited while more than one old lady hugged Patrick for a little too long. He was a Father What-a-Waste, so she could understand, even though she was half-tempted into asking him if he wanted to file a complaint against Mrs. O'Toole.

After everyone left, she waited in the sanctuary until Patrick took off his robes. She didn't take out her phone, just sat in silence and looked at the light dancing through the stained-glass windows.

No one knew why Patrick had decided to enter the seminary after his mother died—not even Chris. When she'd asked, Patrick had said that he felt obligated to. Bridget hadn't been satisfied with his answer, but sitting in the quiet church, she could kind of understand why he seemed to like it. It was a peaceful life, predictable, and he could help and heal other people without letting personal concerns intrude.

She'd tried to do the same thing when she'd sworn off relationships after Chris. And she'd failed—probably because she didn't have vows to God to keep her safe.

Patrick came out and sat next to her. He didn't speak right away. Eventually, she did. "Did Chris tell you?"

"About what?"

"The thing that rhymes with schmaschmortion." She still didn't feel ashamed but didn't think it was right to say it in church.

"Told me ages ago."

She couldn't believe that Patrick sounded so nonchalant about it, given their location and his occupation. "And you aren't upset?"

Patrick shrugged. "It's not really my business. You aren't a believer. And I care about you, but that's because you're practically family. And even if you'd come to me wanting absolution or whatever the fuck you're looking for, I would have told you that you did the right thing."

"You said 'fuck,' and you approved of my abortion?" Bridget shouldn't have been shocked, but she was.

"It's not about approval or disapproval, Bridge." He nudged her shoulder. "How do you feel about it?"

"I always thought that Chris and I would get married and have kids."

"Everyone did."

He probably knew the whole story, but Bridget said the next thing anyway. "The night we broke up, he told me that he'd bought a house."

Patrick nodded.

"He didn't even ask me. I'd never even seen it. I knew when he told me that and just expected me to fall in line that it was never going to work. If I acquiesced right then and there, it wouldn't be my life anymore."

"My brother was never good enough for you." He let out a soft laugh. "He's one of God's children, but he couldn't keep up with you."

They were quiet for a moment then.

"I didn't want to do it alone—having a kid."

"You wouldn't have been alone." He was right. Her dad and brothers would have been around. But if her mother had freaked out even with a co-parent, what kind of hope would she have had when the buck stopped with her? And Chris would have tried—not that he would have been much help.

"Chris and I were done, and I felt like it just needed to be done."

Patrick turned to her and she met his gaze. "Then you did the right thing."

"Really?" This conversation wasn't going the way she'd expected it to. She'd sort of expected it to be awkward. "You're not even going to encourage Hail Marys?"

"Nah. That works with the biddies. It's really more for them."

Wanting to change the subject, she said, "Mrs. O'Toole totally went in with that hug."

Patrick laughed, and it made him look incredibly handsome and incredibly young. She sort of ached for that version of Patrick. His eyes seemed tired now. "I think I'll have a bruise on my ass. She pinches."

"I noticed."

Patrick sobered. "You came here to make sure that I was cool with your life choices."

"Pretty much."

"Anything else you want to talk about? Like, I don't know, a new husband?"

Bridget wasn't about to lie to him after this conversation. "We didn't exactly make a *conscious* decision to get married." She was starting to really want it to last, even though Matt was the last thing she expected. Staying with him forever and ever, amen, would make her life so different from what she'd envisioned with Chris that she was still getting her head around it.

"Jack really likes him."

"That makes me feel better." Her tone was sarcastic, but it did make her feel better that her brother liked Matt. Despite his generally affable demeanor, Jack was fairly exacting when it came to people's ethics and morals. He was loyal and kind, and he expected that from others. Bridget always sort of expected the worst from people. She used to blame that on her job, but it was starting to seem like it was a really shitty outlook on life.

"If you need to talk about it, I'm here." And she knew he would be. She was relieved that this conversation had taken the turn that it had, but she wasn't eager to share what was going on in her head with respect to Matt before she'd sorted it out herself.

"I think you'll assign me a novena if I go into too much detail about Matt."

"Sounds juicy." He stood up. "I heard a rumor that you're going to feed me?"

"Yes, I'm making a chicken."

Patrick pumped a fist. She'd never met anyone who appreciated a home-cooked meal more than him. "My favorite."

"I'll see you in a few hours." She got up to leave because Matt was going to show up at her place shortly to "help" her.

Patrick hugged her before she could walk out, and her heart felt lighter knowing that not everything from her old life had fallen away.

CHAPTER TWENTY-SIX

MATT DID NOT KNOW how to cook. Bridget didn't know why this surprised her, given that he'd grown up with actual butlers. But he was an adult who lived on his own. The fact that he relied on take-out and meal delivery was sort of disturbing. It delineated the differences between them when they needed to find common ground, and it reminded her of Chris's helplessness.

Even though she'd generally rejected stereotypical gender-based tasks, Bridget loved to cook. After her mother left, she was on her own after school and spent a lot of time watching television. For some reason—probably because her sense of home had been so fucked up by her parents' divorce—she'd gravitated toward the Food Network.

Every afternoon after school, she'd done her homework while watching the *Barefoot Contessa*. Each day, she could take a little va-cation to the Hamptons, where everything was easy and beautiful and domesticity was something to be celebrated. Sometimes, she would pretend that Ina Garten was her mother—even though the real Ina didn't have kids.

If Ina was her mother, she would have come home to warm cookies every day and a delicious dinner every night. Her parents— Bridget loved her dad, but Jeffrey would have been a good substitute—would have gotten along. They would have still been in love.

But they were probably still happy after all these years in part because of the no-kids thing.

Eventually, she'd started cooking the meals on the show. Her brothers and dad had appreciated her new hobby, and they never questioned why. They'd even bought her every single *Barefoot Contessa* cookbook. And she'd never resented cooking for people. It was a way that she could share love with them without any sappy, mostly empty words. It was a tangible thing.

She didn't think to hide her cookbook collection, all lined up in a cabinet her father had built for exactly that purpose. But Matt, seated at the kitchen island with a glass of wine, noticed. "Holy shit, you have a lot of cookbooks."

"I guess." She felt her skin heat. It was the sort of thing she'd missed growing up with her first and only boyfriend. There'd been no slow reveal, no gradual increase in intimacy. And even though this was nothing that she had any reason to be embarrassed about, it felt strange to show this little anomalous thing about herself to someone who was still a stranger in a lot of ways. "Do you think it's weird?"

He was paging through *Barefoot in Paris*, the book she needed the chicken recipe from today. "I think I hit the jackpot."

"Don't tell me you think that I'd have a home-cooked dinner waiting for you every night if we stayed together."

Her words must have sounded as bitter and wary as she felt in that moment, because he stopped cold. "I didn't mean it that way."

"What way did you mean it?" She kind of hoped he had the wrong answer so maybe she wouldn't be quite as smitten with him anymore.

"I just meant that it's cool that you are so into this. I know that you work really hard and really late. I'd never expect some *Leave It to Beaver* dystopic fantasy Stepford Wife shit."

"Good answer." His shoulders fell in relief. "Now wash the chicken."

MATT HAD NEVER WANTED to stab a priest before—at least not until Patrick took the last of the chicken-fat-soaked croutons out of the bottom of the pan. Before that, the whole evening had been markedly more relaxed than the dinner parties at his parents' house.

Jack, Bridget, and Patrick had inside jokes that he could only sit back and enjoy vicariously. Hannah had been folded into their little crew, and it seemed like she had always been there.

Even though he knew that they'd be divorced inside a couple of weeks, he wished he could have that. He ultimately let Patrick have the last crouton. It was only fair. Matt had Bridget—for now—and Patrick had taken a vow of celibacy.

When everyone was done eating and the last wineglass was drained, Bridget stood to clear plates. When he jumped up and said, "Sit down," she looked a little startled. Then Hannah gave Jack a pointed look, and he got up to help.

"I have him well trained," she said with a smile.

Jack scoffed. "I showed up trained."

"Ha! You and Michael were like feral cats in high school." Bridget handed Jack her plate with a raised brow. Patrick got up, too, said something snide about still being sore from Mrs. O'Toole, and the kitchen was clean rather quickly.

Since it was a Sunday night, everyone left, and Matt and Bridget were alone. He didn't want to make any presumptions, but he really hoped that he could stay with her tonight. He'd have to rush out in the early-morning light for class, but he knew he wouldn't see Bridget until the rehearsal dinner that weekend. Between school and work, they wouldn't connect. And he needed her.

He should have been terrified by that need, so fast on the heels of his relationship with Naomi. But Bridget felt like home to him in a way that no one else ever had.

"So," he said, facing her in the sparkling-clean kitchen.

Bridget yawned, and he half expected her to usher him out. They'd gotten too close, too fast. And he knew her well enough to know that this was when she'd push him away. Over the past few weeks, he'd come up with a theory. She'd dated Chris and no one else because he'd been safe. He was already a fixture in her life, and she figured that he might not be the best guy for her, but he would never leave. When he did, it had rocked her.

And if she was feeling anything close to what he was feeling for her, she would be afraid right now. She would lock it down because what they had wasn't safe. Physically, it was safe. Just not emotionally.

Because he hadn't been entirely honest with her, hadn't told her that he'd always wanted to stay married to her because he was into

229

her and not because he thought it would get rid of Naomi, she still thought they were having a fling.

And he was going to tell her all of this—he was—but she stepped close to him, went on her tiptoes, and kissed him in a way that told him that she didn't want safe. She didn't want words. And she wanted him.

It was more intoxicating than any wine or any drug, and he knew he wouldn't survive withdrawal. And he didn't want to think about it. He kissed her back instead of giving her the words. A kiss that said they had all the time in the world to tell each other the truth. How he felt about her was completely out of hand. The only place she opened up to him was when he was kissing her. That was the only time that she let him peel back the layers she kept buttoned up at work—and even in front of her family.

He backed her up to the kitchen counter and picked her up to place her on top of it. She made a sound deep in her throat that made him weak. He pulled her T-shirt up and drew back as she raised her arms.

When he'd stripped her down to her pretty pink bra, he let himself look at her face. He wanted to absorb every dimple. And he wanted to commit her kiss-swollen pink lips to memory in case this did end.

She let him look, and he wanted to drop to his knees to thank her—and maybe do a hands-on demonstration that her kitchen counter was now clean enough to eat off of.

"Here?" She sounded soft and vulnerable. Knowing that she never let herself sound like that, it made him feel like he'd found rare treasure without a map.

He pulled his T-shirt off over his back, and she did a sharp intake of breath. He'd do whatever it took to get more of those sounds from her. "Here."

And she lifted her hips to let him strip off her jeans and panties. He kissed her neck and her delicate collarbone and the freckles along her belly.

"I'll have to clean the kitchen again." But she didn't sound that upset, so he didn't stop. And he nudged her to lie down so that he could have all of her laid out in front of him.

He decided to leave all his admissions for after the wedding.

Maybe she would believe him then.

CHAPTER TWENTY-SEVEN

Tuesday 2:30 p.m.

Matt: How's it going?

Bridget: Shouldn't you be in class?

Matt: Professor got the stomach flu.

Bridget: Stay away from the professor. I need you on top of your game for the wedding this weekend.

Matt: I promise I won't get the stomach flu intentionally.

Bridget: Don't get it unintentionally, either. I don't have time to find another date.

Matt: Only useful to you insofar as I look great in a tux.

Bridget: You got me.

Matt: I'll let you get back to work.

Bridget: I don't want to. I'd rather talk to you. I'd rather you were here.

Matt: I want that, too.
Bridget: Talk to you tomorrow?
Matt: Yup.

Bridget almost inserted a bunch of red heart emojis after Matt's last text. But she didn't know if they were in a hearts-and-flowers place or more of an eggplant emoji place.

She'd almost told him that she loved him two nights before at her place. Not even while they were in the throes, but when he'd stood up to clean the table after dinner. She really was easy if that was all it took for her to realize that she was so gone over him. But there it was. Every little thing he did that was nothing like what Chris had done made her realize that Matt was a safe person to fall in love with.

And while pretending that they were going to stay married had really just been a way for her to save face and for him to shake off his ex, her feelings had never been fake. When she looked at Matt, sometimes she thought she could see the same feelings shining out at her, but she couldn't be sure.

She needed to be sure before she told him how she felt because she wasn't going to put herself out on a limb or make assumptions that would bite her in the ass again.

Since she wouldn't see him for the rest of the week, she wouldn't need to worry about it. She could just focus on work and ignore the fact that she was in love with a guy who might just see her as a convenience.

After about fifteen minutes, she was able to focus on the grand jury questions she needed to ask a beat cop the next morning. However, her concentration and peace of mind were short-lived.

Jackie walked into her office. "Good news!"

Bridget hoped it was actual good news, and not the kind of good news that meant she might have to miss her brother's wedding. "Oh?"

"You got the fellowship," Jackie said, clearly waiting for her to get excited about it. "Not that I'm surprised, given how much you taught Matt this summer."

Bridget's stomach sank. She knew that she had to tell her boss that she and Matt had gotten married—probably best to leave out the drunken-wedding part—and that she most likely didn't even qualify for the fellowship anymore because she had marital assets now. Not to mention what kind of conflict of interest would come up because she was married to the son of the people who ran the endowment.

Instead of fessing up, all that came out of her mouth was another, "Oh?"

Jackie was literally vibrating with excitement. "I knew you could get past your misgivings about mentoring Matt . . ."

Bridget's face heated, and she knew she would be bright red if she looked in a mirror. Under no circumstances would she tell Jackie all the ways that Matt had been mentoring *her* on filthy sex. No way could she tell her boss that she'd married him. No way could she turn down this fellowship. It meant that she wouldn't have a ten-ton weight resting on her shoulders for the next twenty years.

"Why aren't you excited?"

"I guess . . . I'm still in shock." Bridget started trying to cover. Maybe the Kidos didn't know that she'd applied for the grant, and maybe they had very little to do with it personally. Some staffer had probably approved it. Or maybe it was a mistake.

"This is a coup for the office," Jackie continued, oblivious to Bridget's confusion and distress. "And for you, of course."

"Of course." Bridget forced herself to respond, but her mind was going a mile a minute. There had to be some logical explanation for this. It couldn't be that she was now the recipient of nepotism—the kind she'd eschewed her whole life. There had to be a reason that the Kido Foundation chose her for the fellowship, and that reason had to be some sort of mistake.

"I think there's been a mistake . . ." She needed to find a way to explain this to Jackie that didn't include admitting that she'd married and had been sleeping with her former intern. She couldn't take the fellowship money, but she couldn't decline in a way that would torpedo her entire professional reputation. After all, without the fellowship money, she'd have to continue working here until she was a crusted shell.

"There's no mistake." Her boss was emphatic. "In fact, Jane Kido wants to take you to lunch tomorrow."

The sick feeling in her stomach told her that it was more that Jane Kido was going to eat her for lunch than tell her that she'd won the fellowship with no strings.

BRIDGET HADN'T BEEN ABLE to get ahold of Matt the night before. She shouldn't have been as pissed about it as she was, but his phone going to voicemail had made her even more agitated. The last thing she'd needed the night before had been agitation. Having lunch with her mother-in-law, the one who'd just offered to give her more than a hundred thousand dollars, was nerve-wracking enough.

She didn't know why, but she smelled something rotten about the whole thing. It didn't sit well. Jane Kido was too sharp not to see the optics of this—it looked nepotistic and corrupt. It would put their name in the same breath as the Chapins. People would talk about how they were corrupt, and it would obviate the whole existence of their philanthropy.

In the back of her mind, she suspected that this was just an elaborate way of getting rid of her. And part of her wondered if this wasn't at Matt's behest. There had been nothing strange about the last time they'd seen each other. He'd kissed her forehead before slipping out of her condo to get to class. They hadn't shared "I love yous," but it had felt like there was more to this than assured closure.

But Bridget had been fooled into believing that she had a future with someone before. Maybe he'd decided that being with her was too much for him or not what he wanted and was having his mother clean things up for him. Maybe she'd been wrong all along and he really was the kind of guy who used his money and privilege to escape hard work or inconvenience.

She didn't think that was true, but she couldn't exactly trust herself.

When she walked into the supremely elegant restaurant, the kind of place where ladies who lunched smiled with their mouths and stabbed with their words, she didn't let any of her anxiety, confusion, or anticipatory grief show. She held her spine straight and put a smile on her face.

She didn't even miss a step or let her smile fade when Jane looked her up and down in the same way she had the first time they met—as though she was lacking. Instead, she extended her hand and made sure it wasn't shaking.

"Please sit." Jane motioned to a chair across from hers. "I took the liberty of ordering the branzino for two."

Fish wasn't Bridget's favorite—it reminded her of Lenten Fridays and sacrifice—but she didn't tell Jane that. This woman didn't get her vulnerabilities in a moment when she wasn't even sure if she was going to blow up her marriage. The one she hadn't known she wanted to stay in until a few days ago.

"Thank you. Sounds delicious."

Jane gave her an almost-indulgent smile when the server came over and poured them both a glass of white wine. Then her mother-in-law picked up her glass as though she was going to make a toast, and Bridget braced herself. "To your new fellowship."

"Mrs. Kido—"

"Please call me Jane."

Now Bridget was in a bit of a cold sweat. "Jane, I think there's been a mistake. I sort of wasn't thinking about the fellowship application when I married Matt, and I know I can't accept it. I shouldn't have gotten it in the first place." Jane quirked her head, and Bridget couldn't seem to keep herself from talking. "How can I fix this?"

After a beat, Jane said, "I'm glad you asked." She turned and pulled a manila envelope out of her shoulder bag. She pushed it across the table. "A final divorce decree. I had to pull a few strings with Judge Dickerson's clerk, but he expedited them for me. We're good friends."

Fucking Judge Dickerson, screwing her over again. Bridget

wanted to throw up. All over the table and all over the *final* divorce decree. "I don't understand."

Jane smiled again. "It's simple. You sign these papers, leave my son alone, and then you get your fellowship. Everyone wins."

"But why?" Everything about herself that she'd ever thought of as inadequate rushed up into the front of her mind. And it was compounded by the woman sitting across the table from her. Jane Kido was head to toe a lady. Her nails were perfect, her clothes pressed just right, and Bridget doubted that she'd ever had a hair out of place.

Bridget knew she didn't measure up, but she hadn't thought she needed to.

"You're simply not the appropriate partner for my son." Jane shook her head.

Even though she wasn't cataloguing the ways that she didn't have rich-girl hair or a taste for gin that the appropriate partner for Matt would probably have, she captured a little bit of anger. "Appropriate?"

"I just don't think that you're a good influence."

"And so you're paying me off like this is some kind of 1980s nighttime soap?" Bridget almost pushed away from the table and left. This was beyond insulting.

"So dramatic."

"I'm dramatic?" Bridget scoffed. "I'd say that you're the dramatic one, lady."

There was no way she could take the fellowship now, under any circumstances. And she wasn't sure how she was going to tell Matt that his mother had tried to bribe her. He would be so hurt by it. But she still didn't know if he shared her feelings, didn't know if he would choose her over his family.

"What happens if I refuse to sign the papers?" Jane was probably prepared for all sorts of possibilities and had contingency plans in place in the event that Bridget told her to shove her divorce papers and fellowship up her well-heeled ass.

"Well, I think I can convince you to take my side."

Matt's mother had another think coming, but she would hear her out. "Let's just say you can't."

"Did you know that Matt's trust fund doesn't vest until he turns thirty?" Bridget was going to get whiplash from the change in subject, but she was willing to see where this went. "Unless he marries, of course."

"So? I don't know what that has to do with me other than that you don't have him under your thumb anymore."

"I would think that you would care more about being married to a billionaire."

Although Bridget was a little bit surprised that Matt was a billionaire in his own right, she didn't care. She'd want to be with him if he didn't have two pennies to rub together, and she was going to tell Jane that. "I think you have the wrong idea about me."

It wasn't as though she was from the wrong side of the tracks. She just wasn't insanely rich, like Naomi Chapin. And she didn't chase status like—well—her mother.

"Don't get me wrong. I think you're a very clever girl. But you're not part of our world. Matt needs to be with someone who has been training to be a good steward of resources all of their life."

This all sounded incredibly archaic, and it made Bridget question whether Jane knew her son at all. "Listen, don't let the red hair fool you. I'm not the fucking Little Mermaid, and I don't *want* to be a part of your world."

Jane looked taken aback for a moment, but she recovered. "I had your credit checked. You're living hand to mouth, practically. Especially after your unfortunate breakup with Chris Dooley—"

"You ran an actual background check?!" Bridget was aware that she was shrieking, the other guests were looking, and she was probably confirming Jane's suspicions that she wasn't appropriate for Matt. But this woman had no idea what was good for her son. Spending twenty minutes with her had Bridget wanting to become a legit socialist.

"Of course. You can't understand what it's like. But we've worked hard to get where we are, and we have to protect our interests." With that, Bridget felt a little bit of empathy for Jane. She respected how hard her family had worked to get where they were, but that didn't excuse her outlandish, controlling behavior.

"I can't know what it's like to be you," Bridget said. "But I have always paid my own way, with minimal help from my parents. I only applied for the fellowship because I don't want my dad to work himself into an early grave trying to pay my way. I'm not with Matt because of your—his—money. And I would never dream of taking advantage of him."

"You really care about him, don't you?" Jane looked surprised.

"How could I not?" Bridget said. "I know what this looks like—he borrowed your plane to fly me to Vegas and married me the same day as our first kiss. He'd been with Naomi for years, and you expected him to be with her, or someone like her, forever. But I'm not the girl you think I am.

"I care about Matt. A lot." She wasn't going to say the "love" word to anyone but Matt. "And I don't want to do anything to hurt him."

"Then you'll sign the papers." Jane pushed the manila envelope an inch farther across the table.

"You're not listening to me, Jane." Bridget stood up then. "I'm not going to let anything hurt Matt, but I'm not giving him up."

CHAPTER TWENTY-EIGHT

MATT HAD SPENT ALL day and evening Tuesday and Wednesday in the library for the first time since his first year. But it would be worth it so that he could spend the entire weekend with his whole focus on Bridget and their future together.

He could barely wait to put the nonsense about their marriage being real behind them. He was ready to tell Bridget he loved her, and he didn't want to do it over the phone or text, so he'd turned those things off while he was working.

As soon as he turned his phone back on, he realized what a mistake he'd made. He had three voicemails from Bridget, each sounding a little more frantic. Shit. He'd never had to be available to anyone before. Not even Naomi.

He still didn't call her back. It was Thursday, and he was meeting Bridget and the rest of the wedding party for a dance lesson. They weren't doing anything elaborate, but Jack had said something about Hannah's inability to take a lead. Besides, anything that would allow him to hold Bridget for two hours sounded like a lot of fun.

So, he was rushing out of the law library when he ran into Naomi—again.

"You look like shit." If only she'd been this honest when they were dating.

He actually didn't feel well, and was sorely hoping that he wasn't coming down with the stomach flu that had been going around the law school. "I'm fine. What do you want to talk about?"

"I just have proof that your wife was only after you for your money." He tried passing her, but she moved to block him. "You want to hear this."

"No. No, I don't." He tried to pass her again, and she huffed at him. All of his trying to move around her made his stomach pitch. "Get out of my way. What's it going to take for you to leave me alone? I get married to someone else, and you're still after me." He ran a hand through his hair and noticed how clammy his forehead had gotten. "Seriously, what do I have to do to be rid of you?"

"Well, you don't have to blow up your whole life so you can be with Bridget Nolan. She was only ever after you for your family's money."

"We've gone over this, Naomi." Matt sighed but realized that a deep breath was a bad move when he tasted bile. "Bridget doesn't give a shit about my family's anything."

"You'll see I'm right eventually."

"The only thing about you I want to see is you leaving any room I walk into." Matt turned and walked away, but Naomi followed him. He was starting to get dizzy and needed to get to his car. Away from his ex. "Get away from me, Naomi."

"Are you okay? Do you need to sit down?"

At that point, he knew he hadn't, in fact, escaped the stomach flu. And he just made it to the trash can to empty his stomach into it.

MATT HADN'T ANSWERED ANY of her calls, and he hadn't shown up at the dance lesson for the wedding party. Combined with the disastrous lunch Bridget had had with his mother the day before, his absence made her mind go to all the wrong, dark places a mind could go. There might be an innocent explanation for it, but she couldn't help but think of all the not-so-innocent ones.

What if his mother had told him she'd accepted the fellowship money? What if he believed her? What if the whole bribe-Bridget-to-go-away plan had been his idea all along? Ghosting Naomi hadn't worked out so well, so maybe he was using his family as cover this time.

Sure, he could have just gotten busy with something at school and not charged his phone, but she didn't feel great about the odds that that was the case.

At the dance lesson, she ended up dancing with one of the instructors, wishing he was Matt the whole time. And she didn't miss the pitying looks from Chris as he squired his very buxom date around the dance floor.

The only lucky thing about the day was that she'd been able to slip out before he could corner her and talk to her. She had enough to worry about without him making snide remarks about her still not being able to keep a man.

Her first stop after the dance lesson was Matt's condo. His doorman let her up, because she was his wife, but he wasn't home. She was close to calling hospitals or the law school, when she grudgingly accepted that she should try his parents' house.

The whole drive over, she had a bad feeling that this would turn out poorly. If he wasn't there, she might get another offer of a bribe. If he was there, it might confirm her worst suspicions about whether Matt was involved in the aforementioned bribery scheme. There was really no way to win this.

She rang the doorbell and didn't have to wait for long. Surprisingly, Matt's mother answered the door.

Jane looked at her quizzically, as though she wasn't sure why Matt's wife might be standing on her doorstep. "Can I help you, Bridget?"

Bridget didn't have the patience to sugarcoat. "Is Matt here?"

"He is, but he can't see you."

Bridget hadn't thought past what she would do if he was here and didn't want to or couldn't see her. "Can't see me?"

"He's indisposed," she said, as though it was some final, definitive answer.

"Listen, I know that we got off on the wrong foot and you don't want me with him, but you have to tell me if he's okay."

She immediately realized her mistake—telling Jane Kido that she had to do anything was the height of stupidity.

"I don't want to have to call security." So, in addition to threatening to ruin her life if she didn't divorce her son, she was going to have her arrested for showing up here? Bridget understood that she was just trying to protect her son, but she was so close to losing her temper that she could taste copper in her mouth.

She wrapped her arms around her waist, partially to keep herself from pushing her way inside the house. "Can you at least have him call me?"

Jane didn't say anything, but Bridget took her sniff as an affirmative.

THE NEXT DAY WAS the rehearsal dinner. Bridget had a list as long as her arm of errands to run for Hannah. Under normal circumstances, she would have been happy to do it. But after Matt's disappearance and last night's confrontation with his mother, she was completely on edge and liable to snap at the person who got the font wrong on the place cards.

"I know my sister-in-law did not order a sans serif font on these things," she said, pointing to the very businesslike font on the card stock.

"Look at the order form." The clerk pointed to a black smudge on a piece of parchment that could have said anything.

"I can't even read that." Realizing that her voice had that high quality that it usually got when she was about to lose her shit, she took a deep, calming breath. "How fast can you fix it?"

"It's not wrong—"

Bridget did not have time for this shit. "You and I both know that this shit does not belong at a wedding. It's so ugly that it doesn't even actually belong on paper. Now, you're going to fix it today, and then you're going to have someone deliver it by hand to the venue in the morning."

"Oh? What are you going to do when I don't?"

Bridget was tempted to say that she'd string him up by the balls, but she decided that she could be more reasonable right now. Her bad mood wasn't this guy's fault. It wasn't even a bad mood; it was existential dread. The kind of thing she'd never felt before getting involved with Matt. When she'd made decisions with her brain instead of her heart or her vagina. She almost sighed with longing for that much simpler, if less sexually gratifying, time in her life.

Instead of any of the medieval torture methods she currently wanted to try out on the husband who'd ghosted her, she said, "My sister-in-law, Hannah, is a wedding planner. Apparently, she recommends you to a lot of her clients. If she's stuck with this bullshit"—she pointed to the offending box yet again—"I don't think she'll be using your services again."

Apparently, all she had to say was "wedding planner" and he realized whom he was dealing with. Hannah had a reputation that garnered both fear and respect. The man's face blanched. "This is for *Miss Hannah?*"

"Yep. Miss Hannah's getting married to my brother."

His eyes got big. "Your brother is a brave man."

Yep, he was. Too bad that the man Bridget had married couldn't even tell her to her face that he'd changed his mind about wanting to be with her.

CHAPTER TWENTY-NINE

MATT DIDN'T SHOW UP at the wedding rehearsal, either. That was when Bridget knew that his mother's "offer" had probably come at his behest. She'd made a mistake in trusting him to be there for her beyond what she could do for him. His summer internship had been about getting away from Naomi. He'd flown Bridget to Vegas so he could get into her pants. And he hadn't told anyone about their divorce so that he could get Naomi off his jock and continue having sex with Bridget for a few more weeks. Once their relationship had served those purposes, he'd scraped her off just like he had with his ex.

Unlike Naomi, she wasn't going to blow up his phone and beg him to reconsider. She had way too much pride for that.

What she didn't have too much pride for was crying at her brother's wedding rehearsal even though they didn't even say any vows. It didn't matter. The fact that her sweet, tender older brother had found someone who could balance him out was kind of a miracle. Hannah would hold the family grudges and be fierce when she needed to be. She would let Jack be himself, and he would give Hannah the attention she needed. That the two of them had found each other almost made her believe in God.

Thus the tears that she carefully hid from her parents, her brothers, and her ex as they went through the choreography of tomorrow's ceremony. Hannah was so excited and happy that she didn't even curse out Matt for not showing up.

In fact, her brother had to ask, "Where's Matt?"

"He had schoolwork." Bridget wasn't about to rain all over the wedding parade by telling everyone that Matt had dumped her. To-morrow, maybe he could be sick. Everyone would know that something more had happened, but they were mostly good Irish Catholics. They could pretend that everything was fine for years before directly addressing a problem.

Still, even though she was probably in the clear with having to explain shit to her family, she rushed out of the church after the re-hearsal was over.

By the time she got to the restaurant, earlier than everyone else, she was wishing that she'd chosen another career—not because she didn't find her job rewarding, but because she wouldn't get drug tested in the private sector and could have gotten super high before having to deal with Chris and her family this evening.

As soon as she walked in the door, she found the bar. "Whiskey, neat."

"What kind?" the bartender asked.

"The brown kind." As Jane had so helpfully reminded her, she was not classy. "It's not going to be in my mouth for very long."

Of course, Chris chose that moment to sidle up to her. "Make that two."

"What do you want?" He was way too close, and she was about to lose it. She gave him a hard look, and he moved away by about an inch. He'd only been witness to her losing her temper once, the night of the shoe throwing, and yet he still knew enough to fear her. He'd said that she had "crazy eyes" and she could kind of believe it.

"What's wrong, Bridget?" He actually looked a little concerned—for her. And that made her even angrier. She had to get away from him, like, right now.

"Nothing. Nothing is wrong."

"Don't bullshit me. We've known each other too long." He started to reach for her but stopped when she looked at his hand. She definitely had crazy eyes at the moment. "Tell me what's wrong."

Thankfully, she was saved by their drinks showing up. She downed hers in one shot, and he followed. It reminded her of all the time they'd spent together at weddings like this, at bars with their college and law school friends on random Saturday nights and the most important occasions of her life.

At that moment, she desperately needed to know why that hadn't been enough for Chris. It was too late to fix things with him, but maybe she could convince Matt not to discard her. Her whole body ached, and her eyes filled with tears. When it came right down to it, she'd spent her whole life trusting the man standing in front of her. For most of her life, she'd let him hold all of her sorrows in his hands. And just because they couldn't work as a couple, and she really hated him right now, she knew he would get the shorthand of her pain. She wouldn't even have to say that much. She could give him the bones and he could build out the rest.

"If you must know, I haven't heard from my husband since Tuesday afternoon. His mother tried to bribe me into divorcing him."

"That sucks." Ever eloquent, her ex-boyfriend.

"Yeah, it does." She lifted the glass of water the bartender had delivered with her whiskey. "At least this vindicates you."

Chris leaned close to the bar. "What do you mean?"

"Matt didn't want to stay married to me. You were right about me not being able to keep him." She made a motion in the air, trying to summon the words. "You were right all along—I am just not lovable. Not in the get-married, have-all-the-sex-and-babies kind of way."

"Jesus Christ, Bridget." He scrubbed a hand over his face. "Is that what you really think?"

"I don't know how I'd think anything else." She flagged down the bartender and signaled for two more drinks.

"You were always too good for me." Chris's admission was quiet, and it shocked the shit out of her. Her ex had the kind of ego that needed constant pumping. He wasn't the kind of guy who would admit to weakness. "And I broke up with you because of my wounded pride, not anything you did."

"Well, you really tried to make it about me." She paused to make sure she recalled his exact phrasing. "You said that I was a 'cold-hearted bitch.' That's exactly what you said."

"And you weren't in love with me, either."

Bridget blanched. Of course she'd been in love with Chris. She'd been infatuated with him since she was capable of infatuation. She did love him. She had—once.

"Think about it, Bridget." He motioned between the two of them. "We had no chemistry between us beyond being horny teen-

251

agers trying shit out. Before we broke up, when was the last time you wanted to kiss me?"

He'd stumped her. She tried to remember the last time she felt the thrum of anticipation before touching Chris. And she came up with nothing. Before Matt, she might have brushed that off and thought she just wasn't the kind of person who felt overwhelming chemistry—at least she'd never been the type to let it take her off course in life.

It had literally never occurred to her until that moment that she'd never been in love with Chris. That maybe she'd only been so dead set on having him because of his distinguishing feature of always being there.

"We could have been happy," she said. "I could have tried harder."

"Look," he replied. "We could have faked it for a while, had a few kids, moved to fucking Skokie. But we would have been just as miserable as your parents."

She knew he was right, and they hadn't worked out because they weren't right for each other, not because she hadn't tried hard enough. But she could only see that because of what she'd started to feel for Matt.

Before he'd ghosted her, she felt light whenever she thought about him. He might not be like anyone else she knew, but he called to her for some reason. The way he smiled at her, wanted to make her happy, all the feeling he poured into every single kiss. All of it made her feel more—like everything she had inside her was bigger than her skin.

She'd never felt that for Chris. Maybe because he was familiar? But something inside her said that she wouldn't have felt the same way about him that she felt about Matt if she was just meeting him now. Not because he wasn't handsome or smart or worthy. Just because he wasn't her soul mate.

"What was the whole thing in Vegas about?" She was curious as to why he acted like a petulant child once she brought someone else around.

His face got a little more ruddy, and he grimaced. Signs for when he didn't want to tell her the truth but was going to anyway. "I always thought we'd get back together. What you did just felt like the definite end."

"It was the right thing to do," Bridget said. "This way we're both free."

"What if I don't want to be free?" She saw something that looked like hope in his eyes, and she should have extinguished it on the spot, but she couldn't bring herself to. She had enough emotional bullshit to sort through in her own head and didn't have the bandwidth to deal with his. "We could try again. Just date and see if we fall in love with each other this time."

"You only want me because someone else came into the picture." Not that Matt wanted her anymore. "I think maybe you should try giving one of your flavors of the week like two weeks and see if it works out."

Chris looked down, but she could see a smile tugging at his lips. He knew she was right. "You always were a whole hell of a lot smarter than me."

"I know." And then they laughed.

At that precise moment, Jack and Hannah and the rest of the wedding party burst through the door and ended her conversation with Chris. She was extremely grateful to not have to deal with his misgivings about their breakup for the rest of the night.

She realized while talking to him that she was done grieving him. Just in time to grieve what she could have had with Matt.

MATT WOKE UP ON the floor of his childhood bathroom with a pit in his stomach. And it wasn't just because he hadn't even been able to keep down water for the past however many hours. He wasn't even sure how long he'd been at his parents' house.

All of his limbs were heavy, and he felt weaker than he ever had as an adult. When Naomi had gotten him here, with him puking out of her car's window at every stoplight the whole way, he'd been grateful. He hadn't been able to think of anything but getting somewhere to be sick in private.

He'd have much preferred if it was Bridget and not his ex driving, but beggars couldn't be choosers. And he'd have much preferred to be on the floor of Bridget's bathroom—she probably would have done more than slide soda water and saltines through a crack in the door like his mother had.

He needed to call Bridget. It took him five minutes to get himself together to stand up, and it all turned out to be futile because his cell phone wasn't in the bathroom or his old bedroom.

All the searching left him sweaty and tired. But at least he wasn't about to puke again—small favors. He called the butler and asked for his phone. When his door opened, he expected it to be Jerome. But it was his mother.

That should have been his first clue that something was terribly wrong.

"I need to call Bridget," he said.

His mother sighed. "You need to get into bed. Your sheets were changed."

"I need to call my wife," he said, knowing that his mother had changed the subject on purpose. She wouldn't meet his gaze, and he knew she was up to something. "Where's my phone?"

"Charging in the kitchen."

Matt was pretty sure he'd fall down the stairs in some melodramatic move, and maybe that would be fitting. This whole thing smelled like the machinations of Alexis Colby. His mother had been a childhood devotee of *Dynasty*, and maybe this was her trying out some Machiavellian tactics from her favorite show.

"Can you just get my phone, Mom?"

Instead she ignored him and tried to usher him over to the bed. "She stopped by."

"And I didn't see her why?" He sat down on the edge of the bed.

"You were asleep, and I didn't think you'd want to get her sick two days before her brother's wedding."

"How long was I asleep?" It only felt like a day since he'd gotten here, but he'd been so exhausted and ill that he hadn't kept track.

"It's Friday night."

Fuck. He'd thought he was only going to miss the Thursday night dance lesson. Now he was going to have to grovel about missing the rehearsal and dinner. That gave him the strength to get up and get to the door.

"You should stay in bed."

He looked back at his mother, who still looked innocent. "Please don't tell me that you did anything to mess things up with her."

She moved toward him. "If anything I can do is going to mess up your *marriage*, then maybe that's telling you it was a mistake."

He didn't really have an answer for that, but he knew she'd done something. He only hoped he could fix it.

BRIDGET CRIED WHEN HER dad made a toast after the rehearsal dinner. She couldn't help it, because she cried every time her dad cried. It was like a reflex, and not at all surprising.

"Molly and I couldn't be happier for Jack and his lovely bride, Hannah." He raised his glass and then quoted a few lines of her favorite Yeats poem—*Had I the heavens' embroidered cloths* . . .

By the time he finished up, tears were full-on running down her face, unimpeded. Her mascara was surely a mess, so she excused herself to the bathroom.

The last thing she expected was for her mother to follow her.

"Now is not the time, Molly," she said. She didn't need more emotion. She wasn't into feelings on a good day, and she was full up.

"You're just like him, you know?" Her mother was clearly dead set on ignoring her wishes. So what else was new?

"Like who?"

"Like your father." Molly brushed the bangs of her thick gray bob out of their perfect alignment. "Both incredibly stubborn, temperamental—"

"Are you done singing our praises? Maybe you want to tell me that both our feet stink. Is that why you left him?"

"We've been over this before, Bridget." Her mother handed her a tissue, which she took because she didn't have it in her to be spiteful, just prickly.

"Yes, we have."

"And I don't want to see you ruin a good thing because you're afraid of becoming me." Then her mother smoothed a hand over the back of her hair.

And it broke her.

All the feelings she'd kept bottled up for years that might have come out of her in anger before came out in tears instead. Even though she hadn't connected with her mother as an adult, and the idea that her mother would try to parent her after abdicating those responsibilities for so long should annoy her, she needed it so much in that moment. She needed her mother to tell her that they were nothing alike—that the genes they shared weren't destiny.

But it also meant that all the care she'd taken to make sure she wouldn't flake out on her life was misplaced. If she was like her father, she was the one who ultimately got left. Her mother had left. Chris had left. And now Matt.

"I'm sorry, Bridget." Her mother had apologized a bunch of times for bugging out after the divorce, and Bridget had deflected those apologies every time. She'd told herself that her mother didn't mean them, that she was trying to get back in Bridget's good graces because she was dating her father again. And Bridget didn't know why this apology was sinking in, why it felt real.

But it did. "It's okay, Mom."

That was the first time she'd called her mother "Mom" since she was thirteen years old.

"It's not okay. I know I'll never make it up to you. I can't, and I've accepted that." Her mother replaced her tissue and started rubbing makeup off her face. "But I'll do whatever it takes to build something new with you."

"I'd like that," Bridget said quietly. And it was the truth.

"Tell me what happened." Her mother leaned against the counter. "Maybe my experience with ending marriages might help you keep yours going."

Bridget laughed at that. Her mother had a terrible record, but she would probably be able to see inside Matt's head more easily than Bridget, because it looked like he was flaking on their relationship.

"Well, he just dropped off the face of the earth after Tuesday. When he didn't show up at the dance lesson on Thursday, I called him. When he didn't answer his phone, I went to his condo. He wasn't there, so I went to his house. And then his mother—"

She hesitated to tell her mother about what Jane had said and about the bribe. She wasn't sure her mother would take her side. After all, she still had to cultivate the Kidos and families like them for donations and sponsorships at the museum. Maybe she would agree that she and Matt were a mismatched pair and she didn't belong with someone like him.

"What did his mother do?" Her mother's brow wrinkled. "She's a legendary bitch. And I mean that as a compliment."

Bridget giggled. Her mother very rarely swore, and she didn't call other women names. "What did she do?"

"Don't get me wrong. She's smart, and I love seeing a woman sitting on top of a huge pile of money for a lot of reasons. But she's downright unpleasant at times, and very touchy about her kid."

She decided it was safe to voice her doubts. "She tried to bribe me with a fellowship that would pay off my student loans if I would sign divorce papers. She doesn't think I'm good enough for Matt."

"Bullshit." Her mother sounded unequivocal, and Bridget was relieved.

Still, she had doubts. "I mean, there has to be a reason I haven't heard from Matt since Tuesday. Maybe he decided that I was too much trouble."

"What happened the last time you saw him?"

Bridget's face heated because she'd been naked the last time she saw Matt. Naked and satisfied.

Luckily, Hannah and Sasha came into the bathroom. Hannah took one look at Bridget and said, "I told you that no family angst was allowed on the wedding weekend. Cease fire. What are you ladies doing in here?"

Bridget's mom met her gaze, and Bridget nodded. Hannah was a safe person to tell. "Bridget's worried because she hasn't heard from Matt since Tuesday."

"What happened on Tuesday?"

Bridget threw up her hands. "Nothing. He texted that his class was canceled, but he had a lot of work to do. But then he didn't show up on Thursday, and he's apparently at his parents' house and refused to see me."

Her mother helpfully added, "His mother refused to let her see him."

"Why is his mother even involved in this?"

Bridget wondered the same thing. "She hates me."

"Well, she doesn't know you well enough to hate you." Hannah pulled a lipstick out of her bag. "And if she knew you, it would be impossible to hate you."

"I don't think it matters anymore. If Matt wanted to see me, what would stop him?"

"What exactly did he say the last time you heard from him?" Hannah held out her hand for Bridget's phone. When Bridget lit up the screen, she saw multiple new notifications from Matt Kido and felt sheepish. She'd turned the ringer and vibrate functions off during dinner and hadn't seen any of them. She'd lost so much hope that she hadn't even checked her phone.

"See? Everything is probably fine."

Bridget wanted to tell her mother and Hannah to leave while she listened to the messages, but she thought better of it. They were invested now and apparently got to hear what he had to say. In part, she was grateful for the support. If Matt had only left multiple "Dear Jane" messages for her, it would be embarrassing. But they'd probably be helpful in drying many, many more tears.

"Bridget—I'm so sorry. I got the stomach flu while I was at school, and Naomi was there." Bridget winced hearing her name, but mouthed, "It's fine," to both her mother and Hannah. Then Hannah grabbed the phone and put it on speaker.

"I passed out after I finally stopped puking, and I just woke up. I know what this seems like . . . I'll be there tomorrow. I promise. And not contagious anymore. Call me when you get this."

The six other messages where increasingly pathetic and worried. She was tempted to call him back right then and there, but she didn't trust herself not to tell him that she loved him and that she would murder him in his sleep if he ever disappeared on her for multiple days again.

"Are you going to call him back?" her mother asked.

"We're not there yet, Mom." Bridget needed to do this alone.

CHAPTER THIRTY

AFTER LEAVING BRIDGET MULTIPLE frantic messages, Matt called a car and went back to his condo, over his mother's fervent objections. It was as though she didn't want to let him out of her sight, and she hadn't been like that since he was a little kid getting picked on in boarding school.

He managed to keep down some lightly buttered toast and liquids, and he'd been able to shower the sick off his body. But those two things had exhausted him. Had he not still been feeling the effects of the flu, he would have been pacing his apartment. As it was, he was lying on his couch, crawling out of his skin.

Why hadn't she called him back?

He could think of all manner of reasons that she wouldn't—the ghosting was the first one. But his brain also went to another place. What if Chris had swooped in at a weak moment, when she was sure that their sham marriage had done its job, and convinced her to take him back?

It was insane, but he couldn't help but think that.

When a key turned in his lock, he was hoping it was Bridget, and he was relieved when it was red hair, not blond, that peaked in the doorway.

"Come here." That wasn't enough, but that was all he could say. He just wanted her close to him.

"Are you sure you're not still contagious?" She looked uncertain, and he wished he could say something, anything, to assuage that. But he'd done the thing that would be most likely to push her emotional buttons—disappearing. Even though it wasn't intentional, she hadn't come to trust him easily, and he knew he would have to earn it back.

"The good news is that I didn't do any puking here, and the bug is out of my system by now."

"That's great." Still, she sat at the end of the couch. If he was at full strength, he would have pulled her into his lap. "Why didn't you call me?"

"My mom had my phone in the kitchen." A muscle tightened in her face, one that he was familiar with. It was the muscle in her jaw that twitched when she was frustrated about something. "I'm so sorry, Bridget. I hope it wasn't a pain in the ass to try to explain things to your family—and Chris."

He hated that he hadn't even been able to fulfill the original intent of them staying married.

Bridget leaned back into the sofa, and he let off some of the tension he'd been holding in his body. She was staying, and he wasn't going to have to run and chase her. "It was actually fine. My mom saw that I was upset." She looked over at him then, and he realized that her skin was scrubbed clean, much more clean than it would have been on a regular night out. He loved that he knew what she looked like on a regular night out. "And we talked. She apologized—again—and I kind of think she meant it."

"Of course she meant it." Matt hated that Bridget had ever believed that she was leavable, unlovable, forgettable in any way. He'd known the day he met her that he would never forget the fire in her eyes. The sway of her hips and the way her hair caught the sunlight were imprinted forever on his mind. And it didn't matter that it felt like she was his to love now. He would never have been able to let go of how she made him feel—like he could be better than the dilettante she'd thought he was—even if they'd never gotten married. She would have been indelible to him even if he'd never kissed her.

"You think?" Bridget bit her bottom lip, and that was when Matt knew he was truly on the mend.

"Don't do that."

"Do what?" She bit that fat, pink bottom lip even harder and he groaned.

"Don't look good enough to eat right now," he said, hoping she would flush pink. She did. "I was just able to keep down toast, and I'm not going to start on you until I know I can gorge."

Bridget rolled her eyes. "Only you would be thinking about sex like a day after the stomach flu."

"That's on you, Little Bird."

It was her turn to groan, and not in the fun, sexy way. "That one's the worst one of all."

"You're going to have to settle on a nickname one of these days." At least that's what he hoped.

"Am I?" Bridget asked. "I thought this was all supposed to be over after this weekend."

He wanted to tell her that he was falling in love with her and that he wanted to stay married to her. "I want . . ." It was harder to get the words out than he thought it would be, but this was a big deal. It was a huge thing to tell someone that you wanted to spend the rest of your life with them. "I think we should stay married."

She paused and looked down at her lap. Her hair shadowed her face, and that was what made him sit up and touch her. He put her hair behind her ear, savoring the silk of it against his fingers.

"I want that, too." She looked at him with her eyes shiny with tears. He hoped they were happy, but he was afraid to ask. "But why?"

"I'm in love with you."

"Good." That was all she said for a minute.

"Good?" He scooted even closer. "That's all you have to say? Good?"

She smiled at him then. "I'm in love with you, too."

"Thank God!" He laughed for the first time in what felt like years. "I thought you were going to say something like you were just going to stay married to me because I'm rich and I have a big dick."

She blanched when he said that, but it was a fleeting thing. "Hey, if you're worried that who I am or who my family is will change your life, don't." She shook her head, but he kept talking. He wasn't about to let her back out of this now that she'd admitted that she was in love with him. "You don't have to go to any charity events or family functions—I mean, it's not like we're the royal family or anything."

"You have always treated me like a princess." The shadows lingering in her gaze after he mentioned his family's money lifted a little bit, and he was deeply relieved. "And we should talk about your family—"

"The last thing I want to talk about is my mother right now."

Matt threw his gaze up to the ceiling. "Can we save it for after the wedding tomorrow?"

"Are you sure that you're going to be up for going?"

"I'd have to be dead or severely maimed to miss out on you walking down the aisle in that dress."

"Remember it's Hannah's day." Her tone was chiding, and he was glad that she had her sense of humor back. He was glad she'd forgiven him, and was over the moon that she loved him.

"I won't even be able to see her."

"You're ridiculous." She slapped his shoulder and then rubbed where she'd slapped. "I'm glad you're okay."

"C'mere," he said.

"I'm right here."

He pulled her close, so that she was lying on top of him on the couch. "Stay, and tell me everything that happened at the rehearsal dinner."

"I thought I was staying forever."

"You are."

BRIDGET HAD NEVER BEEN one for hyperbole. When people said that they felt as though they were "walking on air," it had always earned a healthy dose of side-eye from her. At least until Matt Kido told her he loved her and wanted to stay married to her.

After thinking that she might have lost him forever, the switch to being happily married to him—forever—caused a whole lot of emotional whiplash. But him holding her and asking about the rehearsal dinner, him getting all of the ways her family was nuts, tethered her to the ground.

ANDIE J. CHRISTOPHER

The other thing tethering her to the ground—the issue of his family's money hanging over her neck like the sword of Damocles— was less comforting. Even though he wasn't going to force her to deal with his family, she was going to have to tell him about what his mother had done. One thing she'd learned over the last week was that they had a lot to learn about communication. But he loved his mother, and Bridget didn't want to tell him something that would cause him to cut her off.

Then he would grow to resent her, and their whole marriage could be poisoned by it. She'd seen up close what the slow poisoning of a marriage could do. And even though she'd made some peace with her mother, she didn't want to repeat her parents' mistakes.

Plus, there was the issue of his mother thinking that she was a straight-up gold digger. She didn't think he would believe his mother over her, but his experience with Naomi might have made him more susceptible to the suggestion. Bridget would just rather tell him her-self.

But the point was that he loved her, and that carried her through the doors of the fancy salon where Hannah and her other brides-maids were getting their hair done.

"You look a hell of a lot happier this morning," Hannah said, before downing a mimosa.

Not eager to carry the bride down the aisle, Bridget said, "Are you sure you should be drinking at eight in the morning?"

Sasha piped up then. "That was number one. She needs to have at least one an hour until the ceremony. I have it properly timed out with pastries and cheese so that she won't be too drunk."

"She's a very good friend." Hannah pointed at the chair next to her. "Sit down." She looked adorable and happy in hot rollers with a scrubbed-clean face, wearing a fluffy robe in a salon like she was in her living room. "Is it super selfish if I say that I'm really glad you're not puffy-snot-crying on my wedding day?"

"Not at all. I mean, I don't remember how I felt when I decided to get married, much less right before. But I think it's completely reasonable to want this day to be completely about you."

"I'm really glad you're going to be my sister-in-law." Hannah looked entirely sincere, which was different from how she usually was—cracking wise at everything. Bridget enjoyed her both ways but knew that she needed to listen to what she had to say now. "Even if Jack decides that I'm too much of a pain in the ass to tolerate, you're never going to get rid of me."

Bridget's eyes welled up with tears, and she grabbed Hannah's hand. "Well, for one thing, that's never going to happen. My brother loves you more than he loved *Power Rangers* when he was a kid. And that's saying something." Hannah's lower lip trembled. "For another, I already think of you like my sister."

Sasha was wiping carefully under her smudged eye makeup. "You guys have to stop this. I can only get all smudged up during the ceremony."

Hannah looked at her friend. "You might want to use water-proof. Perish the thought you got all smudged up in front of Father Patrick," she said in a teasing tone.

Bridget was confused. "Patrick Dooley?"

"Yeah, Sasha has a little crush on him. She read this book about a kinky priest—"

"Shut up, Hannah. I will withhold mimosas for the rest of the day, and you will have to walk down the aisle and pledge the rest of your life to another fallible human completely sober," Sasha said.

"You wouldn't do that to me, and it's harmless," Hannah said. "I need more cheese."

Bridget was still a little gobsmacked. "Patrick Dooley. Really?"

"You've never noticed that he's a smoke show?" Hannah said it like she was calling the sky blue.

"But he took a vow of celibacy." Bridget didn't add the part about how he was like her brother, because he wasn't like Sasha's brother. And, hell, if she was into priests, she might be into brothers.

Sasha had apparently decided to give up on not talking about this, because she said, "That just makes it hotter." She shook her head. "I never should have read that book by Sierra Simone."

Bridget thought she might get her hands on that book and a priest costume for Matt.

She must have had a dreamy look on her face because Hannah said, "What happened with Matt?"

"He loves me."

Both Sasha and Hannah stood up and did a little dance. "We knew it."

"How the hell did you know anything?" Bridget didn't understand how Hannah—a former deep skeptic on the topics of love and romance—could possibly suss out that Matt was in love with her. She'd spent no more than twenty-four hours with the guy.

"I knew it when he got up and did the dishes after dinner."

"He's just polite." Bridget didn't know why she was arguing, but she was a little embarrassed that she hadn't figured this out for herself. Sort of like she'd been embarrassed when Chris had told her he wasn't in love with her.

"Nah, a polite guy opens a door for you." Hannah pointed at the man opening a door for another patron. "A guy who is in love with you wants to make sure he's invited back into your home, so he pitches in. Matt did not grow up cleaning up after himself. It's not automatic for him. It's intentional."

"Whatever." Bridget's stylist came over to get her shampooed. She might have been trying to sound nonchalant, but the idea that Matt loved her in a way that was plain for everyone to see kept the smile on her face the whole time.

CHAPTER THIRTY-ONE

MATT WASN'T EXPECTING HIS mother to show up at his house with Naomi in tow. Even though he knew that Bridget was getting glamorous with her future sister-in-law, he'd *hoped* it was her. For longer than he wanted to admit to himself, he'd been hoping she walked through every open door the same way she'd walked into his heart.

Damn, but he was turning into a sap.

When he realized that it wasn't his wife coming back for a pre-wedding quickie, he buttoned up his shirt. "What are you two doing here? Together?"

"You should still be in bed." His mother put her bag on his island and walked over to him. Without him asking, she started tying his bow tie. He didn't slap her hands away, even though he wanted to. That wouldn't help him find out why she was here, placate her, and convince her to leave any more efficiently.

"What are you doing here with my *ex*-girlfriend?" Naomi pouted when she heard that but turned around and started rifling through his fridge as though she still belonged there. He'd never been more tempted to drop a dime on how she'd cheated on him.

"We have some important information to share with you about your current wife."

"Couldn't you have sent an e-mail?" His mother pursed her lips at his joke. "Seriously, I have to get to the church. For my brother-in-law's wedding."

"I'll make this quick, then." Naomi poured herself a glass of his orange juice. "She's after you for your money."

Matt moved over to the kitchen island and met Naomi's gaze. They had a silent standoff for a few beats before she looked away. She really thought that he wasn't going to blow up the quasi-familial relationship between their parents, didn't she?

Before he could open his mouth to tell his mother about Naomi's scheming and lying, his mother piped up. "Did you know that Bridget only took you on as an intern because she wanted the fellowship?"

"Yes. And it had nothing to do with what happened between us after I stopped being her intern."

"Are you sure?" His mother had always asked him that before he made a choice that she didn't one hundred percent agree with. And it always—*always*—made him doubt himself. Including now.

Seeing Naomi, the woman who really had only been with him because of what he could do for her, somehow gave him a sliver of doubt that wedged its way under his skin. Just a stray shard of glass from everything she'd broken—mostly his ability to trust that someone wanted him for himself and not his family's money.

It was small, but the idea that Bridget was playing some sort of long game made its way through his mind because Naomi was standing right there.

He wasn't going to give her the benefit of seeing that she'd gotten in his head, though.

"What does that have to do with anything?" Just because she had student loans and had applied for the fellowship, it didn't mean that anything that happened after had to do with his money. Hell, she'd *made fun* of the private plane and the penthouse. He should be giving her the benefit of the doubt.

"Well, when she heard that she wasn't going to get the fellowship, she married you." Naomi had a smile on her face as she accused Bridget of being what Naomi was. He was so angry that he turned his back on her. It would be better to pretend she wasn't here and was just effective as yelling at her.

"This is a waste of time." His mother hated wasting time more than anything. "We're married now, and I'll pay off her student loans tomorrow. In fact, I can afford it now that I can access my trust fund. She'll probably try to pay me back for the next ten years."

"Are you sure? When I had lunch with her this week, she didn't turn down the fellowship when I offered it to her. And she took the final divorce decree with her."

"Divorce decree?" Bridget hadn't mentioned the lunch, the fellowship, or any *divorce decree* last night when they'd declared their love. And even though this whole thing smelled like a last-ditch effort for Naomi not to lose her golden ticket out of having the last name Kido, Bridget's not telling him about any of this made that glass sliver of doubt a little bit bigger.

"Are you sure that you were both drunk the night you got married?" That question came from Naomi, and it was easy to brush off. The morning after they'd gotten married, Bridget had seemed mortified and hungover. It hadn't been premeditated.

But after? When they'd consummated their marriage—precluding an annulment? Maybe at some point that day, she'd decided that she'd work the situation to her advantage. Using him to needle Chris was sort of a thin excuse. And, even though her ex had been an underhanded dick bringing up her abortion in front of her family, Bridget had handled him deftly.

So, a little bit of what his mom said landed in a suspicious place in his heart that had been previously reserved for Naomi. Even though it was too convenient that Naomi was pushing this theory with Bridget. She was probably projecting. And, regardless of whether his mom's theory of the case on Bridget was correct, he needed to put a stop to the Naomi thing once and for all. "Did Naomi tell you why we broke up, Mom?"

Naomi made a weird squeaking noise. His mom raised one brow in the way that always told him as a teenager that he was borrowing trouble. "No, she didn't. And I don't see why that matters at the moment."

"She cheated on me, in my fucking bed."

"That wasn't—" Matt held up a hand so Naomi wouldn't go in with her excuses.

"I wasn't going to say anything since the Chapins are old family friends and all. But she wouldn't leave things alone."

"Is this true?" This question was directed at Naomi.

"Um. It wasn't what it looked like."

Jane Kido put on her don't-fuck-with-my-family face then. It was everything he'd been trying to avoid since the beginning of the summer, but it was almost a relief at this point. And it took the heat off him and Bridget so that he could figure out that—much more important—situation on his own.

"Yeah, she fucked one of the guys who used to make fun of me at boarding school." He left out the part where she'd besmirched his reputation as a considerate lover because he didn't need his mom knowing about that.

"Why didn't you tell me this before?" his mom asked. "I wouldn't have had her in my house."

"That's exactly why." Matt motioned at Naomi. "I don't need you fixing my problems. I had it handled."

"Is that why you didn't take the perfectly good summer job you had?" She wasn't going to let him off easily. But, fortunately, she wasn't going to let Naomi off easily, either. "I thought your parents raised you better, Naomi. I think you should leave."

"But—" Naomi started to talk, but a look from his mother cut her off. She left her half-finished orange juice and walked out in a huff.

His mother turned her attention on him. "So, you threw away a whole summer and married a virtual stranger so that you wouldn't have to tell me and your father about Naomi?"

"Pretty much." There was no use in denying it now. This summer had really taught him a lesson about being direct and trying to solve his problems. If he'd broken up with Naomi when he'd realized they weren't in love enough to sustain a long-term relationship, maybe she wouldn't have cheated and they could be amicable exes.

But then he might never have met Bridget. He wouldn't have married her, then fallen in love with her. Or maybe it was the other way around? He didn't know precisely the moment when he realized that he couldn't stand the thought of her being temporary in his life.

The idea that maybe she didn't feel the same way lingered, even though it felt like it couldn't be true. He'd thought they'd laid everything out on the table the night before. Her not telling him about the fellowship or the lunch with his mom didn't sit well.

He needed to ask her directly. He also needed to get more information out of his mom, but he doubted the utility of that. She'd made her decision about Bridget, and she would twist the facts to fit that vision—especially if she thought it would protect him.

And he didn't have time to go any more rounds with his mother. He needed to leave about five minutes ago if he wanted to make it to the church on time. Although it wasn't his wedding, it felt like it was. It was the first time he would be in public with his wife with them both knowing it was a real marriage and not just a way to get back at their exes.

Despite any tiny doubts he had about Bridget's motivations, he needed to be there for her when he said he would be. Even if she wasn't in love with him in the way he was in love with her, he wasn't going to be the bad guy by not keeping his promises.

"I have to go, Mom." He tried to ignore her downturned mouth and the wary look in her eye. They could straighten everything out later. "I'm going to be late. Lock up behind yourself."

He'd grabbed his keys off the entry table when his mom called out, "I just don't want you to get hurt again."

He turned around and held his palms open. "Even if she is out to hurt me, that's my problem."

"You've always been too naïve." His mother said that like it was the worst character failing she could imagine—wanting to believe that people were good.

"It's not like you weren't taken in by Naomi." His mother rolled her eyes. "And she was a known quantity. You were blinded by the fact that the Chapins have always been in our lives. You've always wanted me to play things safe, when I can afford to take more risks than anyone."

"But you have a legacy to protect—"

He cut her off before she could continue with the legacy speech. "I love her, Mom. And maybe that's foolish and naïve. But it's the truth. And, maybe for the first time in my life, I'm willing to risk it all for someone."

Even if Bridget wasn't really in love with him, he needed to stand up for himself in front of his mother if he ever wanted any peace. And even if this was mistake, maybe taking a stand now would let his mother know that he could clean up his own messes and protect himself for once.

"I just want to protect you."

"I know," he said. And he believed her. "But you can't protect me from being in love with her. It's too late."

His mother took a moment to compose herself, and it was like a ripple drifting over a pond. In that moment, he knew that she'd accepted his marriage as much as she ever would. Before she left, she took a manila envelope out of her bag and put it on the island. "In case you change your mind."

Thinking that it might contain some sort of documentation that Bridget was after the family coffers—or at least something that would help him make sense of all this—he grabbed it off the counter to read in the car.

CHAPTER THIRTY-TWO

JACK WAS TOTALLY CALM when Bridget went to check on him. Not that she expected him to have a sudden-onset case of cold feet. No, her brother was so in love with Hannah that it shone out through every word he spoke.

She was, however, surprised to find her other brother, Michael, in equally good spirits given his pending divorce. For months, he'd been sulking in a corner at family events. She'd barely seen him at the fateful bachelor/bachelorette weekend. He'd been like a ghost.

But when she walked into the musty room where grooms got to stew in the significance of their decisions and make sure their bow ties were straight, she walked in on a distinctly bro-y hug.

And she might have been mistaken, but she thought she saw Michael wiping under his eyes.

She'd seen her oldest brother cry maybe three times—when he broke his leg skateboarding at fourteen, when his daughter was born, and now. Jack and her dad were the emotional ones.

"Do you want me to come back later?" If they were having a moment, she didn't want to interrupt.

But Jack motioned for her to come in. "Nah, he was only telling me he was proud of me."

"That was private," Michael said in a familiar grunting cadence. "I don't want to get a reputation for being soft."

"Nothing wrong with being soft, bro." Jack gave him another pat on the back. "I mean—emotionally."

Not expecting a sex joke, Bridget covered her mouth to stifle a laugh that would probably reach the sanctuary.

"Shut the fuck up, Jack-hole." There was the familiar brother-to-brother dynamic she had been expecting. If one of them knocked the other to the floor, maybe equilibrium would be restored.

"I came to check to see if you guys needed anything before the ceremony." Once she'd arrived at the church with Hannah, her mom, and the other bridesmaids in tow, things had been hectic. She wasn't going to tell Jack that Hannah had told her to make sure that Jack hadn't *cut and run while he still could.* She didn't think her new sister-in-law would appreciate being ratted out.

"I've been expecting you." Jack walked over to her and slung an arm around her shoulders. She had to do a little maneuvering to make sure that he didn't do any damage to the elaborate updo she was working. Her thick, heavy hair was held together by bobby pins, hairspray, and hope. "Hannah wanted to make sure I was still here."

"It's not like she actually thought you would leave." She didn't think.

Jack made a little, thoughtful humming noise. "It's not like she actually thinks that I'm going to suddenly turn into a runaway groom, but I think she feels like it."

"Dude, she knows that you're butt-crazy in love with her." Michael was spilling all the emotional tea today. Bridget was tempted to check his temperature.

"She knows I'm in love with her, but she always feels like the other shoe is going to drop." Jack shrugged and dropped his arm from Bridget's shoulders. "It's barely conscious, but it's just one of the things I have to work around with her."

Jack was probably the most empathic person she'd ever met. His willingness to read between the lines of what his betrothed said instead of stopping at the surface was unique as far as Bridget knew.

Her brother reminded her of Matt that way.

Just thinking about her husband had Bridget smiling and feeling warm all over. In that moment, she was a little ashamed of how she'd assumed he was a jerk at first. How she'd been the one who had only looked at the surface—the wealthy playboy who had probably never taken anything seriously in his life. She'd almost missed out on a kind and generous friend, a scalding-hot sex god of a lover, and the best person she knew whom she wasn't related to.

"I'm surprised you ventured in here, knowing that Chris might be around," Jack said. "He, on the other hand, has been asking where you were all day."

And she'd been avoiding him all day. She'd made sure that both he and Matt were escorting people to their seats—on opposite sides of the sanctuary—before coming in. Partially because she wanted to avoid any toxic posturing. Mostly because she'd wanted a moment alone with her brothers.

Bridget rolled her eyes. "Why the hell would he want to know where I am?"

"Dude's still in love with you." Michael threw that out there as though he was telling her that the sky was blue or that the Cubs were going to have a losing season.

"No, he's not." Bridget was sure of that. He wasn't as stupid as he appeared to be sometimes. If he was really still in love with her, he wouldn't have been behaving so badly. Chris didn't require a look below the surface. That one thing she'd learned and learned well. If only she'd listened the first dozen times he'd told her that he wasn't ready to talk about their future. She could have avoided a lot of pain. "He's just mad that he can't have me."

"Definitely sounds like Chris." Jack snorted as she pinned on his boutonniere. "Are you sure you're okay that he's back in the wedding?"

Bridget thought about it for a beat. Although at first she'd wanted to stay married to Matt because it would make Chris feel like a chode to see her with someone who was better than him on every level imaginable, she truly wanted Chris there that day for closure. Maybe if he saw the two of them together and married and happy, he would give up on trying to get her back out of some sense of FOMO.

Maybe it was a sign that she'd truly moved on that she wanted her ex to find happiness—with someone else who wouldn't expect as much as she had.

"It's fine. I mean, Matt will be here, too. He's going to see that we're together-together, and then maybe he'll give up the ghost."

Michael went to leave the room and patted her on the shoulder.

"Sure, tell yourself that." Then he turned to Jack. "You ready for this?"

Jack met both their gazes in turn and said, "I was ready for this the night I met her."

Then it was Bridget's turn to get teary-eyed. It was because of Jack and Hannah, but also because now she finally knew how he felt. Still, she covered. "You definitely would have had a runaway-bride situation on your hands had you proposed over tacos."

BRIDGET HAD AN IDEA of how Matt would look at her in her bridesmaid's dress when he first laid eyes on her the first time that day. Not that awed, sort of slack-jawed, stupid, and trying-not-to-cry look that the groom usually had—that Jack would definitely have. After all, Matt had already seen her in her dress, though it wasn't the completed look.

What she hadn't expected was the tight, almost constipated smile that he gave her as he took her arm. She immediately got a sick feeling in her stomach that had nothing to do with the emergency queso that Sasha had ordered for lunch or the champagne that she'd had with that queso. It was the same feeling that she'd had those last few months with Chris—the feeling that something was off and she was in the dark as to what that thing was.

She wanted to stop Matt in the middle of the aisle and ask him about it, but she wouldn't do that. So she settled for going through the previous night in her head and coming up with nightmare scenarios for what might have happened.

Totally reasonable.

Her thoughts about her own marriage stopped when Hannah came into the church. She'd seen the dress of course; she'd helped Hannah put the thing on. But, when she entered the sanctuary, there was a certain impact of the simple blush A-line that skimmed Hannah's curves that couldn't be overstated. The church Bridget had grown up in was filled with white flowers and rich greenery, giving the whole thing a sort of enchanted-forest feel. Unlike on the Sundays of her childhood, there was a hush. Bridget knew for a fact that there were three whole babies in attendance, but not a single one of them cried as Hannah and her mom marched up the aisle.

And Hannah was looking at Jack and smiling like a woman who was definitely sure of her decision. When Bridget glanced at her brother, he rubbed a hand over his short beard. He shook his head slightly, as though he couldn't be sure that he was seeing what he thought he was seeing.

Bridget was more like Michael than she was like her dad and brother on the crying, but she was most definitely getting choked up. But when she glanced over at Matt, he was looking down at the ground as though he wanted to be anywhere but here.

She tried to shake off the feeling that last night was the setup for some sort of hoax but couldn't. Still, she needed to pretend, so she focused on Hannah, Jack, and Patrick, the only people who really had anything to do with this ceremony.

"All right, folks, I'm going to keep this short—just kidding." Patrick paused for laughter, since he was a pro at this. Bridget couldn't help but notice that Sasha laughed a little too loudly at the joke. "This is a Catholic wedding. You knew what you were in for."

After that, Bridget let herself go on autopilot. Kneel down. Stand up. Read First Corinthians. Listen to Patrick give a beautiful homily about the power of love being stronger than the power of anger and fear—with stories about Hannah and Jack and how God was smiling on the latter when blessing him with a woman who wouldn't let him rest on his laurels. And then Hannah and Jack said their vows and kissed for way too long.

It was all very beautiful, and it made it easy to forget that her husband hadn't once looked at her during the ceremony. The most innocent explanation—that he was still too sick and weak to be here but had come anyway to keep his promise—wasn't the one chief on her mind. She couldn't stop thinking about his mother and her offer, which were not things she wanted to think about as a newlywed.

And neither of those things mattered, did they? She'd told his mom to shove it, and she wasn't with him for his family's money. Maybe she should have totally come clean last night, but she couldn't figure out a way to tell him without damaging his relationship with his mother. Despite the fact that she couldn't stand Jane Kido, she respected that the woman loved her son.

Bridget likely imagined the chill that passed through her when Matt took her arm during the recessional out of the church. She peered up at his face, and he had a grin that she would definitely characterize as political affixed to his face.

As soon as they got to the reception, she was going to pull him aside so that they could talk. This sort of icy silence between them was not sustainable. At all.

But the pictures outside the church and at the reception venue—a modernist hotel built in an old church/cult that had to liquidate its considerable property assets—took forever.

And then they were with the rest of bridal party—plus Patrick, who was not dressed as a priest that night—in a hotel suite, toasting the bride and groom during the cocktail hour.

"We're not doing one of those dumb entrance things, Jack," Hannah said.

Jack looked at her with pleading puppy-dog eyes. "C'mon, wifey, let me do this one cheesy thing. I promise I'll do the thing with the thing we were talking about the other night." Her brother waggled his brows, and Bridget most definitely did not want to know what they were talking about.

Hannah got this half smile on her face and said, "The zip-lining thing?"

"Oh yeah," Jack said.

"Fine. You owe me one." Hannah was doing a pretend-mad thing that Bridget knew worked on her brother because she'd taught it to Hannah.

Jack counted something out on his fingers. "I owe you at least five."

"Stop it, you guys." Bridget was actually sort of jealous that the other married couple in the room was cracking sex jokes while her husband was sulking with a glass of soda water in the corner. Maybe he was irritated that he still wasn't up to partying at the wedding. Perhaps she should send him home after the toasts?

"Besides, you're going to scandalize Patrick, and that's really not fair," Sasha added.

Hannah narrowed her gaze at her best friend. "So generous to Patrick."

"At least it got you to stop," Sasha said with a cheeky raise of her shoulder. But then Patrick leaned down and said something close to her ear that Bridget couldn't hear, and she got all red. Hopefully, her little crush went away after the wedding. If it didn't, she was in for a world of celibate heartbreak.

Hannah must have had the same idea because she clapped her hands together and said, "Let's get downstairs."

MATT REALLY DIDN'T WANT to believe that Bridget was after him for his money—the way she'd looked at him right before the ceremony had told him that. And he didn't want to ask her about everything his mom had told him this morning. But he hated that she hadn't told him the whole truth. The beginning of the end with Naomi had been when she'd started lying to him. The lies had been small at first—what she'd been doing when she said she was at home studying, or who she was texting with on her phone.

He'd thought he had a more honest relationship with Bridget, and he desperately needed that to be true. He'd thought that they'd broken through all their bullshit, and he needed it not to be a lie. If things with her turned out like things with Naomi had, he wouldn't be able to shake it off through one impulsive decision. He couldn't run away from what he felt for Bridget, how much he wanted to earn her respect. The feelings he had for her didn't work like that. Even the word—love—felt too small.

While listening to the sermon, he thought about what kind of blessing Bridget had been in his life. He thought about how she expected more from him than just throwing money at problems. How she expected him to be present. How hurt she'd been when he'd missed the rehearsal and hadn't been in touch. And he questioned whether he could measure up.

They didn't know each other that long, only for four months.

And he didn't have the depth and breadth of knowledge of what made her tick that Jack seemed to have of Hannah—he couldn't possibly have that.

By the end of the homily, Matt wasn't sure that he and Bridget should stay married anymore. They didn't know each other; how could they braid the whole of their futures together without spending some time first?

They'd had so many miscommunications over the past few months. She'd thought he was a lazy, rich asshole. He'd thought she was cold. Neither of them had to make any compromises. Hell, they were married, and they hadn't even talked about where they wanted to live.

He had huge confusing feelings for her—but could he really be in love with her in the way that he should be with the woman he was going to marry?

Thinking about all this as they walked out onto a dance floor filled with Bridget's family and friends made him dizzy. He knew, in that moment, that he didn't belong where he was standing right then.

His tux felt as though it was going to smother him, and the thick air, filled with the scents of hors d'oeuvres and gin cocktails, made him sick. As soon as the spotlight hit Sasha and Chris instead of him and Bridget, he tried to slip away. He ignored Bridget's questioning look.

He made it out to a coat closet, but he still couldn't breathe. He even did that cliché thing where he loosened and undid his bow tie. But he still couldn't seem to get enough air.

"Are you okay?" When Bridget's hand hit his back, he jumped even though he'd had warning. When he turned, her eyes were really big. She seemed truly concerned. But how could he know that she was really worried about him and not a big payday? "Are you feeling sick again?"

"Yeah." That was the truth. But then again, he'd only ever barely lied to her to keep her close. The only thing that he'd ever told her that was close to a misrepresentation was that getting rid of Naomi was the only reason that he wanted to stay married. "Why didn't you tell me about lunch with my mom?"

Her face went totally pale—like paler than usual. And then he knew that there was more to what his mom had told him than her not approving of his life choices. Maybe she'd been right to want to protect him from Bridget. His panic fled and he stood a little straighter in that moment.

"I didn't—"

"You didn't want me to know that you were taking money from my family in exchange for breaking up with me?" That was probably—definitely—the wrong thing to say, but he couldn't seem to find the right words. He felt as though he was in some sort of soap opera teleplay rather than his actual life right then.

"I didn't accept her offer."

The only thing he could remember then was how Naomi had kept telling him that her fucking someone else in his house *wasn't what it looked like.* But he knew then that he could trust what he saw with his own eyes. With Bridget, he couldn't square what he'd seen from her since the day they'd met and how his mother's accusations fit in with that.

"I know what this sounds like." His words came out harder than he'd intended.

Bridget looked down at her hands, and it was such a contrast to the usual sure-and-steady way she talked to people that it made him doubt her even more. He didn't want to feel like he couldn't trust what would come out of her mouth next, but he couldn't help it. His mother had never lied to him about anything important before. Why would she start here?

Something about Bridget's posture changed as he watched her thinking. Instead of wringing her hands, she crossed them over her chest and met his gaze. No trace of the watery emotion he'd seen from her during the ceremony. "Are you accusing me of being with you for your family's money?"

"That's what my mother thinks."

The last thing he expected her to do was snort and roll her eyes, but she did. "Oh, believe me, I know."

"What would have given her that idea?"

"I don't know what your mother was thinking when she tried to buy me out of your life."

"She must have—"

Bridget held up a hand. "No, that's exactly what she tried to do. She thinks I'm some tramp, only with you for the precious trust fund. The trust fund that I knew nothing about until she told me."

He realized his mistake then. Bridget barely believed that she was cut out for a relationship. She was afraid that she was exactly like her capricious, social-climbing mother. And the fact that Matt gave any credence to his mother's theory that Bridget was a gold digger hit that sore spot with Bridget harder than she could poke at it herself. He was inflicting a bruise on a bruise.

Instantly, he wished he could go back and approach this differently. He wished Naomi hadn't gotten so far in his head. He wished that he had waited until after the wedding to talk about this.

More than anything, he wished he could pull Bridget into his arms and make things all right.

"I don't believe her, Bridget." It was too little, too late. But he had to try to claw this back.

"Then why haven't you so much as looked at me all day?" Bridget had already turned this around in her head, and he wasn't going to be able to save this. When she'd first walked in, he had her on the defensive—not a position she liked to be in. Now she was fully on the offensive, her home base. And just like an unwary defense attorney, he was toast. "And then you run out of the reception as soon as possible. Were you going to leave without telling me?"

"I was only getting some air."

Bridget gave him a rueful laugh. "So funny that you need air when last night you were in love with me and wanted to be with me."

"It's not like that." The way she looked at him in that moment told him something. It was the same way she'd looked at him on the first day of his internship. As though she couldn't care less that he existed. "I needed a minute to think. My mom came over right before I left to come here and said all these things. I didn't—"

"You didn't know that she was just trying to plan your life and curate who's in it. Just like she's been doing your whole life?" Bridget asked, though he knew it was a rhetorical question. "After last night, when you were so sure that being married to me was the right thing, it was that easy."

He didn't have anything to answer that with. It had been that easy. So easy for him to doubt her. And if so little could make him doubt that she was exactly what she was—tough, kind, generous— and that she loved him, then maybe his big feelings weren't enough to make a go of this.

Before he could open his mouth to speak any words, she did it for him. "I should have signed those divorce papers at lunch."

He couldn't disagree, no matter how much he wanted to. Looking at her, even now when she was looking right through him, made him achy all over. He wanted to touch her, and he knew he'd think about kissing her for the rest of his life. She felt like his match on a deep level, and it wrenched at him that he could be wrong about that.

She must have been going through something similar. It wasn't as though they didn't have palpable chemistry. She stepped toward him and put her hand on his chest. Then she brushed her hand over his chest again and the pocket where he'd put the divorce papers before leaving.

He took them out, knowing that she would think he was the biggest asshole on the planet when he did. But wasn't he?

Even if he'd approached this as delicately as he ideally would have, she wouldn't forgive him for not believing in her.

"You brought them with you." Bridget bit her lip and made a noise that was somewhere in between a groan and a laugh. "Classy."

"It's not what it looks like." He felt sick again.

"That's my line." She tipped her chin at him. "You have a pen?"

"You don't have to do this." He wanted to take it all back and beg for her forgiveness even though he didn't deserve it.

"Yeah, I think I do."

Matt knew when he was fighting a losing battle. That was the one thing he could say for himself. He might not have had the good sense to disbelieve his mother's wild theory about Bridget this morning or the better sense to keep any doubts to himself, but he knew that if he didn't give Bridget a pen right now, she might cut herself open to sign the papers in blood.

So he pulled out his grandfather's pen and handed it to her. She smirked before pulling the papers out of the envelope. It probably took less than a minute for her to sign and initial all the designated places, but it felt like agonizing hours. It felt like she was cutting his heart out while he was awake.

And when she was done, she was out of the coat closet in a flash. He could still smell the faint residue of her perfume in the air, and he tried to savor it for a moment before leaving. She was gone, and he wouldn't get to smell it again.

CHAPTER THIRTY-THREE

BRIDGET HAD NO IDEA how she made it through the reception before losing her ever-loving shit. When she'd walked out of the coat closet a single woman, she didn't feel any different. Except for the gaping hole in her chest that she was walking around with. It was surprising that she could function like that—dying inside—for hours on end.

Everyone had taken her excuse, that Matt was still not feeling up to snuff, without question. Aside from a couple of concerned looks from her parents, everyone bought the fake smiles, the well-timed laughter, and her terrible dancing at face value.

No one knew that she'd just taken a fatal shot to the heart.

It was so different from how things had gone down with Chris. Due to the family/neighborhood grapevine, everyone had known about that inside of forty-eight hours. She didn't have to tell anyone that her life had just blown up. They just knew and adjusted by not inviting them to the same things at the same times. They'd even had the courtesy to blame Chris for the whole thing.

This . . . she didn't know who to blame. The whole thing was a fuckup and a mistake. From the first moment she started thinking about Matt as anything but her intern, she'd set off down this path. Of course it wouldn't end in anything but heartbreak.

As soon as Jack and Hannah left for the airport and their honeymoon, she knew she was only going to have a little bit of time before she fell the fuck apart. The rest of the bridal party was deep in their cups, telling stories at tables scattered throughout the reception venue.

She grabbed her bouquet and clutch and trailed away from the group, allowing her smile to fade as she walked away. She couldn't wait to get to her bed.

Almost home-free.

But it was not to be. Chris, who she thought had left hours ago, intercepted her in the lobby.

"Where's your hubby?" he sneered.

She wanted to kick him in the nuts for being such a douchebag, but she didn't really have the energy. Besides, it wasn't all about him. It was at least a little bit about Matt.

"Not feeling well." She pasted on one more fake smile. "I'd better get back to check on him."

She moved to circumvent her ex-boyfriend, but he grabbed her arm. "I need to talk to you."

She sighed. "Send a fucking text. Better yet, an e-mail so I can ignore it."

"C'mon, Bridge. You're better than this."

"Better than what?"

"Looking through me. Acting like you don't even know me."

Bridget's temper snapped. "But isn't that the issue? I never really did know you. And you never even wanted to know me. You wanted me to fit into your life the way you wanted, and then you were out the second I didn't follow exactly your plan." She made a motion to the banquet hall. "But I was wrong about that, wasn't I?"

"I'm not the only bad guy here," Chris said, and he was right. He wasn't the only bad guy here. She was the one who persisted in throwing away good love after bad with him. And she hadn't learned anything.

"Yeah, my bad that I didn't once question my decision when it came to loving you." Not until it was too late.

Chris paused. He let her go because it was clear that she wasn't going to leave without finishing this conversation. Maybe it was best to rip off all the Band-Aids and light a big enough fire to raze her past and all of her bad decisions.

"I'm sorry, Bridget." He sounded contrite for once, but she wasn't quite ready to just let things go.

"How many times do I have to accept your apologies before you stop hurting me?" It was the first time she'd ever asked that question. She'd always accepted his apologies because he was so sweet when he gave them. Hell, he was just as sweet now. But she was immune to his sweetness now. She'd lost a taste for it, and only had a taste for sweetness from one man—another one she'd lost.

"This is the last time."

She didn't have time to avoid it, but she should have seen it coming. He smashed his lips against hers, and she was stunned for a long moment. It didn't last long, though. Almost like a reflex, she put her hand against his chest and pushed him away. "What the hell was that?" She wiped off her mouth for good measure.

"C'mon, Bridget." He held up his hands as though he'd bumped into her accidentally, not ambushed her with a surprise kiss. "I saw the way you two were today. And we had so much fun last night."

"We had a couple of drinks. And how we were is none of your business." She hated that even her oblivious ex sensed the tension between her and Matt. That meant that she wasn't going to have very much of a grace period with her family. "And, even if we were fighting, it wouldn't be an invitation for you to try whatever *that* was."

"Don't you miss me?" Chris asked plaintively. "I miss you all the time. We had that conversation last night."

"Just because we had a conversation that didn't end in a shouting match or a death threat doesn't mean that I want to try to get back together with you." Bridget started edging her way toward the elevator. "There are plenty of women online who can help you out with a hand job if you're lonely."

"I don't want any of them."

"Well, you can't have me." God, why did guys always have to do this. Make everything about what they wanted and their dick? Even Matt couldn't understand why she hadn't run to him right away about his mother's offer. Sure, it looked bad, but he'd only allowed himself to see it in a way that was all about his ego.

"You're just going to throw away all that history?" Chris sounded so confused, and she wasn't even thinking about him anymore. "Just like that?"

"Just like that." It wasn't as though their history didn't have value. It had taught her exactly what she didn't want and exactly what she needed in a relationship.

The elevator arrived and she turned her back on Chris.

"He really makes you happy?" he asked when she looked back.

"He does," she said with a nod. *He did*. And now she would just have to get over him.

CHAPTER THIRTY-FOUR

BRIDGET SHOULD HAVE GONE to her own condo after the wedding, but she really didn't want to sleep in a bed she'd shared with Chris *and* Matt. She wanted both of those men out of her mind as soon as possible. Scrubbing Matt out of her heart would take a while, but she was determined to do it.

After the wedding, she'd spend a few days in her childhood bedroom, milking her dad for all the scrambled eggs and buttered toast he would make.

Her parents had a hotel room for the night, so the house was empty when she snuck up the stairs and found her faded Northwestern T-shirt to sleep in. It was weird how normal it was thinking about her parents staying together after all these years. Seeing them canoodling at the wedding hadn't turned her stomach once.

It hadn't even bothered her thinking about it later. She was too emotionally exhausted to sustain even that temper tantrum. She'd passed out as soon as her head hit the pillow.

But even though she was past caring that her parents were really back together, she wasn't prepared to have a heart-to-heart with Mommy Dearest the day after her own ill-thought-out marriage fell apart.

And that was actually going to happen, because her mom was perched on the end of her bed. It made her feel like a wayward teen, even though this scene had never played out during her adolescence.

Bridget rubbed the sleep out of her eyes. "What time is it?"

"After noon." Her mother's brow rose. "What are you doing here?"

"It's more my home than yours." That sounded more sullen than she'd wanted it to. It was true, but kind of snitty.

"Why aren't you with your husband?" Bridget didn't like how her mom's eyes got all wistful when she mentioned Matt. It couldn't possibly be that Molly actually cared about her marriage. She was probably just thinking about all those sweet donations to the museum drying up if Bridget and Matt didn't work out.

"Don't worry about it, Molly." She relished her mother's wince, even though it was crappy. "Matt's mother will probably hand over their entire collection of Rothkos now that our marriage was dissolved."

Her mother's face sort of crumpled, and Bridget felt extremely guilty. She felt even more guilty when her mother said, "You really think I was worried about how this would affect my work?"

Not deep down. But Bridget had been resisting getting close to her mother—hell, truly close to anyone—for so long that it was second nature at this point. Pushing her mother away extra hard after she'd pushed Matt away was just all a part of that.

In the cold light of day, she knew that she'd probably made a mistake not trying to talk it out with Matt. But she was so tired of taking care of everyone else's feelings.

When would someone take care of how she felt for once?

And her mother wasn't going away this time. Maybe she was for real about trying to be a family again. Just this once, Bridget let herself hope a little.

"What happened?" her mother prodded.

Bridget already felt hollowed out and empty. What more damage could letting her mother in do? "He thought I was with him for his family's money."

Her mother's eyes flashed with a temper she'd never seen from her, and she stood up, crossing her arms over her chest. "What?"

"His mother offered to pay off my student loans if I signed divorce papers on the spot." That really raised her mother's ire because she ran her hand through the elegant bob that never had a single gray strand out of place. She even made a deeply unladylike grunting noise before Bridget continued, "I told her to shove it up her ass."

That earned her a half smile from her mother. Maybe they weren't as completely different as she'd thought. "I can only imagine the look on her face."

"Barely fazed her." Bridget remembered the slight start that Jane had given when Bridget had started talking in a loud voice in the crowded restaurant. Very satisfying, but she'd decided to double down quickly. "Well, she told Matt that I was all set to take it."

"And he believed her?" Bridget could visibly see her mother's regard for Matt go down as the volume of her voice rose.

"Shh!" Bridget tried to get her to quiet down. The last thing she needed was Sean Nolan coming up here. She only wanted to tell this story once, and she didn't want to have to talk her father out of going after Matt, loaded for bear. "You're going to get Dad up here, thinking he's going to have to break up a catfight."

"He believed her?" her mother asked, more quietly this time.

But it was too late, because her door swung open and her dad entered. This was going to be a huge pain in the ass. At least he'd brought eggs and toast—with bacon.

"Do you need a little hair of the dog?" he asked as he put the tray over her legs. Her heart warmed. At least she'd always had one parent who cared for her. Maybe that had been all she needed. And even though she'd accepted her parents being back together, she still worried about her dad. Who would take care of him when Molly left him again?

"What the hell are you two doing?" Bridget asked, not capable of a filter anymore.

"What do you mean?" her father asked as her mother said, "We're not here to talk about us."

"No, seriously. What are the two of you doing together? Besides the sex stuff that I don't want to hear about."

Her dad shrugged and looked at her mom like he looked at heavily discounted lumber prices. "She's the one."

"But how did you know?" She'd thought Matt was the one, but it had turned out that he was only one of two. "And why did you stay away from each other for so long if she was the one?"

Her mother grabbed her father's hand. "I know because I tried to be without him, and my life didn't make sense."

"For more than a decade and through a whole other marriage, your life didn't make sense?" It just wasn't logical. All those years that her family was right here waiting for her, and she'd always seemed happy when she took them to lunch or brought presents over for birthdays and holidays. "I thought you didn't want us."

"I made a lot of mistakes." Her mother came back to sit on the bed and grabbed her hand. Bridget wanted to pull it away, but part of her was so starved for maternal tenderness that she didn't. "The biggest one was that I didn't make sure that you and the boys knew how much I loved you."

"You said it." Even Bridget could admit that her mother had never treated them like a burden when she was around—it was just that she wasn't around a whole lot.

"But I should have shown it more. I just—I didn't feel like I was a good mother when I was here. I hated the day-to-day of it all, and I didn't want my resentment to spill out and ruin everything. I'd never had anything of my own my whole life. I left my parents' house, became a wife and mother, and I never knew who I was. I never knew what I had in your father and you and your brothers, either. If you give me a chance to be in your life—really—again, I promise that I won't take any of you for granted. Not for a second."

And for what felt like the millionth time that weekend, Bridget's eyes filled with tears. As they fell, her mother wiped them away. And Bridget let her. "I should have been here to do that when you were first falling in love with a boy."

"It wouldn't have changed anything. I decided I was in love with him when I was four."

That's when her father piped in. "When he whipped his johnson out and pissed in your wading pool? That little son of a bitch is lucky that they'd started frowning on corporal punishment by then."

"He was always a little shit," her mother said on a laugh. "I would have tried to talk you out of him."

Her father grunted. "I would have wished you luck with that. The girl always was as stubborn—"

"As you are?" She had to admit that it was comforting to watch her parents bicker in such a nonmalignant way.

Her father just grunted again. "Eat your eggs."

Bridget followed instructions, eating her breakfast while her parents gazed at her with worried looks on their faces. "You guys don't have to do this."

"Do what?" Her father had the audacity to look innocent. "Just when I think I get all three of you knuckleheads out of my house for good, your dumbass brother gets a divorce and you get married and divorced in a butterfly's lifetime."

Her father made the way she'd blown up her whole life sound almost poetic.

"It's not her fault." Her mother was trying to defend her? Maybe she was living in an alternate universe.

But her mother was wrong to defend her on this. She'd made a decision in the heat of the moment and decided that Matt couldn't possibly love her because he was having doubts. Totally natural doubts given what he'd gone through with Naomi and the fact that they barely knew each other before getting married.

"Mom, did you ever think about coming back?"

Her mother looked back to her. "Every day."

"Why didn't you?" Bridget asked.

"Pride. I didn't think your father would take me back. But mostly I didn't want to admit that I was wrong."

Bridget set aside her eggs and threw her arms around her mom. "I don't want to make the same kind of mistake."

Her mother pulled back. "You couldn't possibly."

"I already did," Bridget said. "I stayed with Chris for a decade because of my pride. I think I got married to Matt in the first place because of pride."

"I think tequila might have had something to do with that." Sean Nolan, one hundred percent reliable in keeping it real.

"Word." Bridget looked down at her hands, the left ring finger still holding the engagement ring that Matt had given her. Something that felt so flashy and audacious at first now felt like it had always been there. She should take it off; it didn't really belong to her anymore. But she couldn't bring herself to do it. Not until she knew they were done for real.

She'd let her pride and temper get the best of her. All her life, she'd thought she was her father's daughter with her hot, long-burning temper. This morning, she realized that she was a mix of her father's temper and her mother's pride. If she didn't get her head out of her ass, she would end up letting the best guy she'd ever met think that he didn't mean everything to her. She would go years and decades without the only guy she thought she could be happy with if she didn't swallow her pride and apologize for her temper.

Still, there was the fact that nothing about her and Matt's lives fit together. The fact that they came from two different worlds would always trip them up—just as much as her pride and temper. As much as Matt's unwillingness to stand up to his parents.

But she could say the same thing for her parents now. Despite the fact that they came from the same neighborhood, her mother was a museum curator who bumped elbows with famous artists and celebrities, and her father was a contractor who cussed, drank cheap domestic beer, and worked with his hands. And they looked at each other like the other held their heart. After thirty-five years, three kids, and two divorces between them—a lifetime.

Bridget wanted that. All that messy. All that good.

"I want to be married to him," she said quietly. "He's my one."

"His mother owes you an apology," her mother said.

"That's—"

"What did she do to Bridget?" Her father's face was getting a little red.

"I have to figure this out myself, you guys." But she needed a little time to figure out how.

MAYBE I'LL BUY A *boat. I can quit law school and sail around the world. Maybe I'll just fuck off to the Greek islands for a while. Really lean into what Bridget thought I was. Live that Leonardo DiCaprio life with twenty-one-year-old models until my dick withers and falls off.*

It was about the thirtieth idea that Matt had come up with to escape his life. The best one so far.

But it still felt hollow because he would be sailing around the world without Bridget. And, call him weird, but he only wanted to share any of the ideas he had—hike the Andes, start an orphanage somewhere, sail around the world—with the one person he couldn't have.

He was certain of only one thing. Now that his trust fund had vested—because it turned out that he didn't have to stay married to get access—and he was out from under his parents' thumbs, he was done doing what they wanted him to.

His mother was still trying to run a power play, though. That's why she'd kept him waiting for fifteen minutes in her office.

"Shouldn't you be in class right now?" She made a show of checking her watch.

Matt stood up and kissed her cheek. Once she'd rounded her desk and was about to sit down, he dropped the bomb. "I quit school."

"What?" Not very many people surprised his mother; she was far too shrewd for that. Despite the fact that marrying his father had given her more access to resources, she'd been successful because she was always the smartest person in the room.

And that was probably why she didn't like Bridget—both of them were usually the smartest people in the room.

"I didn't want to be there." It was true. That morning, he'd walked on campus for the first time after Jack and Hannah's wedding, and he'd realized that there was no point. He didn't want to join any of the firms that his father or mother employed regularly. Nor did he want to be groomed to lead either one of his parents' companies. He had more money than God at this point, and he'd never really decided what he wanted to do with his life.

"What are you going to do?"

He shrugged, knowing it would drive her absolutely nuts. "I guess I'll figure it out."

She stood up then. "Is *this* about that girl? Did she convince you to throw your life away?"

"Don't be so dramatic, Mother." He stood up, too. He needed to leave. "She signed the divorce papers and so did I. I think she's done with me. This is about me."

"You'll regret this."

He shrugged again. "Maybe." There was a lot he regretted about the past week. Dropping out of law school wasn't currently one of the things in that group.

Losing Bridget, however, was.

He started walking out of the room, but his mother's voice stopped him. "Where are you going? We have to figure this out."

"*We* don't have anything to figure out." In that moment, he felt sorry for his mother, being so driven and direct and having a sensitive dreamer for a son. Still, he knew enough to know that he needed to make a boundary now, before their roles hardened and they felt real resentment toward each other. "I have to go see a guy about a boat."

He wondered what the Greek islands were like this time of year.

CHAPTER THIRTY-FIVE

DESPITE ALL OF HIS grand plans of escape to the Greek islands, Matt did not have the motivation to seek out a boat *and* a crew. He could have done one or the other, but that would have been disastrous with just the boat and silly with just the crew. Turns out that once it really sank in, a broken heart had sapped almost all of his appetite for anything but the remote and his couch.

He didn't expect to hear from Bridget, but he expected to feel more relief than dejection at this point. It had been *days*, and all he could feel was sadness. He seriously hadn't been in love with Naomi if this was what losing someone he loved felt like.

It was difficult to describe. It was as though the adrenaline rush of Bridget signing those papers and shoving them at him had gotten him through dropping out of law school and confronting his mother. But then it had faded, and he was just existing.

Every so often, he had to check his pulse to make sure his heart was still beating. Everything he'd thought about doing or buying while he was still strung out on fight-or-flight hormones made him feel even more dead inside. Every adventure he could have or thing he could see only reminded him of how he wanted to see or do them with Bridget.

It was almost ironic that the one thing he wanted—a second chance with her—was the one thing he couldn't buy. Especially when he'd assumed that she could be bought.

One thing Matt definitely did not expect was his ex-brother-in-law showing up at his place when he was supposed to be on his honeymoon.

"Why aren't you in the Turks and Caicos?" Matt opened the door even though he was fairly certain Jack would try to kick his ass. Matt would let him—just so he could feel something.

"Hannah missed the dog." Jack shrugged with a goofy smile on his face. "Said that we could have sex in our apartment. So we came back."

"She really likes that dog." Matt led Jack into the kitchen, where he got them both beers. Jack looked at the bottle and nodded in approval.

"Not as much as I hear that our dog likes you." Jack laughed and winked, and Matt let his guard drop a little. This didn't feel like an ass-kicking visit.

"Tell him that I still feel violated." Matt took a sip that didn't taste like anything even though he knew for a fact that it was very good beer.

"I'll try to get him to send you flowers, but he's a real cad, our Gus." Jack narrowed his gaze at him, and Matt realized that his whole nice-guy routine was a front. It became immediately clear why people gave him scoops on big stories. Dude was disarming. "Were you just being a cad with my sister?"

Matt thought about it for a long moment. Although he'd been the one accusing her of using him, he wasn't innocent. He'd been willing to have a fling with Bridget without really caring about what it might do to her career. He'd stayed married to her because he wanted to sleep with her but lied and said it was to get Naomi off his jock. He'd told her that he was in love with her—and he'd felt it—but he hadn't shown it.

He looked Jack in the eye and said, "I love your sister."

"I believe you." Jack took another drink. "What are you going to do to get her back?"

"Does she know you're here?" Matt hoped so. If she was sending emissaries on her behalf, maybe she felt more than she'd let on.

Jack actually guffawed. "She would tear me a new asshole if she knew I was here. You really don't know my baby sister that well, do you?"

"Wait a second. I know plenty about your sister. I was just hoping for a miracle."

"Good. I was hoping she wasn't in love with yet another idiot."

"You talk that way about your friends?" Matt didn't want to know how Jack talked about *him* when he wasn't around.

Jack looked at him soberly and said, "With our friends we tell the truth."

"Seems about right." Matt nodded. He agreed that any man who let Bridget get away was an idiot. He just didn't know how to avoid being an idiot in that moment. "How do I get her back?"

"Well, word on the street is that you told her that you thought she was with you for money." Matt nodded, and Jack sneered a little. He deserved that. "Also, you sided with your mom over her?"

"Yep." Hearing it in such stark relief had him wanting to kick his own ass. "I really fucked up."

"Listen, the best of us fuck up." Matt trusted him. He'd heard the whole story about how he'd initially started dating Hannah for a story at his old job, and then he'd done a bunch of terrible shit to her in the name of finishing that story. "Hannah threatened me with an ice pick when she found out about my fuckup."

"I was actually there earlier that night. With my ex."

"The cheater?" Jack asked. Man, the Nolans were bigger sharers than Bridget had advertised. He wasn't sure he could get used to it. But he would try if it meant that he could get her back.

"Yeah, the cheater."

"Listen, I don't know anyone with a bigger heart than my baby sister, but she keeps it all locked up."

"Because your mom left." Matt understood why Bridget was hesitant to open up or commit. After he met Chris, he'd understood her efforts to keep him at arm's length.

"Yeah, and Chris was a fuckup." Jack looked at Matt as though it was his fault, which made Matt angry.

"I'm nothing like him."

"Nah, you're more like Bridget," Jack said. "Stubborn."

"She never changes her mind." Matt had changed his mind about the possibility that Bridget was after him for his money an instant after he'd entertained it. But he'd held the thought too long for Bridget. "And I can't see how she's going to change her mind now."

"She changed her mind about whether she wanted to be in a relationship, didn't she?" Matt nodded, and Jack continued. "For your ass. What makes you think she won't change her mind about you being a douche canoe?"

"For a hot minute," Matt said. "I don't know what I can do to convince her to give me another chance."

Matt didn't trust the smile that crossed Jack's face. "Luckily, if you have more beer, I have ideas."

BRIDGET SMELLED FOOD COOKING from inside Matt's apartment. It almost made her turn around. What if she showed up to apologize—to eat shit and see if he would forgive her—and he was here with another girl?

But she realized that it didn't matter. They'd left words unsaid. If she just let him go without fighting for him, she would regret it for the rest of her life. And she'd racked up way too many of those as an adult.

So she knocked on the door.

When Matt opened it, he looked delicious. Disheveled, but she still wanted to put her mouth all over him. They'd only been together a handful of times, but he looked like home to her. His hair was tousled, his T-shirt had sweat stains at the pits, and his face was flushed. Which somehow made him more charming. If she didn't already love him, she would hate him.

"You're early," he said, but he was smiling, so she didn't think it was a problem.

"I can come back later if you have someone in there." She started to back away, but he grabbed her arm and pulled her in the door. When he closed it behind her, she was about an inch away from him.

"You're the only one here and the only person I was expecting." It was just a sentence, but he said it like there was some sexy double meaning that she couldn't begin to understand. Her body understood it, though. And it made her want to forget about apologizing to him and kiss him.

But that wouldn't solve any of their problems—they needed to be better at communicating and they couldn't do that with their mouths attached to each other. So she needed to step back and change the subject to something safe. "It smells good in here."

He let her go, but he waggled his brows and that almost reeled her back in. "I'm glad you think so."

"You didn't have to cook me dinner." She didn't need to be filled with hope like this. It felt entirely too normal for her to just sink in. "You have every right to be mad at me."

When he didn't respond, she looked down at her feet. "Take off your shoes and stay a while." His words made her want to stay even more. "I made a chicken. It was my first time, and I hope I didn't mess it up too much."

Once her shoes were off, he grabbed her hand and pulled her into the kitchen. "You didn't have to cook me dinner. I came by to talk."

Matt shrugged. "We'll talk. Over food." He boosted her up onto one of the stools around his kitchen island and handed her a glass of wine. He turned back to the stove where something that looked like brussels sprouts was cooking. "It's been breathing for a while."

"I came over to apologize." This was entirely too romantic, and she didn't deserve it. He was acting as though she hadn't tossed divorce papers in his face and stomped out in a huff less than a week ago. "Aren't you mad at me?"

That stopped him, and he turned off the burner and turned to her. "I was mad that night, but mostly I've been sad."

It hurt her heart that she'd made him sad. "I'm sorry I didn't tell you about your mom's offer and the lunch. It was just awful, and I didn't want to damage your relationship with her any more than I already had. Plus, I kind of thought—for just a minute—that you were behind the whole thing."

He nodded. "I get it, and I'm sorry I didn't believe you right away. I think the thing with Naomi messed me up more than I wanted to admit. And I hadn't realized that my mother had gotten so involved with trying to control my life."

"She really did go overboard there."

Matt rounded the counter and cupped her face. "But you never gave me any reason to doubt you." He ran his finger over her lower lip, and she just fought the urge to lick him. "I really want to kiss you right now."

It pained her to say it, but she did. "I think we should talk more."

He groaned and looked to the sky. "You're really going to make me work for it, aren't you?"

"When haven't I?" They might have graduated to jokes, and her will to talk things out before jumping his bones might be slipping, but she wanted to do things right if they had hope for a future. She was using her stubbornness for good.

Luckily, the timer on his oven went off, saving her from relying on willpower alone. When she went to get up and help him, he put a hand on her shoulder. "Nuh-uh. This is my show."

"It feels weird not to help." It was killing her not to do anything. She always felt like she had to be doing something for Chris. If Matt didn't need her help, then what would he need her around for?

"I wanted to do something nice for you. It would hurt my feelings if you didn't let me."

ONCE MATT TALKED BRIDGET out of taking over dinner prep and got them seated, he let himself really look at her. He was glad that he'd lit candles, because she was so beautiful and lush to look at in candlelight. It danced over her freckles and made her look almost otherworldly.

When Jack had suggested this, it had seemed too simple. But he should have known that simple wouldn't mean easy. Convincing the woman in front of him that she didn't need to do anything to earn his love was much more difficult than one would think.

Every time she'd thanked him—for the wine, for carving the chicken, making sure she got her favorite cut—it made him angry. Like, it was nice that she was grateful, but couldn't she see that she deserved to be treated like a queen?

"It's so good," she said, barely finished chewing. "I don't know how you had time to do this."

"I quit law school, so I've had a lot of time on my hands." Best to get the thing that might piss her off the most out on the table first.

"You quit?" Her eyes bugged out of her head, but she didn't choke, which was less of a reaction than he expected. "Why?"

"I didn't really like it, and—thanks to you marrying me—I'm rich now and I don't have to do pretty much anything I don't like." And the only thing he'd really like to fill his time with was making Bridget Nolan happy.

"But you were almost done."

"That's not a reason to do anything." He poured her more wine.

314

"Besides, I paid Brent's tuition, so I felt good about it. He won't have student loans for his third year."

"One of the other interns?" Bridget seemed a little shell-shocked. "I don't know what to say."

"You don't have to say anything." She hadn't walked out, and that was enough.

"What are you going to do?"

"Not sure yet." He took a bite of chicken. "That all depends on you."

"How so?" She took his cue and ate another bite. "I didn't know you hated it that much."

"I didn't hate it; it just wasn't for me." That was the truth. He had the freedom to decide, and he'd decided that he wanted something else—something with Bridget.

Bridget snorted. "Not all of us can be quite that capricious."

"You can." Now that she wasn't so shocked that she couldn't use sarcasm, he needed to drop the second bomb. "Your loans are paid off, so you don't have to do anything you don't want to do ever again."

Bridget stood up then. "I didn't ask you to do that."

"And I did it anyway." He sat back in his chair. Even if she didn't want to be with him, he wasn't going to take this back. "What are you going to do?"

"After I kill you?" She looked like she was ready to, with balled-up fists and a red cast to her face that made her look like fire. He liked fire, though.

"My parents should have given you the fellowship last year. I'm just doing my part now."

She shook her head. "You didn't have to do this."

"But I wanted to." He stood up and walked over to her. "I want to do things for you. Because I love you, and I want you to be happy."

Palpably, her anger dissipated from the room when she laughed. "I'd never thought about love as something that would make me happy before."

He cupped her face with both hands, needing to be as close to her as possible. He touched their foreheads together, and her hands came around his waist. "That's what love is for. You make me happy just by being who you are."

"You're going to make me cry." Sure enough, a tear rolled down her face. He kissed it away.

"I never want to make you cry."

"You're going to fail at that if you keep being so sweet." He'd gladly fail at it every single day. "This is Ina's chicken, isn't it? The engagement chicken?"

His hope was suspended in between them like a physical thing— the fact that she got what he was trying to say through his actions feeding it. "It is."

"Did you file the papers?" She raised his hands and clutched his wrists.

"I did." He risked a kiss on her forehead. "I'm sorry."

"It's okay."

When she said that, his blood ran cold. Maybe this wasn't going as well as he'd thought. "You don't want to be married to me anymore?"

"That's not it." She pulled back to lock gazes with him. "I just think that we should start fresh, so it's not so messy. Besides, I'm coming around to the idea that the second time might work out better than the first."

"You want me to ask you if you want to get married?"

She shook her head, and that left her neck open to kiss, but he waited. "Not yet."

He cupped her jaw, running one of his thumbs over her lower lip. "What are we going to do?"

"Love each other." She pushed up on her toes and kissed him. He caught her up in his arms and they forgot about the chicken dinner.

EPILOGUE

ALWAYS A BRIDESMAID, NEVER a bride" would be a fitting epitaph for Bridget Nolan if it didn't have the wistful connotation of an old maid wishing that she could still be married. There needed to be a colloquialism for the woman merrily schtupping her ex-husband, with whom she was very happily in love, while serving as maid of honor in her parents' second wedding.

Molly and Sean Nolan got remarried in the backyard of the house where their children had grown up. Their daughter-in-law, Hannah Mayfield, had transformed the space into a fairyland, if one could ignore the sounds of traffic wafting over the assembly from the freeway a few blocks away. Father Patrick Dooley performed the ceremony, even though he could get in trouble because you technically can't perform a marriage ceremony for two people who were divorced—even from each other—in the Catholic church. But he seemed totally copacetic about it.

"You look beautiful, Mom," Bridget said as she grabbed more smoked salmon from the buffet table.

Her mother stopped and dropped her new/old husband's arm, so he stopped, too. "How much champagne have you had, Bridget Mary Nolan?"

Bridget looked at her half-empty glass and did some quick subtraction in her head. "Two and a half glasses. Why do you ask?"

That's when she noticed that her mother's eyes were glossy with unshed tears. "You called me 'Mom' again. I'm not sure I'll ever get used to it."

Although she really didn't want to get into a teary scene now, she couldn't think of a better time to tell her mother, "I've been thinking it consistently for a while now."

She didn't have to look at her father to feel that he was pleased with her, but that's not why she'd said it. After almost losing Matt, Bridget had forgiven her mother. She'd realized that she'd had a blind spot when it came to empathy with her for years and years. She didn't have to forgive her—after all, Molly had made some grievous errors in how she'd lived her life—but it made her father happy.

Over the past year, since she'd gotten back together with Matt, she'd actually opened her heart to her mother again. She decided that she'd rather have the woman who'd given birth to her in her life than hold her choices against her forever.

If Molly bugged out again, though she doubted that would happen, it would hurt a lot. But she would still have her father and brothers to fall back on—and now she had a partner.

Her mother still looked as though she was going to start crying, and that simply wouldn't do. There was no way that their makeup could withstand another onslaught of tears. "Don't cry, Mom."

Her mother reached out for her hand. "There's one thing we

definitely do have in common," Molly said on a sob. "Neither of us likes people telling us what we can and cannot do."

Bridget was only saved from crying by Matt wrapping his arms around her from behind. "Music's going to start soon, and I need to dance with my best girl."

"I like 'my best girl,'" Bridget said.

"It's sort of a mouthful." Her parents wandered off to talk to other guests, but she barely noticed. She didn't clock much besides the man who turned her in his arms and smiled down at her.

"Well, it sort of fits because I'm kind of a handful."

Matt laughed and moved them both toward the dance floor. "You can say that again." He then squeezed her butt, which made her squeal and look around for where his parents were hanging out.

"Your mother is going to tell me that I'm eroding your morals." She didn't slap his hand away, though. "Again."

She and Jane had come to an understanding after joining forces to convince Matt to go back to law school. After Bridget had screeched about how wasteful it was not to go back when he wouldn't have any student loans, Matt had capitulated.

And after they'd discovered a shared interest in elaborate skincare regimes Jane had stopped calling her a gold digger under her breath. A few months after that, Jane had shocked the shit out of Bridget in suggesting her as a candidate for a legal position at a national reproductive rights organization.

Since her family's foundation bankrolled a lot of that organization's initiatives, it was a very friendly interview process.

Even with all the progress they'd made, Bridget didn't want to tempt fate with lewd displays in front of the woman. Matt was undeterred, though. He leaned over and whispered in her ear, "If I can't play grabby hands with my ex-wife without getting yelled at by my mom, what am I even doing with my life?"

That, they hadn't figured out. He'd graduated from law school and taken the bar exam, but he hadn't said what he was going to do with his life. "I think we're all waiting to find that out."

"Are you worried that you'll end up with an unemployed slob sleeping on your couch?" Matt teased.

"Well, we don't live together, so you can be a slob on your own couch." After fast-forwarding the beginning of their romantic relationship, they'd elected to take things slow. But for the past month, since he'd finished the bar exam, there had been a feeling like they'd been dancing around the next step in their relationship. She could kind of see why Matt didn't want to suggest anything drastic. After all, she'd broken up with someone for buying her a house once.

He took her in his arms and pulled her onto the dance floor that had been constructed over the grass. Bridget breathed in, comforted and aroused by his scent. She let her hands creep down his back and squeezed his ass.

"Now my mother is definitely going to tell us both off."

As they swayed to the sounds of the band playing Sinatra, she kind of didn't care. "If I can't grab my ex-husband's ass at my parents' second wedding, what am I even doing with my life?"

"That's the spirit." He was quiet for a few more moments, and everything felt perfect. Except for the question that his parents— and increasingly her parents—had started asking them: What were they doing with their lives?

They were committed to a future together, but they'd been in a sort of stasis since Matt had gone back to school. And it was all great. They loved each other. But, still. Unlike when she'd been expecting a proposal before, she felt the anticipation of Matt asking her to move in or get married like an itch that she couldn't quite scratch.

If she reached for it first, would he pull away? She didn't think so, but what she had with him felt too important to risk.

She was going to pull back and say something because tonight felt like the right time to ask, and then they could tell everyone and really mess up her mother's makeup. But he beat her to the punch.

"I've got a question for you, Muffin."

"I still hate that." She tried to look serious but failed.

"No, you don't," he said, in a stern voice that wasn't really all that stern. And he was right. She just had to say she didn't like it because it was their thing. They had couple things. She never thought she'd have couple things with anyone ever again. "But seriously, I have a question."

"You didn't buy me a house, did you?" It never hurt to make sure.

"No, we're going to pick that out together." His wry grin said that he was deeply satisfied to be smarter than her ex-douche, even if that didn't take much. "Can I proceed?"

"You may."

He laughed, because she sounded testy, but he didn't miss a step. "I think I want to be your ex-ex-husband."

Even though excitement bubbled up inside, she wanted him to ask her instead of making a vague suggestion. It was important. "That's not in the form of a question, Counselor."

Then he missed a step to get down on one knee. "Will you marry me?"

"Again?" She didn't know why she asked that, but it was probably out of embarrassment because everyone at the wedding reception was staring at them. She broke eye contact with Matt to seek out her mother and mouth, "I'm sorry."

Luckily, Matt didn't rescind the question right then and there. "Yes, again."

Bridget's heart stopped beating for a split second before it started up again. She was surprised that she loved this so much, that she wanted to be married to Matt Kido so much. So much that she didn't care that it was a cheesy move to propose at someone else's wedding.

"Yes."

He stood up then as he slid the ring she didn't even look at on her finger. He kissed her and picked her up off her heels. She didn't care what anyone thought. Didn't care if his parents or her parents approved or if Chris was there or jealous. All she cared about was the man swinging her around the dance floor.

ACKNOWLEDGMENTS

First of all, I need to thank Kristine Swartz for helping me turn a collection of scenes and characters into an actual book. I also need to thank my agent, Courtney Miller-Callihan, for fielding all of my frantic e-mails and calls. I am so grateful to work with the entire Berkley team on this book—Jessica Brock, Jessica Mangicaro, Erin Galloway, and the sales team. Thank you to Colleen Reinhart for creating the work of art that is this cover. And thank you to Alyssa Furukawa for their nuanced read of the characterization.

Writing books isn't easy, but it's made much more pleasant when you have romance-writing Valkyries in your corner, cheering you on. Sarah MacLean, Kate Clayborn, Adriana Anders, Katee Robert, Sierra Simone, Kennedy Ryan, Nisha Sharma, Charlotte Stein, Talia Hibbert, Jen DeLuca, Kerry Winfrey, Alexa Martin, and Kristen Callihan are all A-plus friends. Thank you to Kristan Higgans for dispensing advice and making me cry every time you talk about my work. I would be remiss if I didn't thank Jenny Nordbak, Sarah Hawley, and the entire *Wicked Wallflowers Club*. I am happy to be the podcast's Joan Rivers. Christina Hobbs and Lauren Billings—thank you for being you. Jasmine Guillory—I hope we get to share many stages and many tapas together.

Thank you to Nicole Cliffe; your friendship has become invaluable to me. The only thing I regret about not going to Harvard is that we could have been friends for almost twenty years by now. Laurel Simmons, you are a supermom, a super friend, and every time I hear your voice, I feel as though I've been to church. Michael Angelo, Nick Christianson, and Kim Miller, thank you for all the wine and *Real Housewives*.

Thank you to my number one fan, my mom, who would run over anyone who hurt me with a car. (But probably wouldn't try to bribe anyone out of marrying me?) Thank you for sharing your best friend, Kyoko, with me. I like to think that Jane contains a little of both of you.

And, finally, thank you to my readers. To everyone who connected with my complicated, salty heroines and everyone who is waiting for a Jack or Matt of their own. <3

USA Today bestselling author **Andie J. Christopher** writes edgy, funny, and sexy contemporary romance featuring heat, humor, and dirty-talking heroes that make readers sweat. A graduate of the University of Notre Dame and Stanford Law School, she grew up in a family of voracious readers, and picked up her first romance novel at age twelve when she'd finished reading everything else in her grandmother's house. It was love at first read. It wasn't too long before she started writing her own stories—her first heroine drank Campari and drove an Alfa Romeo up a winding road to a minor royal's estate in Spain. Andie lives in the nation's capital with her French bulldog, Gus, a stockpile of Campari, and way too many books.

CONNECT ONLINE

AndieJChristopher.com

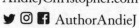 AuthorAndieJ

Ready to find
your next great read?

Let us help.

Visit prh.com/nextread

Penguin
Random
House